Lonely I

by

David Williams

Find out more about the author and upcoming books online at www.lonelyballerina.com
Also at Twitter: @DavidWi18997774 Facebook: www.facebook.com/davieg25

Produced in United Kingdom.

Editorial services by www.bookeditingservices.co.uk

Contents

About the Author

David was born in Leeds in 1963, the second of four children in a single-parent household. He was educated at All Saint Junior and Middle School and Crossgreen Comprehensive. He left school with few qualifications to start work at sixteen in the family roofing business and attended Leeds College of Building. He returned to academic study in 2010 and attained a BA (Hons) degree with the Open University six years later. He is married with four children and lives in East Leeds.

Acknowledgements

Many thanks must go to a number of people, without whose assistance would have made the completion of this work much more difficult. Your help was greatly appreciated. Wife, Yvonne. Children, Roseanne, Gheorghe, Harvey and Scarlett. Karen Williams, Jamie Chambers, Carole Robinson and Gary Cavanagh. I know I plagued you all for many months, but many thanks for your encouragement, time, patience and assistance. Mr Cowans whose remarks on my All Saints Middle School report emboldened me to venture into the unknown, forty-five years after they were penned. To those who doubted the integrity and motivations of the project, I thank you for bolstering my determination to get the work over the finishing line. Last, but not least, a dedication to my parents, Trevor Llewellyn and Shirley Williams.

Within the Darkest Depths

The Irredeemable Fester

CHAPTER 1

June 2016

'Come on, old love, let's get this 'un done wi', then we can get usselves off,' said Jock in a thick Leeds accent as he threw his folded newspaper onto the dashboard and jumped out of the driver's side of a Ford pickup truck. The fifty-eight-year-old, a carpenter by trade, was currently employed as a general operative by East Park Building Ltd. He had spent the last half an hour engaged in a ranting monologue as to how voting OUT, in the forthcoming EU referendum, would be of great benefit to the British public.

His real name, David Strappe, had been modified, not by deed poll, but by the quirky humour of his workmates in an environment where near-the-knuckle wit was not only widely prevalent but cold-bloodedly demanded. Jock was single-minded in his political evaluation, having been born in post-war Britain in the north of England at a time when the economic effects of the Second World War still held sway over many working-class families.

His leathered forehead and determined eyes discouraged his co-worker to interrogate the discourse which spewed from his lips like a bubbling brook of bullshit. Nathan grinned, totally rejecting the tirade as racist-fuelled crap. In any case, all his energies were being channelled towards the afternoon's Euro 16 group game taking place in Marseilles between England and Wales. A faltering start for England's prima donnas had cranked up the tension with the game taking on extra significance for supporters of both nations. He was looking forward to finishing early and taking in the game with the special blend of like-minded associates and copious amounts of alcohol in the vibrant Leeds city centre, known by Leeds Loiners simply as 'Town'.

'Right,' pronounced Nathan with a surge of energy as he bounded out of the cab. 'C'mon, ya taffy bastards, bring it on!'

'An' I'll tell ya summat else an' all, old love, shall I?' said Jock, pointing a thickset finger at the younger operative. 'That fucker Cameron won't last two minutes if they lose. I'm telling ya, he won't, he'll be gone... An' his little slimeball sidekick Osborne! What a twat that bloke is. I can't stand 'im.'

'Aye, all right, mate,' replied Nathan, opening the palms of his hands and with a shake of his head. 'Chill out.' He was only interested in getting the job finished, getting home and preparing for the match. He heaved the double extension ladders from the truck and slid the top section up to the first-floor level with consummate ease.

'It's about time we got a grip o' these foreigners – Eastern Europeans, Poles and Muslims piling into 'country... We can't afford 'em... Taking all us bloody money...an' houses... Hospitals are full of 'em... Look after yer own first, that's what I say. There's fuckin' Mosques cropping up all over 'place, and then there's Isis trying to blow the whole country up and we can't even deport the bastards... Let 'em get their own countries in order before we let em in 'ere, that's what I say.'

'Aye, you're right, Jock, spot on, mate,' said Nathan dismissively as he grabbed the cordless drill and got on with the job in hand, that of removing the plywood security boarding from a back-to-back mid-terrace house in the East Moor Park area of East Leeds. The arrival of the estate agent was imminent with the property on the market for sale by auction.

Jock, leaning on the tailgate, rolled and lit a cigarette from his battered Union Jack baccy tin and continued to spout his views on the political relationship between the UK and Europe and the troubled lands beyond.

The younger colleague dutifully carried out his obligations with a quiet smile in anticipation of the high-octane football match that afternoon. That, and the prospect of a dozen pints of cider with the lads.

*

Reginald Street, in the East Moor Park district of Leeds was one of thousands of rows of back-to-back terraced housing in the northern provincial city. They were originally built to accommodate a rapid increase in the city's population of working classes during the Victorian and Edwardian periods. Although some terraced housing could be three or four bedroomed with small gardens and yards, the style of the smaller back-to-back properties, such as those in Reginald Street, were more basic. Typically, these consisted of a ground floor living room with a tiny side kitchen, often termed as the scullery by older generations. A tin bath would have originally hung behind the cellar door, and on the first floor there would have been two bedrooms, one a tiny box room. In addition, an outside communal toilet 'block' or 'yard' often served up to half a dozen families. Much of this type of housing had been demolished during the slum clearances which had continued well into the 1970s but, nevertheless, many thousands of these dwellings remained in the city which, with modernisation, still provided good housing stock for many a family unit. However, by 2016 the East Moor Park district had seen better days and it was now looked down upon by those of a self-styled superior extraction.

Reginald Street was located towards the bottom end of, and dissected by, East Moor Drive, which ran for about a quarter of a mile from Ascot Terrace at the top and direct to the park at the bottom. 10 Reginald Street was in the smaller section of the street, which was in effect a small cul-de-sac, being enclosed at one end by a low stone wall. The smaller second bedroom of the house had been converted into a bathroom, and a much larger bedroom was added by utilising the loft area through conversion to a slate-cladded, flat-roofed dormer. This was typical of the improvements completed on many of the properties in Reginald Street and the surrounding area. Not all renovations had been carried out in accordance with good working practices, nor building regulations, for that matter, which had the effect of creating a shanty town appearance in some quarters of the now impoverished district. The road was a patchwork quilt of shoddy tarmac with the occasional pothole exposing the original layer of stone cobbles. The pavements on each side of the street consisted of three-inch thick Yorkshire-stone flags worn away by over a hundred years of human industry. These were edged with huge kerbstones, their solidity a testament to the craft and toil of long ago manual labour.

*

Light rain fell from the dreary Leeds skyline onto the slate roofs of the back-to-backs as a white van edged its way along the kerb edge until it reached number 10 Reginald Street. There were no gardens here, no yards, no forecourts where little ones could invent their innocent adventures, just the three-foot-wide uneven pathway between the road and the front doors of each property. Dog excrement and the rotting remains of fast food littered the once smart and proud little street. 'Cooper Electricals' was emblazoned on both sides of the vehicle with colour-coded e-mail address, telephone number and website, giving the prospective customer a multitude of information should they ever require the services of a fully qualified electrician.

Phil Cooper was in his late twenties, thickset and housed the initial swellings of a beer gut. He had an obsession and affinity for Leeds United. Like many others in the city, and many expatriates with roots in West Yorkshire and beyond, the club along with its capricious history was central to his identity. According to Phil, United was a worldwide brand which would undoubtedly, if ever roused from its temporary inert state, unleash an all-powerful force again in European football within the minds of millions across the world. For now, though, they lived off past glories and grainy TV images of Billy Bremner and the boys bossing the likes of Barcelona, the Lancashire powerhouses and the London Mob. In many ways, the current fortunes of the club reflected the mood in Reginald Street on that rainy summer's day in the middle of June. Downcast, depressing, devoid of excitement and devoid of hope.

A striking magpie swept down in front of the vehicle, cackling in anticipation of a rotting morsel of fodder and a potential meal. The iridescent, shining black and white plumage contrasted against the dourness of the little street like a cluster of pearls in a bucket of coal. The bird hacked into the complimentary KFC whilst keeping a close, cold watch on the new visitors through gloss-black eyes.

If Phil's expression was one of enthusiasm and hope, then Zoe's disposition was of the complete opposite.

'What the fuck...? You are fucking joking?' she said whilst surveying the street though narrow, sceptical eyes. She turned towards Phil and stared him square in the face.

'What d'ya think, babe?' he asked as her gaze switched again to the desolate street.

'Is this it? Forty-five grand for this?'

'Yeah, what do ya think? Where else could you get a two-bedroomed 'ouse in Leeds for forty-five grand?'

'It's shite! I'm not living 'ere.'

'C'mon, love, there were others after it y'know, we coulda lost it, and we got it at five thousand under guide price.'

'We got it? You mean you got it!' snapped Zoe. 'It's a right fucking dump. I wanna go back to me mam's.'

'Well, y'know, we can't go back there, love, an' whose fault is that?' Zoe flashed a quick glance at her partner. 'An' stop swearing in front o' Sophia, will you? Come on, love, you haven't even seen inside yet. It's got loads o' potential. C'mon, let's go an' have a look.' He jumped out of the van and as he did so, the magpie ducked and swooped upwards and away with an unmistakable guttural chacking cry. 'Look, Sophes, it's a magpie,' cried Phil to his six-year-old daughter as her mother unbuckled her from the booster seat strapped to the middle seat of the cab.

His positive outlook was mirrored in his huge smile, his white teeth shining through a dark, bushy beard.

It had no effect on Zoe, who carefully lifted a bemused, blonde-haired Sophia down to the pavement.

'Is it the one from Nanna's, Daddy?' she asked in all innocence, pointing towards the fleeing magpie.

'I think it is, sweetheart. I think he wants to come and live here with us,' replied Phil, laughing.

'Is this our new house, Mum?' asked the little girl. 'Where's the garden?'

'There isn't one,' returned Zoe, her voice barely audible under the sheer weight of disbelief.

'No, but there's a lovely park just around the corner with a playground and fields and dog walks.'

'But we haven't got a dog, Daddy.'

'No, but now we're moving away from Nanna's house we can get one... And you get your own room.' Phil picked up his daughter and gave the broadest of smiles as he stared into her captivated sparkling blue eyes. 'What d'ya think, sweetheart, no more sharing a room with Nanna and listening to her snoring and trumping.'

The girl chuckled. 'Can we call her Princess, Daddy?'

'Who, your nanna?'

'No, the new doggie, silly.' She smiled.

'Ha, ha, yeah, of course, love. You can call her what you want. She'll be yours, and you can both share your own room together—'

'There'll be no dogs in any bedrooms,' interjected Zoe, her plain features soured by her negativity, giving her a face like a dour solicitor. She stood facing the house with folded arms clamped firmly to her skinny body, her thin, painted lips and mascaraed eyes unable to disguise her utter contempt. The drizzle continued. Her denim slacks and pink T-shirt contrasted starkly against the backdrop of the grim little house that was to become her home. It had been bright and sunny as they'd left her mother's gardened council house in Seacroft just a few miles away that morning. The aviator sunglasses still clung desperately to her forehead. 'Half of 'em are boarded up,' she said as Phil lowered Sophia to the ground and fumbled around his pockets in search of the keys.

'No, don't exaggerate, love. There's one...two...three... look – oh, and four if you count the end 'un there. And look, we've got an off-licence at that end o' 'street.'

'Well, a lot of 'em are boarded up anyroad... Anyway, come on, then,' she snapped. 'Open the bloody door and let's have a look. I an't got all day – I've gotta life to lead. I can't believe you've gone and bought this at auction without me seeing it. I don't believe it.' Zoe's voice tapered away to a whisper as she shook her head.

Phil unlocked the wrought-iron security grill which protected the front door and matched those on the downstairs windows. He inserted the key into the mortice door lock and slowly turned it clockwise until he heard a muffled click. He then pushed a smaller key into the Yale lock and with just a slight diagonal pressure from the grip of his thumb and forefinger, the door opened, just an inch. He looked behind with a huge grin. 'Ready, girls?' he said.

'Yes, Daddy, open the door,' shouted Sophia. Zoe remained unresponsive.

The family trudged through the door in single file. The air was still, the atmosphere silent. A smell of musty dampness laced with a faint tinge of alcohol and a distant odour of stale urine immediately penetrated the three pairs of twitching nostrils, causing Sophia's snubby little nose to crinkle up. They looked around in silence with the girl seeking out her father's hand for reassurance. It wasn't what she'd expected.

'I don't like it, Daddy,' she whispered. 'It's smelly.'

Zoe and Phil exchanged glances, and for the first time Zoe detected a wavering of enthusiasm from Phil. He was still smiling but this time the smile was less than authentic.

He picked up his daughter and held her at eye level. 'Ah yes, sweetheart, but what about the doggie?'

She instantly broke out in a broad smile and squealed. 'Oohh, the doggie, yes, I like it, Daddy... It's nice.' The spell was broken as father and daughter erupted into spontaneous laughter with Phil swinging her back down onto the floor.

'Hey, why don't you go and explore. Your room's right at the very top of the house. Go on up, you'll be fine.' He nodded towards an open door in the far corner of the room.

'Wait for me,' said Zoe. 'You don't know what's up there.'

'She'll be fine,' said Phil holding her back by the shoulder. 'I've already checked everything out. You go on, sweetheart, explore as much as you want.'

There were two steps inside the living room space up to the door, which, as it was above floor level, made it look a little odd, as if fixed halfway up the wall.

He opened the door fully and flicked on an old brown Bakelite switch located at the bottom of the stairs. 'Go on, love,' he said as he winked and ushered Sophia towards the door.

She bounded through and excitedly tackled the steep wooden staircase on all fours, disappearing as the stairs wound around at the top to a small landing area and out of sight.

'Don't forget the doggie, love,' shouted Phil, laughing.

Zoe remained unmoved at what she perceived to be his pathetic attempts at bribery. 'You sure she'll be OK?'

'She'll be fine, love. Don't worry – there's nothing untoward. The place is structurally sound, and there's no danger... Stop worrying.'

She scrutinised the small living room. Previous attempts had been made at removing an old ceramic-tiled fireplace, but the work had been abandoned halfway through. A cheap, foam-backed carpet, no doubt vibrantly coloured when new, was now heavily soiled and frayed around the edges. The dark wallpaper was a pattern of bold green and brown floral designs on a flecked cream background. It had peeled away on the front wall above the window where the plaster had deteriorated to a crumbly powder, the residue of which now littered the rotting carpet beneath.

Zoe let out a heavy sigh. 'It's lovely, in't it? I don't really know what to say, Phil. I don't...really.' She shook her head and continued to survey her new home.

Phil slunk his arm around her fragile shoulders. 'Give us a month, love, an' I'll have it looking like a palace. I've priced everything up, and all you have to do is choose the carpets, kitchen and furniture. It'll be great, trust me... I'm tellin' you.'

They continued to assess the front room, which was empty save for the moulding remnants of an uneaten sandwich still in its plastic packaging and a couple of empty drink cans. There was a grey dust-covered blanket in an alcove by the far corner of the room opposite the staircase door. As Phil reached over to pick it up, Zoe flinched and gave out a little cry.

'What's up, love?' he asked as he swivelled around and squared up to her. 'What's up?' he repeated.

'Er...nowt. I...I thought—'

'What?'

'Oh forget it. Nowt...forget it. There's not much life around here, is there? It's like being in a morgue. Just stop and listen.'

They both listened intently, standing perfectly still and modifying their breathing to eliminate all possible internal and external bodily sounds. No life, no pitter-patter of footsteps, no traffic, no bird call, even the magpie from earlier had disappeared. They looked at each other but before either could muster another word, a thundering blast shattered the silence causing the whole building to quake. Through the drizzle and mist and even though they were a full sixty miles from the coast, for all the world it sounded like the foghorn of a huge ocean liner, right there on their doorstep. Both jolted backwards, their senses nullified, followed by a stunned silence.

'What the hell was that?' whispered Phil.

'What the fuck?' mumbled Zoe.

They remained in a state of bewilderment before the blast was repeated, although this time from slightly further afield, less harsh than the first. A shaken Phil racked his brain for a rational explanation whilst Zoe racked hers for an irrational one. Phil's logical thought process gradually took stock of the situation as a look of realisation descended onto his sheepish face.

'Bloody hell,' he said with a sigh. 'It's the bloody railway line. There's a railway cutting at the bottom of the street. Here, come and look.' He marched over to the door and beckoned Zoe, his beaming smile returning to its usual glory. He pointed. 'Look, see that old stone wall at the bottom of the street? Well, over it is a row of allotments and then a sixty-foot drop to the main East Coast Railway line. It must have been a train passing through.'

'I nearly had a friggin' heart attack,' cried Zoe, planting the palm of her right hand in between her still heaving small, firm breasts. 'We've gotta put up with that every five minutes, 'ave we?' She released a sigh, and they both smiled and re-entered the house.

It was the first time since the visit that Zoe had expressed anything but resentment and bewilderment; she almost broke into a laugh. Her ice-coldness towards the house began to evaporate as she realised how much the project meant to Phil. They'd lived with her mother for the last three years, but that arrangement had ended abruptly, so they needed somewhere to live as quick as shit. He'd done his best, she reasoned, and maybe she should cut him a little slack. After all, he'd worked every hour possible in order to realise their dream of owning their own place as well as trying to establish the business.

'You're much better looking when you're a happy bunny, you know,' said Phil with a mischievous grin.

Zoe was unable to hold back yet another smile, but, wary of showing her full hand, she quickly turned a cheek while raising an eyebrow. He knew which buttons to press, that was for sure, and his persistence and constant positive manner were beginning to forge impressions into the often cold and mysterious psyche of the one he loved.

'So, this is the kitchen then, is it?' said Zoe as she stepped over towards the entrance which was immediately to the right of the front door. Although the timber frame and architrave were present, there was no door. It was just an opening where a heavy curtain had at one time formed a divide between the 'scullery' and living area. She poked her nose into the tiny room which was empty other than a chipped ceramic Belfast-style sink with antiquated taps positioned directly under the window. She looked at the walls. *Fuck me, dark green. What the fuck were they thinking in those days?* 'I hope these bare pipes and wires are safe, love,' she said while gingerly placing a foot onto the ragged sputnik-patterned oilcloth and leaning further into the room.

'It'll be reet, love,' replied Phil, now on all fours inspecting the condition of the brown-painted skirting boards in the living room.

She leant over and tentatively tipped a dirty mug which was standing upright in the sink to inspect its contents. She curled a lip as she swiftly let go, unimpressed by the unidentified vestiges welded to the inside. 'Me mother's outhouse is bigger than this.' She wasn't far wrong. The footprint of the kitchen was barely thirteen feet long by six feet wide.

'Use your imagination, love,' replied Phil, peering over her shoulder. 'I know it's small, but we'll fit it out with a nice new kitchen. We can have the hob and oven on that wall, and then down here we can have a worktop, cupboards and wall units. And there's still room on that back wall to fit a big American fridge-freezer you're always going on about.'

Zoe looked at Phil with an air of suspicion. She didn't share his optimism but decided to keep her opinions to herself on this occasion. 'Hmmm,' she mused as she backtracked and turned to face the living room again.

The rain had started to fall more intensely and tapped against the window. The skies were now a slate-grey, casting an even gloomier setting to the inside of the tiny house.

Phil flicked the light switch which powered a single low-wattage bulb hanging from the original plaster cast ceiling rose.

Zoe wandered to the open front door and once again looked out onto the dreary little street. The only sound was the constant pattering of rainfall and the rainwater leaching through a rotted gutter from an adjacent property as it gushed onto the stone pavement below. She looked up and down the street. There were no cars, no movement. *Surely these bleedin' hovels should be knocked down, demolished, never mind buying one as a doer-upper. What was he thinking, the fucking numb-nutted numpty?* As she turned to re-enter the room something caught her eye. She instantly twisted her head around. A movement, something. Just like a twitcher searching for that elusive bird in the bush, Zoe searched for that twitch, a flicker, a suggestion of human existence. Nothing but drizzle and blackened clouds. The rain began to spatter her face, so she moved back inside not wanting to displace her carefully administered cosmetics.

She turned to face Phil just as he cried out, 'Zoe, look at this! I didn't see it when I came last week.' He lifted away the dusty blanket to reveal what looked like an old-fashioned, cream-coloured vanity case.

'What is it?'

'Well, let's have a look then, shall we?' He bent down and wiped away a layer of dust before releasing two slightly rusted latches which sprung open the lid. 'Oh look,' he said. 'It's an old portable record player. I bet it's worth a few quid.'

'It looks like a pile o' junk to me,' said Zoe.

'No, it might be worth summat... And look, what's this?' he continued as he fully opened up the case. 'They're old records, like them your mother has in her loft.'

Zoe looked on, unimpressed.

'Who've we got here, then?' said Phil as he stood up with a handful of around half a dozen sleeved vinyls. He brushed the covers with the outside of his hand. '"Lonely Ballerina". Who the hell? By Man-tov-ani... Never heard of him... And who's this?' he continued more to himself rather than to a disinterested Zoe. 'Slim Whitman – "Rose Marie". Never heard of these lot, love... Ronnie Hilton. Dickie Valentine. Bloody 'ell. Maybe they're worth summat, eh? What d'ya think?'

'Nowt much,' replied Zoe, her initial objectionable manner seeping back to the fore. 'Just some old records. Sling 'em. I'm not having any junk in the house,' she snorted, rolling her eyes in damnation of the decrepit property soon to become her home.

'Maybe your mam'll want 'em?' enquired Phil with unshakeable eagerness.

'No, don't think so,' said Zoe firmly. 'They're junk. Just sling 'em.'

'Hang on, let's see if it works,' he said, trying to locate the plug. Having done so, he searched for a wall socket. He found one at skirting board level in the alcove where the blanket had originally been found. As he attempted to connect the plug, there came a high-pitched scream from upstairs.

Both Zoe and Phil froze before Sophia cried out, 'Daddy!'

Phil dropped the cable and leapt towards the stair door. 'Sophia, what's up?' he shouted as he flung open the door and bounded up the stairs.

Zoe was in close pursuit moving almost as fast with adrenaline flooding through her overly sensitive nervous system. 'What's up, love?' she screeched.

The steps were steep. Both used their hands and feet to expedite a hasty ascent before turning to the right onto a small landing. The immediate door to the left opened up to the converted bathroom, and the slightly elevated door to the right led up to the attic dormer bedroom, but it was the main bedroom straight in front that led them to their distraught daughter.

Phil raced in and grabbed her by the shoulders. 'What's up, love?' he demanded while looking around the empty room.

With tears tumbling from her glistening eyes, she blubbered, 'Daddy, there, look.' She pointed towards the fireplace.

'What is it, sweetheart?' he asked just as Zoe burst into the room, breathing heavily.

'What? What's up, love?' she rasped as she wrested the child's shoulders from Phil and grabbed them tightly herself.

'Look, Mum.'

Phil and Zoe looked towards the original cast-iron fireplace which had long since been blocked off with a flimsy piece of painted hardboard.

'What is it, love?' probed a flushed-faced Zoe, desperate to make sense of her daughter's distress.

'I just moved it a bit, Mummy, and...that fell out,' to which she burst into hysterics again.

Both parents looked down to where she'd pointed

with Sophia now encased within her mother's arms.

'Ugh, what is it, Phil?' asked Zoe.

Phil crouched down to closely inspect the object, which at first sight appeared to be the skeletal remains of some small, alien-like creature. After a couple of seconds, he stood up and shook his head. He smiled at first, but then engaged a more serious countenance for the benefit of his daughter. 'Don't worry, love,' he said. 'It's just a dead bird. It's a magpie. You know, like the one we saw outside when we first came. Do you remember, the one from Nanna's, it swooped down and then flew away?'

'Yes,' said a still teary little girl, 'but it looks like a skeleton.'

It was a gruesome spectacle, so it wasn't hard to see why a six-year-old would recoil in horror at such a disgusting sight. Due, probably, to some atmospheric condition, half the body of the bird had been perfectly preserved, but the other half had completely rotted away, revealing a stiffened, emaciated and whitened skeleton including beak and claws. Easily identified by virtue of the iridescent dark blue and green wing and tail feathers, some still in perfect condition, and a white belly. The pitiful creature had squawked its last caw many years ago, the remains having been incarcerated within the dusty, dark tomb of the chimney breast.

Phil was reluctant to dwell on such an unpleasant situation, particularly in the middle of his 'hard sell' of the house to his small family.

'Is it just a bit alive, Daddy?' asked Sophia, her eyes welling up and her cheeks flushed.

'No, sweetheart, it's just a dead magpie,' he replied before quickly lifting the dead creature with forefinger and thumb and proceeding to transport it, at arm's length, to the outside bin yard further down the block.

'Ugh, put it down. It'll have all sorts on it,' protested Zoe.

But by that time Phil was halfway down the stairs, swiftly taking control of the situation.

Zoe comforted Sophia with a firm hug. 'It'll be all right, love, don't worry,' she said, stroking the child's forehead. 'Daddy's gonna make this place lovely for us all, and your room is upstairs. Come on, show us up there, let's go see.'

Once in the attic, Sophia wasn't quite tall enough to see out of the dormer window, so Zoe held her up tightly with the little girl's elbows resting on the grubby window board as they surveyed the bleak panorama of the street. Although the rain had now stopped, it was still overcast with the ill-tempered clouds holding court over the neglected little Edwardian street.

Zoe scanned the scene for life – not a glimmer. Even though it was mid-afternoon, the street was dark. The little dismal cells, those not otherwise boarded up, were bereft of activity, light and life. However, Zoe painted a rosy picture to the impressionable Sophia, priming her pitch with visions of doggie walks in the sunshine and ice-cream vans jingling at the end of the street with the nice, smiling ice-cream man offering free chocolate flakes, raspberry sauce, and hundreds and thousands. She spoke of picnics in the nearby East Moor Park, on the daisy-carpeted meadows surrounded by borders of sweet-smelling roses. She knew all too well of the colourful reputation of the park, of the high-profile murders and rapes, of the rumours of dogging and other such unsavoury social pastimes. She didn't mention her fears of spent hypodermic needles in the sunken sandpit or the broken glass strewn over the adventure playground. In any case, she thought, they're only rumours. She hadn't actually ever been to the notorious park, but now she'd be living barely a hundred yards away from it.

Her positive pitch had the desired affect; the smile and colour returned to the cherubic cheeks of the little blonde-haired six-year-old.

Again, Zoe's attention was diverted, but this time towards the house directly opposite. This time she interrogated her senses more thoroughly and with more scrutiny. She fixed her stare in the direction of number 11. *Nowt, not a thing... No...hang on... Surely not.* Her eyes narrowed. *Have I just seen...? Yes!* The distinct form of a human, an old woman passing the inside of the darkened window. A vague impression, but clearly it was...a person – a life form.

As the figure moved out of focus, a dim light appeared from the back of the room. Zoe's heartbeat increased, spellbound and oblivious to Sophia's enthusiastic chatter of doggies and ribbons and ice creams. She crouched lower and stared fixedly, eager to glean any information available as to the nature of the creature in the house opposite.

She tried to figure out the layout of the room, but even with the addition of the dim lighting it was indiscernible. She angled her gaze and tightened her eyes to increase the intensity of her focus, whilst all the time Sophia continued to jabber on about ice creams and playgrounds.

Suddenly, a figure appeared in full focus in the middle of the window, causing Zoe to jerk backwards. *Where the fuck did that come from?* It didn't appear to come from the left, or the right, or from below or from above. But there it was, in full fucking view, holding aside the net curtains and glaring outwards onto the pitiful street of death, white-haired with large, malicious, bulging eyes.

Zoe attempted to back away, but it was too late. The figure was now returning her own focused stare, which momentarily paralysed the young mother. Although eye contact lasted only a second or so, it seemed much longer as the bulbous eyes of the white-haired old woman transmitted an embittered communication – a malevolent communication.

Zoe ducked down just for a second and by the time she'd popped her head back above the level of the sill, the woman had released her grip on the net curtains and hastily swished the draw curtains closed.

The street was as it had been just a few seconds previously, lifeless and dreary, with the only sound being the rainwater from the rotten guttering as it continued to spurt water onto the Yorkstone flags.

Zoe, unreceptive to the babbling Sophia, shook her head. *Did that really happen? Did I just see an old woman in the house opposite?* She began to question everything about the house, the street and the idea of moving there.

'Can Princess sleep in my room, Mummy?' asked Sophia, oblivious to the fleeting state of hypnosis the mental shock had triggered in her mother.

'What?' replied Zoe sharply.

'Can Princess sleep in my room with me?'

'Who the hell's Princess, Sophia? What are you talking about, love?' she objected, unable to process the girl's incessant chattering on top of her own raging emotional state.

'Princess...the doggie – the one Daddy said we could have,' she protested, her soft, innocent voice rising in tone as if chastising her mother's silliness in forgetting about the promised puppy. 'The one we're going to take for walks in the park, silly.'

Zoe sighed and then smiled as the realisation of the situation struck a chord in her negative mindset. She realised that her lack of enthusiasm was borne out of the prevailing circumstances. A small, run-down house in a deserted street on a dismal, wet Friday afternoon. Of course she'd be feeling a little negative. Was there really a sinister touch to the white-haired lady? Probably just an old lass who'd lived in the street for donkey's years merely closing her curtains and probably being just as shocked to see her. *Let's face it, there can't be much activity in this street to get excited about.*

Zoe closed her eyes and arched her slim neck. She then gave out a large sigh before relaxing her shoulders and slowly sinking to her knees in front of Sophia. She cupped her daughter's flushed cheeks and kissed her on the lips before breaking into a broad smile. 'The doggie...? Of course she can, my darling.'

At that moment, the clouds parted and the elusive sun directed a stream of brilliant light onto the opposite row of houses.

'Yay,' pronounced Zoe. 'Sunshine and light. Look, Sophia, the sun's come out to play!'

A little bemused, Sophia joined in with her mother's enthusiasm. 'Hooray,' she countered, 'the sunshine.'

Both started to chuckle – Zoe because she realised how ridiculous her behaviour had been and Sophia because her mum was chuckling.

'Come on, sweetheart, let's go see Daddy,' said Zoe, grabbing hold of her daughter's hand and making her way through the door and towards the steep and winding staircase.

As they struggled downwards, with Zoe almost descending backwards in her attempts to make sure Sophia followed her safely, a slow melody softly radiated upwards from downstairs.

'What's that?' Zoe murmured to herself, to which Sophia immediately repeated the question. 'I don't know, sweetheart. Let's go see.'

They continued their descent with the soft music slowly increasing in volume. As much as the initial ambience of the house had had a negative effect on Zoe, this smooth, canorous harmony was having the opposite effect. She found her soul being uplifted with the mesmerising resonance. She stopped, just for a moment.

'Phil,' she uttered, 'is that you?' They continued their descent and turned the winding corner at the top of the lower staircase.

Sophia clumsily kept pace, anchored to her mother's iron-like grip.

Zoe saw the door leading to the living room slightly ajar. The music increased in volume and with it a continuous soft, crackling sound. 'Phil, Phil! What's going on? What is it?' As they reached the bottom steps, Zoe pushed the door open to find Phil on his knees crouched over the old record player.

'Look, love, it works,' he exclaimed as he turned around with a beaming smile. 'It actually works... Look, it's the "Lonely Ballerina",' he said, waving the record sleeve in the air, 'by Man...to...vani. Ha, ha! Who'd have believed it? It actually works!'

Zoe stood there wide-eyed. Her emotions welled up and for once her hard features softened. She gently released her grip on Sophia's hand and stared straight ahead, her focus in another dimension. 'That's lovely,' she murmured.

'Well, what ya crying for then, ya silly bugger?' retorted Phil before removing the stylus and standing up to embrace his emotional partner. 'What's up, love?' he asked.

She slipped out of her transitory state of hypnosis and gazed towards Phil. 'I don't know; it's just this house. Up one minute, down the next. The music... The bloody sun coming out... It just...got to me. Bloody hell, Phil. I hope you know what we're doing.'

'We'll be fine, love. Don't you worry – we'll be fine.'

'I saw an old woman from over the road, with white hair and pop-out eyes. I don't know who wa' more bleedin' scared, me or her?'

Phil looked down at Sophia, he tutted and shook his head. 'Your language is getting worse than your mother's,' he said, only half joking. Linda, his mother-in-law, had a turn of phrase much coarser than most and didn't differentiate between recipients, including her granddaughter. Zoe, although not quite as candid with her own language, was susceptible to the odd use of an industrial expression, or two. Phil didn't press the issue too vigorously; his easy nature enabled him to overlook this minor imperfection.

'...And then when we came down and heard the music, it made me feel happy... But at the same time...sad... It just got to me a bit. It was lovely.'

'Well, it's only a record, love. Come on, let's play it again,' said Phil as he crouched over the record player and carefully repositioned the stylus onto the already spinning Decca-labelled record. 'Come on, love, let's dance,' he cried and grabbed Zoe by the elbow, but she was having none of it.

'Geroff,' she growled, shrugging him off. She'd already let her guard down once and had commenced the process of steeling herself back into her default persona.

'Can I dance with you, Daddy?' asked Sophia.

'C'mon then, sweetheart,' cried Phil. With that, father and daughter waltzed around the room to the crackling composition of the 'Lonely Ballerina' by Mantovani and his orchestra amongst the dust, the damp and the decay.

By now the clouds had thinned, allowing the summer sun to strut its stuff and swathe the row of houses opposite in bright light. This heightened Zoe's outlook. With the soothing tones of 'Lonely Ballerina' permeating deep into her soul, she enjoyed a brief moment. The feeling of sadness and empathy generated by the recording radiated an austere but warm feeling inside.

*

As the little family drove out of the street contented, for the time being at least, with their acquisition, a magpie sat in a gap behind the set-pot chimney stack of number 10. The stare of his beady black eyes converged with that of the bulbous-eyed, white-haired old woman who, again, peeked out of the gap in her heavy Dralon curtains.

CHAPTER 2

September 2016

I t was a warm September afternoon as Zoe marched down East Moor Drive on the homeward-bound school run from All Saints Primary School. Sophia lagged behind as she endeavoured to keep pace with the purposeful stride of her mother.

Fifty years earlier, East Moor Drive had been the hub of community activity with the majority of street corners given over to a wide and varied spectrum of shops and small business enterprises. Occasionally, larger stores had spanned the whole end of the block, the width of both back-to-backs, but most had been single units, positioned side by side, with the proprietors often occupying the overhead living accommodation. These had been local people serving the local community. In the days before supermarkets dominated our shopping conventions, in the days before it was financially viable to scoot to town and back in minicabs, and in the days when the utterance of a foreign tongue would cause commotion amongst the whole neighbourhood. Only in exceptional circumstances would one have to seek elsewhere those provisions needed for everyday life in East Moor Park. There were two fish and chip shops, three butchers, a greengrocer, two general grocers, a clothes shop, an off-licence, two newsagents, a sweet shop, an electrical appliance and hardware store, a doctor's surgery, a dentist, a barber shop, a hair salon, a chemist and a post office. The Slip Inn stood at the head of East Moor Drive and with over a dozen other pubs located within a ten-minute walking distance, there'd been many a drunken altercation to brighten up an otherwise dour East Moor Park evening.

By 2016, the twilight altercations in and around East Moor Park were a tad more sinister, involving drugs, knives and car theft. And the number of tills ringing on the Drive had gradually whittled down to just the one: a double-fronted off-licence, East Park Wines and Spirits whose proprietor was Saleem Patel. The old corner shops had long since been converted into squalid living quarters for the cheap rental and DHSS markets. Bollards had been placed across the road every fifty metres as a deterrent to the local joy riders, and the nearest pub still open for business was the, ironically named, Hope Inn, almost a mile away.

'Come on...pick your feet up, young lady. Your dad should be home by now, and he's got a surprise for you.'

Sophia struggled with the multitask of half running, half walking and half conversing with her mother. 'What? A surprise, Mum? What is it?'

'You'll find out. Now, come on... I an't got all day – I've gotta a life to lead.'

'What's the surprise, Mum? What is it?'

'We've just got to nip into the offie,' replied Zoe, ignoring the Spanish Inquisition and whisking her daughter by the hand into the off-licence, which stood near the bottom of East Moor Drive where it dissected Reginald Street.

The PVC door swung open to the traditional jingle of the shop-door bell. Although the establishment predominantly offered liquor for sale, it was packed with all manner of items ranging from maple syrup to lipstick, stamps to sanitary wear and soft porn to pineapple chunks. The proprietor, Saleem Patel, mid-fifties, known locally as Sally, was a well-nourished, fully bearded character who tendered Zoe his customary welcome.

'Ey up,' he gushed with a huge smile. 'How are you, love? Have you settled in, then?' Before she could reply, he moved on to the little girl. He peered over the counter. 'And how's little Sophia, then? Have you had a good day at school, luvvie?'

A bemused Sophia nodded without a sound.

"Ere y'are, sweetheart,' he said, reaching down to hand the girl two chocolate mice from the 'penny tray', even though all the sweets were priced at five pence each or three for ten.

Sophia took the chocolate and looked up to her mother who sanctioned the backhander with a slight nod.

'What do you say?'

'Thank you,' said Sophia quietly, unable to withhold a shy smile.

'That's all right, luvvie. You're worth it with that lovely little smile o' yours,' returned Sally with a grin as wide as a car bonnet. 'Oh, and by the way, Zoe, ask your husband to nip in, will you, love? I owe him a bit o' cash for that little job he did for us.'

By this time, Zoe had turned her back on him. After a brief search and grabbing two small tins of dog food and a packet of dried puppy food, she turned around. 'Put that in a bag for us, will ya?' she said quietly before nodding towards Sophia.

'Ah...I see.' He smiled and took the items, carefully

placing them inside a plastic carrier bag with an exaggerated wink and a tap on the nose.

'Yeah, I'll tell him,' she said stiffly. 'But he's not me husband; we're not married.'

At that moment, Mrs Patel eased her way through a door positioned directly behind the counter which led to a back room living space. The entrance to the door was stacked with boxes of goods, forcing her to squeeze through a narrow gap. 'Ah, missus,' said Mrs Patel. 'Are you well? Have you settled in?'

Zoe offered the slightest of acknowledgements with a nod.

Dressed in flamboyant and colourful silk sari, with greying hair immaculately brushed back into a bun, Mrs Patel kept up the charm offensive. 'And hello, little one.' She smiled, looking down at Sophia.

'Have you got doggie yet?' Sally interjected with a manufactured cough and glare at his wife who, in turn, glanced at Zoe and then back at Sophia before realisation set in.

'Ah, OK, OK, I see... In any case,' she said, once again turning to Zoe, 'tell husband to come in for payment for job.'

'I told her already,' snapped Sally, his eyes widening.

'He did very good job,' continued Mrs Patel.

'It's all been arranged, missus. Stop interfering, will you? You're always bloody interfering.'

'Oh, keep this out,' replied Mrs Patel, tapping the side of her nose. 'And don't tell me what to do. I don't know you think you are.'

'How much do I owe you?' pressed Zoe, sensing the rising of tensions between the squabbling proprietors.

'Er, just four pounds sixty-five please, love,' replied

Sally.

Zoe handed over a five-pound note. Although her lips didn't move, she uttered a barely perceptible, "Kin' hell,' under her breath. She hadn't meant to produce an audible sound, and wasn't sure whether she had or not, but she couldn't help sometimes speaking aloud her innermost thoughts. In any case, neither Sally nor Mrs Patel reacted, so she assumed she'd got away with it.

'There y'are, love,' said Sally, handing over the change after rummaging through a primitive 1970s till.

'Thanks, see you later. Come on, Sophia,' replied Zoe, grabbing hold of the girl's collar before marching out of the shop with her young daughter following like a fluffy duckling on a piece of string.

'Bye, love,' said a smiling Sally.

'See you later,' called out Mrs Patel.

The door closed to the jingle of the traditional bell.

'She miserable cow,' said Mrs Patel. 'I never see her smile, not even once.'

'Leave her alone. She's just a lass with a young 'un to look after. Probably got a lot on her mind wi' just moving and all that. You're being too harsh on her.'

'Ah, listen to you, mister. Maybe you have eye on her. A mean spirit cow, I say. Husband is OK, but not her. And another thing, you stop giving sweets away to kids. We run business here you know, you forget?'

'Oh, stop interfering, missus. I'm the gaffer around here. If you carry on poking your nose into my affairs, you'll be on the next flight out to Bombay. You'll be back wi' your mother washing 'pots up in 'street! I'm telling you.'

'Ah, listen to you. In your dreams, mister,' she replied. 'My mother worked in office for government, and if I could afford ticket to Bombay, it will be YOU on flight, not me! And a bloody one-way ticket, mister. And don't forget your father started business selling chicken on street corner. Too big for boots,' she muttered as she squeezed back through the door into the back room and out of sight.

'Too big for boots,' mocked Sally, rolling his eyes and mimicking his wife's Indian accent, nevertheless making sure she was well out of earshot before he did so.

*

It had been six weeks since the 'Coopers' had moved into the house at Reginald Street after Phil had spent almost two months renovating. He'd kept to his word and had created a comfortable, modern-styled home for his small family.

The dilapidated house had been completely trans-formed. New carpets for the stairs and upper two floors, and a good-quality laminate for the living room and kitchen. The whole place was decorated. Also, new electrical wiring, a new central heating system and a complete new bathroom and kitchen. Zoe had added the finishing touches with modern furniture, rugs and colour coordinated fixtures and fittings. The place had had a complete makeover from the one she'd first stepped into during that dour summer's day back in June.

It turned out that they even had neighbours to complement the bulbous-eyed mystery woman. According to Zoe, at least three of the back-to-backs were occupied by Poles. Although, as far as she was concerned, they could easily have originated from any Eastern bloc country. She'd neither the inclination nor confidence to delve any further into their backgrounds and was just grateful that she and the old bird opposite weren't the only occupants of the street. The laid-back Phil would have offered an 'Ey up, old lad, how's it going?' had it been Nelson Mandela, Donald Trump or the Yorkshire Ripper living by the side of them.

But he had more important things to deal with, having recently secured a two-year contract for the upgrading of electrical wiring on behalf of a nationwide chain of estate agents. Although this took him away from the family, including occasional weekends, he was contented that things were going well. He'd managed to get his foot on the property ladder without a mortgage, and now the business was beginning to flourish. He was as happy as a piglet in a pie shop. It seemed that nothing and no one could extricate him from this positive, outgoing mindset.

As well as the three Polish families, there were two groups of Syrian refugees, an Iranian couple, a Bangladeshi family and a gay couple, one of whom was a non-English speaking biracial Italian. His partner, a smartly dressed Indian, possessed a command of the English language bettered by not one person in the street, nor probably, for that matter, anybody in the whole of East Moor Park.

In the end house, which was attached to the railway on the Coopers' side of the street, lived a white single mother with four children of varying skin colour and heritage. Although they were not the best dressed or cared for children in the neighbourhood, they displayed impeccable manners and appeared happy with their humble background, always smiling whenever confronted.

Zoe labelled the children 'The Bottom House Kids'.

Little 'un, Big 'un, Middle lass and Middle lad is how she identified them. The little 'un, a dark-skinned boy, was about the same age as Sophia. Zoe had suggested to Phil that the mother might be on the game, judging by the number of male visitors that she'd covertly observed frequenting the property. Phil was unperturbed, but Zoe was loathed to let Sophia anywhere near the house.

Other than the Bottom House family and the 'Poles', Zoe pigeonholed the remainder of the inhabitants as Pakistanis. Apart, of course, from the reclusive, bulbous-eyed, old woman whose path she hadn't yet crossed on the street. She knew it wouldn't be long before the inevitable face-off, but for now she wished to avoid it at all costs.

The security grill and front door were wide open as Zoe and Sophia reached home. Phil greeted them both with a smile and a kiss as they entered the house.

'The conning bastards,' proclaimed Zoe.

'Daddy, what's the surprise?' interjected Sophia with the flushing eagerness of innocence.

'Nearly five quid for a bit o' do… For a bit o' food,' continued Zoe.

'Whooah,' exclaimed Phil with a grin. 'Ladies, ladies, one at a time, please.'

'Mummy said you'd got a surprise for me,' gushed the little girl.

'Well, I have,' replied Phil. 'But first I've got to tell Mrs Cooper off about her bad language, haven't I, sweetheart?' said Phil, nodding down to his daughter.

'Yes, you have, Daddy,' replied Sophia, staring at Zoe.

'I'm not Mrs Cooper, and in future we'll be buying off the internet. I'm not paying those prices. Anyhow, did you get it?'

'Yep, I did. Now you two sit down on the sofa and close your eyes.'

Sophia dived onto the sofa and clamped her little hands over her face.

Zoe eased the schoolbag, coat and carrier bag onto the coffee table and sat next to Sophia with arms folded, reluctant to enter into the spirit of excitement and anticipation that Phil was attempting to cultivate.

'Close your eyes, Mrs Cooper,' urged Phil.

'I'm not closing me bleedin' eyes.'

'Close your eyes, Mum,' demanded Sophia.

'Oh...all right, all right.' Zoe tutted and placed one hand loosely over her face. 'Come on then, get on with it.'

'Right then, no opening before I say, OK? OK, Sophia?'

'Yes, OK, Daddy.'

'Zoe? Zoe?' repeated Phil.

'What!'

'No opening before I say, OK?'

'All right, all right, just get on with it, will ya? I'm losing me bleedin' patience now,' she fired.

Phil turned his back on them and opened the new bi-folding door which now separated the living area from the kitchen. He reached in and picked up a cardboard box from the worktop before turning back towards the room. He stooped to place the box onto the coffee table and paused, further cranking up the tension before offering up yet another huge toothy grin. 'No peeping now, girls.'

'Oh...just get on with it, will ya?' Zoe sighed, at which point the bottom of the box collapsed and out dropped a scraggy little puppy which fell on its side sending papers, bags and cups scattering as chaos descended on the small living room. The puppy immediately started yelping and darting over, under and around the table.

Sophia squealed with delight. 'Daddy, Daddy...a puppy!' she cried.

Zoe screamed at Phil, 'What the hell! Get away, ya little bleeder... Get it, Phil... Phil, sort it out!' she shrieked as the puppy took a flying leap onto her lap, did a three hundred and sixty degree turn and jumped off again while Sophia tried to grab hold of it. 'Arrggh, Phil, get it off... Piss off, ya little twat!' she cried as Phil, laughing uncontrollably, tried to recapture the turbo-animated little canine.

The yelping was constant, and Sophia joined in with her father's hilarity as the puppy scampered at full pelt around the room to the backdrop of Zoe's constant screeching.

At first, Phil's cumbersome attempts at capture were no match for the energised little animal, who was already displaying a mischievous character through cheeky little glinting eyes, but after a while fatigue set in and he was able to trap her under the table. He lifted her up and cradled her, gently stroking and calming down the excitable little bundle of energy.

Sophia stood up and beamed with her arms held aloft. 'Daddy, Daddy, can I hold her, Daddy?'

'Yes, sweetheart. Sit down, then,' said Phil before gently lowering the puppy into the arms of his doe-eyed daughter.

A bond was immediately struck as the puppy looked up at her doting new mistress and began licking feverishly at Sophia's flushed little face.

She giggled, unable to conceal her obvious delight, but Zoe interjected, 'Urgh, don't be letting her lick your face, love, it's not hygienic.' But even she couldn't hide the genuine humour of the moment as a smile, albeit a slight one, transformed her usual sour countenance. The smile turned into a chuckle. 'Well, you did a good job there, didn't you? Smashing job, Phil. Well done, you.'

'Ha, ha, yeah. Look, it must have peed in the bottom, it's all wet,' he replied, looking at Zoe through the bottom of the box.

The family spent a good hour, a happy hour, getting acquainted with Princess, as she'd been christened by Sophia. Both parents agreed that Princess could share the attic bedroom with their daughter, and, for a while, they were as contented as any family could be in the whole of East Moor Park.

Phil came down from the attic having arranged a litter tray and newspaper onto the carpeted floor of the bedroom with two small dishes, one of water and the other with food. He'd left Princess fast asleep in her new doggie bed, but as soon as his back was turned, Sophia had retrieved the puppy and gently laid her onto her own bed continuing to caress, cuddle and explore.

'Well, what do you think?' said Phil, smiling at Zoe.

'Well, she's not a Yorkie, is she?'

'What do you mean? What's wrong with her?'

'I thought you said she was a Yorkshire terrier?'

'Well, Andy said her dad was a Yorkie,' replied Phil.

'Hmmm,' mused Zoe. 'I dunno about that one. How much?'

'Two hundred quid.'

'Well, definitely not a Yorkie, then – not at that price,' countered Zoe. She was happy with Princess and relieved that Phil hadn't been suckered into paying full whack for a pedigree Yorkie. She wouldn't have put it past him.

'What we having for tea?' asked Phil.

'I dunno, but I'm not going back round to Sally's. I'm

sick and tired of 'em asking if we've settled in! For fuck's sake, we've been here six weeks now, an' every time I go in it's, "'Ave you settled in then yet? 'Ow are ya? 'Ow ya settling in?" I wish they'd both just shut the fuck up, to be honest.'

'Right, so what we having for tea, then?'

'An' the prices they charge.'

'Tea?'

'An' they're always bickering. He seems all right, but she's a right false bitch. She's smiling at you one minute, then her face drops an' she scuttles off into 'back room.'

'Fish 'n' chips or pizza?'

'Pizza. And by the way, they said you've to go in for your money for the job you did for 'em.'

'Well, I wasn't gonna charge 'em owt. It was only a couple o' sockets, and they didn't cost me owt. I already had 'em.'

'What? Course you've gotta charge 'em. You're running a business, aren't you?'

'Yeah, I know, but I was only there half an hour, and they're always giving Sophes free sweets an' stuff.'

'Free sweets!' snapped Zoe. 'Free bleedin' sweets? Not a bad trade-off, is it? You do all their electrical work for nowt, and she gets a penny mouse every other fuckin' Friday! They've seen you coming, mate.'

'No they haven't.'

'Yes they bloody have. You're such a muppet sometimes, Phil, you really are. Grow a pair o' balls and go in for your money. If you don't want it, I'll have it.'

'All right, all right. I'll nip in tomorrow and pick it up,' said Phil. 'You're full of it tonight, aren't you? You're that way out, I can tell.'

'No I'm not,' countered Zoe.

'Well, am I picking the pizza up or are we getting 'em delivered? You choose.'

'Oh, please yourself,' chided Zoe. 'I've got a friggin' headache now.'

'Well, I'm not surprised, love. You get all worked up over the least little thing. Just chill out a bit, will you. I'll get us a bottle of wine to have with us pizza before I go up to 'Devon. I'm meeting the lads for the Leeds game.' After a short pause and a cursory glance towards Zoe, he continued, 'Unless you wanna come as well? We can drop Sophes off at your mother's.'

'I'm not going to the Devon wi' you and your mates, all getting pissed up. I'll stay in, as usual.'

'Aw, come on, love. I've been working all week, and it's a local derby. They're playing Huddersfield – I'm buzzin',' contested Phil.

'I couldn't give a toss who they're playing,' said Zoe. 'Just go if you're going...why not? Just get me some wine. If you get it from Sally's, you can pick your money up... That's if you dare ask 'im for it.' Zoe slumped back into the sumptuous new sofa which sat against the wall opposite the fireplace. She picked up a glossy magazine from the floor, displaced during the rumpus caused by the impromptu delivery of Princess, and began scrolling through the pages.

'Right, I'll telephone the order through, and then nip round to Sally's.' Phil sighed. 'Where's the menu thing?'

'I dunno,' replied Zoe, continuing to flick through the magazine. 'It was on the table. It could be anywhere by now. You'll have to look for it.'

Just as normality was slowly descending over the household, and as Phil searched for the menu 'thing', a new disaster erupted with the sound of Sophia screaming accompanied by the clatter of a hasty descent down two flights of stairs.

'Daddy! Daddy!'

'Christ, what's up now?' exclaimed Zoe, closing her eyes with a sigh.

By the time Phil had reached to open the door, Sophia stood on the third step from the bottom with tears streaming down her cheeks.

'What is it, love?' asked Phil.

'What's up, Sophia?' demanded Zoe. She was now standing next to him and facing her distraught daughter who had climbed down to the bottom step.

'It... It's...Princess...' she gushed.

'Princess, love, what's up with her?' asked Phil. 'What's 'matter with her?'

'Well...she...she...'

'Go on, love, calm down. What's up?' said Zoe.

'Well...it's Princess...'

'Yeah, well go on, love. Is she all right?' continued Zoe. 'What's up with her?'

'Well...she...'

'What?'

'She...'

'Go on... What?'

'She's got a cock, and she rubbed it up against my leg,' replied the little girl, bursting into a fresh tirade of tears.

Phil and Zoe were dumbfounded. Without moving an inch, their eyes met with incredulity as the gravity of what they had just heard from their six-year-old daughter slowly sank into their stunned heads.

'She's got a what?' was the first utterance that automatically formulated from Phil's lips.

'A cock,' repeated Sophia, in a matter-of-fact manner.

'A what?'

'A cock, Daddy!' cried Sophia as the sobbing increased amidst a cacophony of confusion for the little girl.

Zoe slapped Phil across the back of his shoulders. 'We know what she said, you bleedin' idiot. Stop getting her to repeat it.'

'Where did you learn to use language like that?' cried Phil, shaking his finger at her. 'That's a naughty word, Sophia. Who's been telling you to use words like that?'

'I...I...don't know,' answered the tearful youngster.

'Well, never mind that,' charged in Zoe. 'What about *you*? Didn't you think to check? Or ask? Didn't you look? Did it ever occur to you?'

'Well...no...not really. I never thought...' replied Phil, scratching his head.

'You never thought... You never thought! You never bleedin' do, do you? I can't believe you, Phil... You never bleedin' thought.'

'Well, it was Andy. I'm sure he said—'

'Andy my arse! It's you, you big gormless get. You've got a mind of your own, an't you?'

'Anyway, that's not the point,' Phil defended. 'The point is that both you and your mother have got mouths like cesspits! Neither one of you can string a sentence together without effing this or effing that, blinding this and blinding that. That's where she's picked it up from. Her own mother and nanna. Six years old and swearing like a trooper... Six years old!'

'I've never used that word in front of her, and don't you dare drag my mother into this after all she's done for us,' declared Zoe. For once, she was careful to choose her words under such highly charged circumstances. She turned to Sophia. 'Now, young lady, you tell me where you've been hearing words like that?'

'It was Dexter,' sobbed Sophia.

'Who's Dexter?' asked Phil.

'Who's Dexter?' repeated Zoe, but with more authority.

'From The Bottom House Kids...'

'I knew it! The bleedin' hillbillies,' exclaimed Zoe. 'What's he been saying? Is it the little 'un or the middle 'un? You don't go anywhere near them kids anymore, do you understand, Sophia? Do you understand?'

'Yes,' blurted out the little girl before running and diving onto the sofa, burying her face into the soft velvet cushion.

'All right, love, never mind. We'll sort it out,' said Phil, stroking her back. 'Come on, sweetheart. Don't be upset. We'll sort it.'

'No, *I'll* sort it!' countered Zoe. 'Cos I can't rely on you, can I? The dirty little bastard. I'll rub its fuckin' nose in it.'

'Rub its nose in what?'

'Well, I'll rub its nose in summat,' replied Zoe after a slight hesitation. She rushed towards the door and stormed her way up the two flights of stairs and into the attic bedroom.

As she entered the room, Princess looked up from the comfort of her bed and gave a yelp accompanied by an enthusiastic wiggle of her scruffy little tail.

'You can wiggle that all you like, you dirty little twat,' fired Zoe. 'You'll be getting no fucking change here, buster.' She grabbed the puppy and sat on the bed turning the dog on its back in between her own legs. 'Sexual predator, eh? I'll predator ya, you mucky little fucker. Who d'ya think y'are, Jimmy bastard Saville?'

Oblivious to the gravity of the situation, Princess yapped and wagged and licked and squirmed. The evidence was obvious. A small, tightly packed package of maleness. Princess had turned out to be a Prince.

'Princess?' muttered Zoe shaking her head. 'What a fucking prat.'

Both parents agreed that Princess could no longer share the attic bedroom with their daughter, and, for a while, they were as discontented as any family could be in the whole of East Moor Park.

*

The meal of pizza and wine went some way to calming down the tensions that had befallen the small family over the Princess shenanigans. Phil had accepted Sally's offer of two bottles of wine in payment for the work, but felt it best to keep the details of the transaction away from Zoe, for the time being anyhow, as it looked as though he'd gone the extra mile in purchasing two bottles instead of just the one.

However, the anticipated avalanche of brownie points never materialised. They ate in silence. Zoe's eyes shifted towards Phil as she tackled a floppy section of meat feast pizza. Only when her gaze shifted back towards the TV did Phil return the gesture and slyly glared back.

'What time will you be back tonight?' asked Zoe without moving her head.

'Dunno, about twelvish.'

'Well, can you make sure you're quiet when you come to bed? I'm sick and tired of you waking me up every night with your grunting an' groaning and clattering about.'

'I don't grunt and groan,' defended Phil.

47

'Well, I say you do, especially when you're half-cut and stumbling up the stairs.'

'No I don't,' insisted Phil.

'You do,' pressed Zoe.

'Don't.'

'Aw grow up and just be quiet when you come home... bloody baby.'

Phil expressed no interest in continuing the dead-end passage of conversation and remained silent.

'And another thing,' said Zoe unable to hold back the impulse now that she was on a roll.

''Ere we go,' said Phil with a sigh. 'What now?'

'Can you start washing your hands when you come home from work cos I'm sick of having to go round and clean your grubby prints from the walls and doors?'

'It's always the first thing I do when I get in. What you on about?' replied Phil.

'All in the kitchen, on the fridge, the living room walls, on the banister, all over.'

'No I don't,' insisted Phil.

'Well, I'm saying you do cos I've got to clean it up,' pressed Zoe. 'Just wash your hands when you come home – it's not rocket science.'

Another period of uneasy silence ensued. Zoe again fired a glance over at Phil as she finished the last morsel of pizza. He stared straight ahead towards the TV. She looked away and then looked back.

'Can you hear the music?' she asked.

'Music, what music? What you on about?'

'Music – I can sometimes hear it, day or night, in the distance sort of, not clear but... Have you heard owt?'

'No not really.' He reached over for the remote and pressed the mute button. Both listened for five or six seconds. Stillness. The cackling of the resident magpie broke the silence as it swooped down onto the road directly outside the living room window. 'I can't hear owt,' said Phil looking towards Zoe.

'No, neither can I,' she conceded quietly. 'But sometimes even in 'middle of 'night I can hear it...from far off...when I get up for the toilet and even during the day when I'm sat in the room and it's quiet. I can hear it.'

'Well, according to you there's plenny o' weirdos living round here, so it could be anyone. All the houses are back-to-backs, so it could be coming from anywhere. Don't worry about it, love, it'll be nowt.'

'I'm not worried. It's just a bit strange, that's all. It must be some poor sod either pissed up or drugged out of their minds playing sad music at all hours.'

'Sad music? Why is it sad? What kind o' music is it?' asked Phil.

'I don't know if it is sad but...maybe because it sounds so far off it just sounds sad,' said Zoe, deciding against admitting to Phil that the music she thought she'd been hearing sounded much like the stuff he'd played on the portable record player that first day in the house.

'Here,' Phil offered with a sigh, 'have a top up.' He reached over and filled Zoe's glass with the cheap red wine he'd 'purchased' from Sally's. 'Well, I can't hear owt. Maybe it's just someone who has their tellys on all night and day. Don't worry, love. We won't be here for the rest of us lives. It's just a stepping stone – a couple of years, and we'll be moving on. It's already worth more than what we paid.' Phil grinned, his beaming smile softening the uneasy disposition which lay rife in the little sitting room.

'Hmm...' she replied.

*

It was only a couple of days after the Princess debacle that Zoe and Sophia arrived home from school to find Phil outside the house on all fours, facing the underside of the living room window with a tape measure at hand. It was a fine and warm late September afternoon.

'What yer doing, love?' she asked.

'Ah, you might well ask,' he replied. 'Hi, sweetie, had a good day at school?' he said to Sophia as he stood up to kiss her on the cheek.

'Yes, Daddy. Look what Mum got me.' she said holding up a white chocolate ice cream.

'Oohh. Did she get me one?' asked Phil.

'Ha, ha. No, only me!' The little girl laughed. 'What you doing, Daddy?'

'Well, look here, love,' he said, turning back to Zoe. 'Look at all the other houses in the street and then look at ours and tell me what you see.'

'Eh?'

'Go on. Just look up and down the street and then look at ours.'

'I dunno,' Zoe replied, surveying first their row of houses and then the opposite row before re-scrutinising their own property. 'They all look the same to me. Just a row of houses. What am I supposed to be looking at?'

'Well, look at our front room window against next door's front room window, for instance.'

'Yeah, well what about it?'

'Well, look underneath both windows and what have you got?' continued Phil.

'Ah, I see,' said Zoe. 'They've got a window going under the path, and we haven't... So what?'

'We haven't now, but once upon a time we did. Look, it's been bricked up.'

'Oh yeah. OK...well... So what?'

'Well, it's a cellar window. I've spoken to a couple of the neighbours, and they all have cellars. Look, all of 'em have either got the original windows in place or they've been bricked up like ours. So we must have a cellar! I never even thought of having a cellar, but we must have one.'

Zoe remained bemused and wondered what all the fuss was about. Sophia became bored and wandered inside to find Princess.

'And look here,' continued Phil. 'See this metal grate thing here. It's stuck and rusted up now, but years ago it would've just lifted up and they'd pour the coal down there, into a cellar.' He couldn't contain his excitement.

'Well, I'm not bothered about a cellar, Phil. They're usually mucky an' full of spiders anyway. Who wants a bloody cellar?'

'Me! I could tank it out and make a games room for me and the lads, or a music room, or a playroom for Sophes – it'll be great. Look, come inside, I'll show you.'

Zoe tutted and sighed but followed into the living room to appease him.

'Look,' he said as he opened up his tape measure. 'Hold this against the back wall.' Zoe did as she was told. Phil then extended the tape to the front door casing. 'That's fifteen foot nine inches,' he said. 'Now, come into the kitchen.' Again, he asked Zoe to hold the end of the tape against the back wall whilst he reached over the sink to the windowsill. 'Thirteen foot three inches! That's a two foot six difference, which is exactly the width of the staircase. There must have been a doorway right there leading down into a cellar!' he said, pointing to the back wall where the American-style fridge-freezer stood, the one Zoe had always wanted. 'What do you think?'

Zoe shrugged her shoulders. 'Well, OK, I think you must be right, but you're not thinking of knocking it through, are you? We've only just decorated the place.'

'Too right I am, me old flower,' he said. 'An extra room down there can double us living space. Just think, all that extra space. I can do it out no problem. The thought of a cellar never even entered my mind.' He shot out of the door and began rummaging around in the back of the van. He couldn't wait. He was like a deranged chicken let loose in the store rooms of Gritland Emporium Inc.

Zoe shook her head and ghosted upstairs to the sanctuary of her bedroom – it was all too much for her.

Fifteen minutes later, and after much banging and clattering, came a holler of triumph from the excitable Phil. 'Zoe! Zoe! Come and look… I was right, there is a stairway, look!'

Zoe, unable to find sanctuary in the bedroom, had already returned downstairs and wandered into the kitchen. 'What?' she fired.

'Come here, look,' cried Phil. There was now a hole the size of a fist which had been knocked through the back kitchen wall. An original cellar-head doorway had been blocked up in lightweight concrete blocks, so it hadn't been difficult for Phil to drive a lump hammer straight through it. 'Look, love, you can even see the old light switch on the wall.' He passed Zoe a small torch.

She peeped through the hole to see an old Bakelite switch almost directly opposite with a void of around two and a half feet between the existing back kitchen wall and the original party wall, which separated theirs from the property that backed onto it. She could see the newly revealed brickwork that had been whitewashed at some stage. 'Ugh!' she cried. 'There's a right draft coming from down there, and it stinks.' She turned to Phil and handed him the torch. 'I don't like it, and I hope you're gonna clear all this mess up.'

'Yeah, I will, love,' gushed Phil. 'But I'm gonna take it down first.'

'When? Now?'

'Yeah, why not? It'll only take me half an hour now I've got a start. I'll get all the crap into the van and clear it all up so you don't have to worry about owt.'

'Oh fuck this. I'm off to me mother's,' she said. 'I'm not hanging around here with all this mess. It's ridiculous, Phil. Just look at it already, and there'll be just a big hole in me kitchen. Why don't you wait while the weekend?'

'Cos I'm away at the weekend, that's why. And in any case, I'm doing it now. I can't wait – there could be owt down there. Why don't you just go get some fish 'n' chips for tea while I crack on? Then after we can go down and explore,' Phil replied, grinning.

Zoe knew that her resistance, in this instance, was pointless. So, with a shake of her head, she picked up her handbag, popped on her jacket and headed off to East Park Fisheries to collect dinner.

By the time she returned, Phil was still busy carting the spoil from the kitchen into the back of the transit. 'That's the last, love. Just got to give it a quick sweep now.'

Zoe entered the kitchen, which was now full of dust. A displaced American-style fridge-freezer and a ragged, gaping hole the size of a small doorway dominated the tiny room. The original brickwork of the party wall was now fully exposed, revealing flaking whitewash paint. A constant draught filtered aloft, along with a stagnant odour that seemed to fill the whole of the ground floor.

Phil's enthusiasm was unrelenting. 'I haven't been down yet, love. I wanted us to do it together,' he said. 'We'll take a look after tea, OK? Are you excited?'

Zoe didn't bother to reply. She decided their meal would be eaten direct from the cardboard trays, and with fingers, thus avoiding any preparation or washing up from within the kitchen area.

Sophia's delicate nature had meant that she showed no interest in the 'smelly' cellar, pronouncing that she 'didn't like it'. Even Princess cowed against the mess and mayhem preferring to stay safe and curled up in his basket.

Phil golloped down his food as the family ate in silence. Once he'd finished, he jumped up. 'Right, c'mon then, love. Let's go see us new cellar. I've got us both a torch. Are you ready?'

'I don't even wanna go down there,' replied Zoe. 'You go down.'

'Aww come on. Here, take this,' he said, handing Zoe the larger of the two torches, as if that would offer superior protection against whatever it was they were about to discover.

'Come on.'

Zoe got to her feet, reluctantly grabbed the torch and slowly followed Phil into the kitchen.

'Are you ready?' he asked, but before she could answer there was a knock at the door.

'Who the fuck's that?' said Zoe shaking her head.

'I dunno, just answer it,' he replied, eager to embark on the exciting underground expedition.

Zoe opened the door and was shocked to see the middle lad and the middle lass from The Bottom House Kids.

Grubby and unkempt, the middle lad looked up at Zoe and smiled. 'Can Sophia come out to play, Mrs Cooper?'

'No!' she replied in a curt and brusque manner.

'OK, thank you.' The boy smiled as Zoe slammed the door shut.

'That was a bit harsh, love. They're only kids,' said Phil.

'I've told you before, I don't want Sophia messing about with that lot. Anyway, never mind that. Are you gonna go see this cellar or what? Cos if you are, get going. I an't got all night – I've gotta life to lead.'

Phil shook his head but walked back into the kitchen and entered the gaping doorway, carefully stepping onto a stone landing area at the top of a small flight of worn stone steps. He flashed the torch downwards and could see the basement below. He began to descend the stairs.

Zoe followed cautiously, aiming the beam of the torch directly where her next step would be and placing her free hand on Phil's shoulder. She looked above at the underside of the stairway, which was strewn with webs and age-old muck.

The temperature dropped and the pungent air increased in concentration as they reached the bottom. Phil flashed the light in all directions trying to make sense of the subterranean time capsule that now lay before them. Neither spoke. The ceiling was low, and the floor was of earth and scattered cinder – probably as it had been for a hundred and odd years. Zoe felt for Phil and grabbed onto his T-shirt.

'Wow!' said Phil. 'Look at this.'

'It's horrible,' replied Zoe.

'What's horrible about it? Look here, this little offset room is directly under the kitchen, and up there where you see daylight is where that little metal grate thing is next to the path. This bit must be where they got the coal delivered – look.' He shone the torch towards the ground and, indeed, particles of coal and dust covered the far corner. The tiny room was empty apart from what Phil suggested was the original door to the cellar-head, which looked to have been dumped there many years ago. 'What do you think, love?' asked Phil.

'I don't think owt,' replied Zoe. 'It's cold, damp and it stinks. I don't like it.'

'You will, when I've finished with it.' He swung around to the right and entered the main area of the cellar taking bold strides into the centre before bumping his hip against a hard, immovable object. 'Ow!'

'What is it?' said Zoe.

'Aww look, it's one of those stone table things,' said Phil as he lit up the object with his torch. A large table-sized slab of stone, at least four inches thick, stood solid in the middle of the room. It was waist high and supported at both ends by rough coursed brickwork. 'It's like an all-purpose workbench. They probably cut meat up and made cheese on it or summat, I dunno.'

'Made cheese? It looks more like a mortuary slab,' said Zoe. 'It's fuckin' horrible.'

'Oh look, what's this?' He picked up a small piece of dust-covered card from the table. He turned it over. 'Look, it's a photo of an old woman and a young lass. I wonder if they used to live here?'

Zoe offered no interest.

'Shelves,' said Phil, dropping the photograph back

onto the slab and moving on, oblivious to his partner's negativity.

There were two rows of empty timber shelves supported by rusted cast-iron brackets running the full length of the room directly under the fireplace in the living room above. The remainder of the walls were covered in various rusting hooks, brackets and iron rings.

Phil shone the torch along the wall, ceiling and floor before something caught his eye in the opposite corner. 'What's that?' he said, striding over to further investigate a small article which lay glinting in the torchlight amongst the dust and crushed cinder base.

'Don't you leave me, Philip Cooper,' said Zoe, clinging on for all she was worth whilst shuffling along behind him.

He crouched down to pick up a small shiny object half covered in grit and grime. 'Look, love,' he said as he slowly lifted the object to reveal a thin silver chain and, as it was carefully pulled through the debris, a small cross attached to it. 'Ha, ha, look, it's a cross. It looks silver, love. Here, d'ya want it?' he said whilst closely scrutinising it.

'No I don't,' returned Zoe. 'What's a bloody cross doing down here? I don't want it, no. It's creepy, put it back.'

'I'm not putting it back. I'll keep it – might be worth summat,' he said as he stuffed it into his trouser pocket. He swung around to his left and shone the torch onto the area below where the living room window was. Even Phil was shocked at the sight that lay in front of them, shocked enough to trigger a faltering step backwards. 'Whooah! What the fuck!' he cried.

'What the fuck is that?' shrieked Zoe, immediately slinking behind Phil, her grip on his T-shirt tightening as she cowered in the shadows.

Stunned and shocked, the couple stood in disbelief before the rationale in Phil's mindset finally kicked in. He sighed. 'It's just an armchair, love, calm down,' he said, still reeling from the initial shock. 'It's a big bugger, though… I'll give you that. But it's just an old leather armchair, just sat there in the dark… Wow…look at it… it's a right beast.'

'It's bleedin' horrible,' blurted out Zoe. 'Fuck this, I'm off.' She released her grip on the T-shirt and shuffled towards the stairs using the jerking beam of the torch as a guide.

'Aww…come on, love, just—'

But before he could finish, she'd already scuttled halfway up the steps before turning the corner at the top and disappearing from sight.

Phil took a step forward to inspect the armchair which had obviously sat untouched and unseen for many years. 'How the hell did this thing get down here?' he said to himself quietly. 'Couldn't have got down the narrow steps, and not on your nelly could it have come through the window.' He mulled over the ambiguity.

The sound of Phil's heavy work boots scrunched on the cinder and echoed around the silent chamber. The dried-out dark leather of the armchair was a fusion of splits and cracks with encrusted segments peeling and curling off at odd angles, almost sharp to the touch. It looked to Phil as if the chair had been fashioned with different types of leather, of differing quality, textures and colours. It was covered in a thick layer of dust and grunge with one of the arms and half of the backrest ripped open revealing rusting springs and original horsehair stuffing. The brass studs that would have once perforated the front of the chair in strict formation were now tarnished, loosened and in disarray. The padding to the seat cushion was worn and compacted, lacking lustre and vigour. The musty smell of ancient leather combined with the essence of rotting timbers and fibres gave the impression of a faraway ancient time and age. A time and age unfamiliar to modern-day East Moor Park. A time and age when, perhaps, circumstances had been different.

*

Phil had bought new light bulbs from Sally's, one for the cellar-head and one for the central light above the stone slab in the middle of the cellar. Zoe refused to go 'down there' in order to see the room in this new light, in spite of Phil's insistence. He saw the cellar as an opportunity for renovation: he saw the walls plastered and painted; he saw the room carpeted and kitted out with modern furniture; and he saw warmth and laughter, a place where the family could make happy memories.

Zoe had an alternative vision. She could see only darkness, the unknown, coldness and damp. Never were the opposites of optimism and pessimism highlighted so starkly in the way this couple looked upon the newly discovered and mysterious little vault lying directly beneath their own sitting room.

Even in the bright, harsh light, the leather chair still created an austere and ominous spectacle. Phil inspected it. He moved it to find nothing but debris, stuffing and fragments of rotted rope and rusted chain links underneath and behind. He prodded it and poked it, he stroked it and sniffed it and even sat on it.

He mulled over forcing his fingers down the back crevice of the cushion but thought better of it – his imagination presenting all manner of beasties and creatures lying in wait to pounce. Instead, he took a screwdriver and scraped it along gouging out decades worth of grime, grease and grit.

With his senses on high alert, his finely tuned hearing detected the soft sound of metal upon metal. He assumed he'd run across one of the metal studs, some of which were lying loose and stranded on the earthen floor. Forcing the screwdriver further, the slight resistance eventually gave way to release a heavily soiled, rounded, flat object. He picked it up and rubbed it between his fingers. It was a dirt-encrusted coin. Placing it in the palm of his hand, he spat on it. After rubbing it further, he discovered that he was holding an old shilling coin. He wiped it dry on his T-shirt and lifted it to eye level for further analysis.

'ONE SHILLING. FID DEF. 1953.' He turned the coin over. 'ELIZABETH II DEI GRATIA BRITT OMN REGINA.' He shouted for Zoe. 'Hardly gonna set the British Museum alight, but a find's a find,' he said quietly to himself before shoving it into his pocket along with the silver chain and cross he'd found earlier.

*

With Phil out of the house and on his way to yet another jolly boys' evening out, *buzzin'* with the lads at the Devon, Zoe's mood began to deteriorate. Her eyes were fixed to the TV and the on-screen adventures of the cast of *Game of Thrones*, but her mind was possessed by the sight of the battered armchair amongst the shadows of the dark cellar.

With Sophia tucked up in bed and Princess in his basket, she was, in effect, on her own in a house she didn't really want to be in. She stood up, wandered towards the kitchen door and peered over to the plywood boarding now blocking the opening to the cellar-head. A tingle ran up the back of her neck before the bifolding door was hastily rammed closed, shutting away the scene, closing it off, out of sight.

She slumped down onto the sofa and looked towards the living room window and the floor area directly beneath. Again, she mulled over the leather armchair. She imagined the individuals who had used the chair in years gone by. She pondered their existences, contemplated their everyday issues and problems. She envisaged the clothes they wore, their personalities, habits and idiosyncrasies. Married with children or lonely eccentrics? Good or bad? Sincere or cunning? Her head was filled with dread. Rational thought was not the way in which Zoe made sense of the world around her.

Picking up her iPhone, she pressed the on button. Ten to nine. She sat back down on the sofa and thought about the cross and the shilling attempting, but failing, to visualise the cellar as Phil had tried to describe it – with light and happiness, laughter and love. She couldn't. A mental block.

She picked up her iPhone again. Nine o'clock. Suddenly there was the sound of a car pulling up and the subsequent stark honking of a horn in the cool night air. She jumped up and ran towards the window to peel back the curtains. A gleaming black BMW 3 series stood outside, blacked-out windows, engine purring. It was a visit she had been expecting.

CHAPTER 3

July 1975

'Miss! Miss! Will you tell Wally Jackson?'

'Tell 'im what? Why, what's he doing?'

'He's picking on me, Miss. He won't leave me alone. He keeps pushing me.'

'Well, stop teasing him, then.'

'I'm not, Miss, honest.'

'Y'are. I've been watching you... You and that Danny Smith... If ya get thumped, then it'll be your own fault. Now go on, away wi' ya.'

'Aww... Miss—'

'Away wi' ya, I said, go on.'

A disgruntled Master Spink scowled as he retreated to his pal Danny where, between them, they began plotting the next move in their ceaseless onslaught to displace the affable nature of the oversized Wally.

The playground was buzzing with the reverberations of two hundred children enjoying the freedom of their lunchtime break. They were being supervised by Susan Wilson, employed part-time by All Saints Junior and Middle School, as a dinner lady and one of four regulars. There were three dinner ladies on duty at any one time and on this warm, cloudless summer day, Mrs Lowry's and Susan Wilson's tour of duty took in the larger top playground, which catered for all but the very youngest of students.

It was almost the end of the school year as they marshalled the gravelled playground from opposite corners, occasionally being drawn into the middle to convene over unofficial tribunals and preside over minor playground misdemeanours and skirmishes. The single-storey school was barely five years old, replacing the old All Saints Church of England School, which had been central to the close-knit, working-class neighbourhood for well over a hundred years. The new school had been built on land reclaimed by the slum clearance of terraced back-to-back housing and was adjacent to the busy A64 York Road on the edge of the East Moor Park district.

Two 10-year-old girls ran towards Susan Wilson, their favourite dinner lady, each grabbing and hugging one of her arms. She looked down at the two youngsters and offered a coerced smile, her forlorn expression lost on her doting charges. No words were spoken.

A group of four or five boys formed a lateral line with arms around each other's shoulders as they meandered around the playground to the boisterous chant of 'All-join-on-to-the-little-boys-gang! All-join-on-to-the-little-boys-gang!' Groups of girls honed their cartwheeling techniques on the grassy verge in front of the caretaker's bungalow. Others practised handstands against the wall at the rear of the detached science block. The oldest boys played the more vigorous game of British Bulldog, where participants ran from one end of the playground to the other, the aim to avoid being tagged. The tagged were converted to reluctant taggers until the last man standing was declared the winner. 'All-join-on-to-the-little-boys-gang!' came the chant from the expanding convoy of meandering youngsters as they strayed into the path of Mick Dixon, a robust school rugby league player who was attempting to escape the clutches of his teammate John 'The Rock' Ryder.

'Get out o' 'fucking way, ya doylems!' (idiots), growled Dixon. But it was too late, his conversion to a tagger was duly rubberstamped as The Rock grabbed him by the collar of his grey school shirt and swung him around by the neck. 'Cunts!' he snarled, firing a menacing glare towards his clumsy, younger subordinates.

'Miss, Michelle Cannon's showing all the lads her knickers, Miss,' puffed a red-faced eleven-year-old as he ran straight up to Susan Wilson and stood facing her with upturned palms.

'Good for her,' replied Susan Wilson.

'Mii-iss...she's showing everything she's got,' he replied with hands now firmly clamped to his hips.

'Well, ya shouldn't be looking then, should ya? Now go on, away wi' ya.'

'Aww Miss,' replied the diminutive whistle-blower. Although his dismay at the failed attempt to tarnish the integrity and reputation of the young Miss Cannon was short-lived, he immediately spun away, jumped upon the back of an unsuspecting classmate and screamed into his ear, 'Ey, Jenno, d' y' wanna see Michelle Cannon's knickers?'

Jenno replied in the affirmative, and, with widened eyes, the pair sprinted towards the rear of the science block and out of view.

Susan Wilson remained unmoved and shook her head. She took comfort from the affection shown from 'her' children who were oblivious to the turbulence that ran amok inside her head. She appeared much older than her twenty-seven years, with drawn and tired features and a posture more befitting that of a fifty-five-year-old. There was no sparkle in her grey eyes, no joy or happiness.

She stood in her corner of the playground with an orange headscarf tied tightly under her chin and, despite it being a warm summer's day, she wore a tired anorak and cheap slip-ons. Her narrow shoulders stooped forwards, laden with unseen, sullied merchandise. Just two months after the unplanned birth of her six-year-old daughter, the father had done one; life had been a struggle ever since.

The only family she could turn to when things got really bad had been her mother and stepfather, but even this, her only source of support, had been taken away under tragic circumstances just a few weeks earlier. With the burden of parental responsibilities and little income, she was acutely aware of her descent down the slippery slope of desperation and doom, with little prospect of an upturn in fortunes. The comfort and love gleaned from her 'schoolchildren', her second family as she looked upon them, was invaluable to her during this testing and turbulent period. Her own daughter stood in the furthest, most secluded corner of the school grounds, subdued, alone and friendless.

'Miss,' shouted a particularly vociferous young student. 'What are the coppers 'ere for?'

'What coppers?'

'There, look,' he continued, pointing towards the wrought-iron entrance gates, which fronted onto Pontefract Lane, and from which a driveway stretched up to the school car park and reception block. 'What do they want?'

She turned around to see a police car roll up the drive and come to a halt in front of the school steps.

The vocal young student ran towards the edge of the playground to get a closer look.

'Ey, come here, you,' said Susan Wilson. 'It's nowt to do wi' you lot...'

The two girls released their grip on the dinner lady and followed the vociferous student which, in turn, attracted even more children.

By the time Susan Wilson had reached the edge of the playground, there was a small group of kids straining necks, ears and eyes. There was nothing to see.

Two uniformed police officers slipped out of the car, climbed the five school steps, pushed open the glass doors and continued into the reception block out of sight.

'C'mon, you lot, get back to the playground,' yelled Susan Wilson. 'There's only ten minutes to the bell, so you'd better make the most of it.'

'You can't tell us what to do,' shouted John Pollard, a slightly cross-eyed and bespectacled eleven-year-old. 'You're not a teacher.'

'Away wi' ya,' she continued. 'Any more chelp from you, lad, and you'll be going straight to Mr Harris – and you know what 'appened last time.'

'Humph,' replied the tearaway, but he took note of the warning in any case, twisting away not wishing to push his luck any further.

The crowd gradually dispersed in accordance with Susan Wilson's instructions.

Conscious that the lunchtime period was rapidly coming to a close, the children continued to play, laugh, mock and run in seemingly uncoordinated lines and circles.

A cluster of gleaming white gulls circled and soared

through the vastness of the blue skies, like a cast of graceful airborne ballerinas, their distant screeching audible to only the most attentive over the vibrant buzz of the playground.

The little boys' gang reconvened and continued their recruitment push. The girls resumed their quest to fine-tune their gymnastic routines. And the older boys knuckled down to their hearty, full-bloodied activities. It was a happy playground. Most wore a smile and engaged themselves in unashamed laughter and enjoyment, content and safe within the security of the local community school. Just one rogue cloud hung over just one corner of the playground where stood just one Susan Wilson.

Her wait for Mr Gomersal, the deputy head, which would spell the end of her shift and duties for the day, was duly upon her. At a quarter to one, with timely precision, he entered the playing arena.

Dressed immaculately in full suit, collar and tie, he stood tall with chest expanded and arms held firmly behind his back. With an unnerving manner, he cast his eye across the landscape like a radar encompassing every moving object, every living being, every sight and sound.

A discernible drop in the volume descended over the playground. But instead of the usual military drill of hustling the students into line amidst vigorous whistle blowing, he sought out and slowly walked towards Susan Wilson.

The children watched as he placed his hand on her shoulder and leant over to speak to her behind a cupped hand.

She stared intently as the deputy head conveyed his message before he nodded and lightly patted her arm.

They parted, walking in opposite directions, with Susan Wilson trudging her way to the general office in the reception block.

Mr Gomersal rubbed his hands at the prospect of organising the rabble that presented themselves before him. He relished the task.

*

Susan Wilson looked a worried woman as the young WPC led her into interview room number six at the newly opened state-of-the-art Milgarth Police Station. Situated on the outer edge of Leeds city centre, it stood in the shadow of the huge grey edifice of the once revolutionary, but now crumbling, Quarry Hill flats. The colossal seven-storey frontage to the flats, known locally as the 'Great Curve', stood sentinel over and dwarfed the architecturally monotonous red-bricked police headquarters. The HQ would later undergo structural reinforcement in order to hold the sheer weight of paperwork and case files as Peter Sutcliffe gave northern police constabularies the runaround during the Yorkshire Ripper murders.

For now, it was just a single folder and the name of Susan Wilson that focused the attentions of DS Bob Manley and DC Barry Taylor. The smell of new paint and industrial quality carpet along with brand new furniture and fittings were not perceived by Susan Wilson. She saw only narrow, oxygen-sapping corridors of sinister authority. The WPC left the interview room and closed the door behind her.

'Thanks for coming, Susan. Sit down, love, and don't look so worried. We've just got a few questions we'd like you to help us with in connection with an ongoing enquiry,' said DS Manley, a slightly overweight, clean-shaven and smartly dressed forty-odd-year-old.

Susan Wilson obediently sat down opposite the two detectives, an empty table separating the occupants of the room. Her eyes fleetingly scanned the two burning pairs in front of her before fixating them onto the tabletop. Her palms and wrists were clammy, and large red blotches began to manifest on her slender neck and throat. Her heart pounded as she placed her shopping bag on the floor beside her. 'Why…what's up?' she asked, her thin fingers shaking like a Rizla paper in a windstorm.

'Well, just calm down, Susan,' continued DS Manley. 'My name's Detective Sergeant Bob Manley, and this is my colleague, Detective Constable Barry Taylor. It's about your stepdad, George Wilson.'

'George? What about him? What's up with him?'

'We just need to ask you a few questions about him.'

'What questions?' she replied, rolling the drawstrings of her anorak between forefingers and thumbs.

'Well, we'd like to know a bit more about him. About your relationship with him. About the last time you saw him, you know, that kind of thing.'

'Well…is he all right?' she asked.

Both detectives stayed quiet. Both stared intently at the nervous interviewee. DC Taylor's grim, laser-like stare cut directly through to her innermost raw emotions.

'When was it you last saw him, Susan?' continued the detective sergeant after a brief pause. 'We need you to help us, Susan. Where was he when you last saw him?'

She hesitated. Her mind was numb. It wasn't that long ago that she'd been shocked to the core at the discovery of her dead mother, sitting upright, on the settee. She'd only been buried three weeks since, and now they were questioning her over her estranged and missing step-father. 'I've absolutely no idea,' she said looking at DC Taylor.

The granite-faced detective gave away nothing other than a cold, hard stare.

She looked back to DS Manley, whom she considered the kinder of the two officers because of his slightly less fierce countenance. 'Er...about two months ago. I don't know... Summat like that. He doesn't even know about me mam yet. I don't think he does, anyway. No one's seen him,' she said whilst wiping the palm of her hand across her moistening forehead. Her gaze flicked from interrogator to observer and back to interrogator. There was no reaction to gauge.

'You've just lost your mam, haven't you?'

'Yeah, I think it was at me mam's when I last saw him, a few weeks before she died... I suppose... I think.'

'You'll have to be more specific than that, Susan. We need to know the exact date and time. Where exactly was he when you last saw him? We need the truth, Susan. What frame of mind he was in? I understand he and your mother didn't get on too well. Is that right?'

'Well, they'd split up just before she died... She kicked him out...'

'Why did she kick him out?'

'I don't know. She wouldn't say... Just that they hadn't been getting on...'

'Do you get along with him, Susan?'

'Yeah, he's allus been all right wi' me. A bit quiet, but...'

'What state of health was he in, Susan? What state of mind were you in, Susan, when you last saw him, at your mother's, you say? You haven't been well, have you?'

'What d'ya mean? What's that supposed to mean? Is he all right or what? What's up with him? What's happened?'

'That's what we need to find out, Susan. What happened to him?'

'I-I don't know what you're on about... What? What do you want me to say? I'm bad wi' me nerves. I don't know what you want from me.'

'We need the truth, Susan. We're not messing about, love. This is serious. We need you to identify a body.'

CHAPTER 4

April 1975

'Well, I'd better be getting off now, Mam. 'Bus is due... Are you sure you're all right?' asked a concerned Susan Wilson as she emptied half a mug of weak tea into a sink full of dirty crockery. 'You don't look too good to me. C'mon, you,' she said, holding a hand out to a subdued little girl, her six-year-old daughter, who'd spent the previous night at her grandparents' back-to-back at 10 Reginald Street in East Moor Park.

'Yeah, I'm all right, love,' replied Stella, her breathing slightly laboured. 'A bit o' fresh air and I'll be champion. Don't you be worrying... It's a bit of a cold, that's all.'

Susan Wilson looked down at her mother and gently shook her head. 'Go and give your nanna a kiss,' she said, lightly pushing the girl forward.

The girl walked towards her grandmother with her head bowed avoiding eye contact, but she still received a warm hug and a kiss to her cheek.

'See you next week, me lovely. I'll have *The Dandy* and *Beano* ready for you when you come... All right, sweetheart? And some pop and crisps.' Her voice was hoarse but nevertheless laced with a genuine love for her granddaughter.

With arms hanging loosely by her side, the girl stood

motionless staring at the floor, offering only the slightest of nods.

'And yer granddad,' urged Susan Wilson.

The girl remained steadfast facing her grandmother.

'What about Granddad George? Go on, give him a hug, and 'urry up cos we've got a bus to catch.'

The girl slowly turned and walked towards her grandfather.

He softly embraced her. 'Right y'are, love, see you next week,' he said in his quaint, high-pitched tone. He cupped her flushed cheeks in his large rough hands and kissed her on the forehead.

His tender smile was disregarded as the girl remained unresponsive. She stared down at the cheap, floral-patterned carpeting in the tiny living room and didn't budge an inch.

Susan Wilson tutted and rolled her eyes. 'Bloody hell, I don't know what's got into her. She's like this all the time. I've got enough on me plate without all this—'

'Oh, she's all right. Aren't you, love?' interjected Stella, her voice deep and rasping as she offered a weak, unreciprocated smile. 'She's just going through one o' them stages, aren't you, me lovely?'

'She's just that way out, that's what it is... Well, she'd better not start wi' me this morning, that's all I can say. I'm at the end of me tether.'

The doting grandparents could see no wrong in what they perceived to be merely the timid mannerisms of their only granddaughter. But after a further passage of uneasy silence, the patience of Susan Wilson had run its course.

'Right, that's it, we're off!' she snapped as she grabbed the girl's arm and bundled her out of the already opened front door. 'Come on, you, out! See you later, Mam... See you next week, George.' She fired a look of disgust as she turned and stormed past the living room window en route to the bus stop, dragging the girl behind her. 'Ungrateful little brat,' she seethed.

'See you later,' replied Stella and George in unison.

Susan Wilson, embarrassed at the lack of interaction her daughter had shown towards her grandparents, walked in short, determined steps gripping her daughter's wrist tightly. 'I don't know what's got into you...ya little bleeder,' she muttered. 'Showing me up like that. I'm sick of it, I'm telling you. They do all sorts for you, and you can't even be civil to 'em or thank 'em for having you. They're your bloody grandparents, for God's sake.'

Through the crimson mists of frustration and anger, Susan Wilson was oblivious to the silver coin, covertly released from her daughter's clenched fist, which silently rolled into the gutter of the newly tarmacked surface of East Moor Drive.

As Susan Wilson continued to scold her daughter, frog-marching her up towards the bus stop, it was no less tense than the frosty ambience back at number 10...

*

Stella sat down on the settee and lowered her head into her hands, rubbing her ashen cheeks and bloodshot eyes. She took several deep breaths.

'Are you ready?' asked George. 'We'd better be setting off – it's nearly half past.'

'Just give us a bloody minute, will you?' snapped his wife as she snatched a packet of Woodbines from the coffee table. 'They've only just gone.' In spite of the shakes, she managed to dock the butt of the cigarette into her dry lips before taking three attempts to light it with the lighter. The first lungful of smoke and toxins immediately steadied her nerves as her shoulders relaxed and her breathing became less erratic.

'I'm just saying,' replied George, 'it's getting late. Have you taken your tablets?'

'Aye! And it's nowt to do wi' you anyway. I keep telling ya. You just keep yoursen out o' my business. I'll take me tablets when I take 'em. It's nowt to do wi' you.'

'Right y'are, love, I'm just saying—'

'Well don't just say. I don't interfere wi' you an' your bloody animals, do I? All that time you spend down there, bloody feeding 'em and clearing the bloody mess up. It stinks to high heaven every time you open the cellar door... Stinks the whole bloody house out... It's nobody's business.'

'All right,' said George, sighing. 'They're not doing you any harm, are they?'

'Doing me any harm? They bloody stink, and I bet the cellar's full o' fleas... You an' them bloody animals... You think more o' them than you do o' me, you do. Bloody rabbits an' ferrets, an' you've started bringing pigeons in now. You'll be fetching bloody pigs home next...'

'It's not a pigeon, love. It's a magpie with a broken—'

'Magpies, pigeons, ducks – they're all the bloody same... Anyroad, whatever it is, I want it out... D' y' hear? Out. Bloody bad luck are birds... Allus have been... You don't have birds in yer 'ouse... Me mother never would. It's bad luck.'

'Right y'are, love... Are we ready yet?'

'I'll right y'are, you,' replied Stella. 'Never mind right y'are. Just keep your nose outta my affairs. I'll take me tablets when I take 'em... Nowt to do wi' 'likes o' you.'

She struggled to her feet and poked her face into a wall mirror positioned above the fireplace. As she crouched over, attempting to straighten her back as best she could, she smeared orange lipstick onto her thin lips and grabbed a headscarf from the settee. 'Pass us me coat,' she ordered.

'Which one?'

'I'm not bothered…just pass us one,' she snapped, continuing to survey her reflection. She saw an old woman, a haggard woman, a sad woman. She saw a woman with eye bags like racing dog's bollocks, with a sallow, sagging complexion. A woman who had once been effervescent, stylish and outgoing. A woman who in times past had relished the prospect of waking up on a morning to face a bright and beautiful world, a world spilling over with endless opportunity. But not now. The days of a vivacious personality and smouldering gorgeousness that had reduced many a potential suitor into a rambling imbecile were a long and distant memory. *And this is where I am now, in East Moor Park, married to a shithouse, and looking and feeling like an old, sad slut.*

'The blue one wants cleaning,' said George.

'Well, give us the other one, then.'

'Well, that's got a stain on it as well.'

'What's wrong with ya? Just give us a bleedin' coat, will ya?'

George handed her the blue coat, a shabby anorak but which, he reasoned, was the less dirty of the two.

Stella fired a sinister glare as she snatched it from him. Both were in their early fifties, although Stella looked fifteen years older and had the posture of an eighty-year-old. She was slight in build, undernourished, and even though she smoked thirty Woodbines a day, her nicotine addiction was hardly her most damaging vice. With the grubby anorak, roughly administered make-up and cheap headscarf, she knew that she'd stick out at church like a nun in a Grimsby drinking pit.

All Saints Church was about a mile walk from Reginald Street, and she knew the score. She knew her station and how her life was slowly dwindling away – out of her control. She knew how she was perceived by the so-called respectable fraternity, but she wasn't giving up yet. She still held the faith. The Church and God were her only salvation; she knew that. It kept her going – that, and the prospect of spending a few hours with her beloved granddaughter once a week.

George was a large, overweight man, a six-footer, who moved in a slow and lumbering manner. Of an easy-going nature, he was softly spoken with a somewhat higher than average pitch of voice, which some thought slightly odd for a man of his size – slightly effeminate. With a balding pate and greying back and sides, he shaved once a week, on a Sunday morning. On church day, he'd don the only suit he owned including collar and tie and Sunday best navy blue raincoat. Well-worn oxblood brogues completed the outfit. However, the smart Sunday exterior was compromised once he opened his mouth or smiled, as his teeth, the few that were still present, were crooked and discoloured. And those unfortunate enough to suffer a face-to-face encounter were engulfed with a repulsive burst of rancid halitosis. Perhaps that was the reason he was known as a man of few words – that, or the oppressive nature of his wife. For the remainder of the week, George dressed less elegantly, as his job, a plumber for British Rail, required the use of heavy work boots, branded donkey jacket and boiler suit. Even the job description of plumber was tenuous because he was predominantly used to clear drains and clean out toilets – in effect, being up to his elbows in shit for most of the working week.

After calling into Jack's paper shop for extra strong mints, the odd couple made their way up the long incline of East Moor Drive towards Pontefract Lane and the 140-year-old stone-built and steeple-towered All Saints Church. They linked arms, not through a close affection for each other, but more as a technique to keep Stella upright as she stumbled her way up the hill. She wiped the perspiration from her forehead and constantly complained about not feeling well.

'I told ya you should've had summat to eat,' George rebuked.

For once the embittered, breathless woman couldn't muster the energy to reply. Her feisty temperament took a back seat as she battled both physical and mental demons in the pursuit of her attendance to the fortnightly Sunday morning service. The damp conditions which hung thickly over East Moor Park that morning provided a grim backdrop to the pitiful sight of Stella Wilson as she staggered up East Moor Drive on the arm of her reluctant husband.

*

With the service at an end, the congregation filed towards the back of the nave. Those with children attending Sunday school turned right and progressed into the small community hall. The remainder turned left through the entrance porch and out into the church grounds. The last thing George wanted, his wife being in such a piteous state, was to dally. So, with his head down, he lumbered up the aisle by her side, keeping quiet.

It was a miracle that Stella had made it through the service. Her forehead had streamed with perspiration with her throbbing skull heavy and cranked up with pressure. With a palate as dry as oven-baked sand, her stomach had churned like a washing machine loaded with evil toxins hell-bent on procuring a premature and malicious exodus.

She'd prayed hard to God that morning that he assign her the strength and fortitude to get through the service. Now she desperately clung onto George as they slowly walked in line past the ancient wooden pews towards the exit. The congregation shuffled its way out against the composition of the organist, who revelled in his attempts to recreate an ecclesiastical masterpiece.

With the irregular tones of the organ pounding in her eardrums, Stella's heart hammered like a steam-fired piston as the congregation bottlenecked. With her personal space and air now compromised, she became crowded in, just as the finishing post loomed. Her prayers were almost answered in full, but not quite. With the large oak doors of the porch now just a few steps away, she lurched in between the last two rows of pews and began violently throwing up.

The organist stopped dead through sheer shock at the intensity of the reverberations echoing around the ancient stone walls. The guttural retching sounded as though derived from the very bowels of the earth, from the larynx of the horned demon of the deep. The procession ground to a standstill as an air of disquiet fell upon the congregation. The vicar and his verger rushed to provide assistance.

'What the devil? Is she all right?' asked an ashen-faced

Father Venables as he stooped over her.

'She'll be fine, Father,' murmured George whilst hovering over the situation, without offering much practical support. He'd been through similar episodes many times before, although not inside a church, their local church, All Saints Church.

Father Venables quickly ordered Mrs Betts to fetch a glass of water as a small cluster of rubberneckers formed, eager to glean a first-hand account of a month's worth of salacious gossip.

The hard-nosed and more dignified continued to file past, ignoring the situation before donating their fortnightly offering of coins and coppers into the collection dish.

Stella was sitting up and breathing heavily by the time Mr Betts returned with water. The violent retching had only produced an evil bile, but the sheer intensity had rendered her semi-conscious. Warm urine stemmed from between the beleaguered woman's legs and dripped onto the worn pine floorboards. The small pool of amber liquid agitated age-old dust particles before seeping through to the very foundations of this ancient house of God.

Whilst Father Venables and Mr Betts fussed over Stella, holding and tapping her hand, George had shuffled his way through the porch and into the church grounds where he gulped at the cold, fresh air. Many offered sympathy and words of comfort; others tendered a compassionate handshake, an arm around the shoulder, a knowing nod. There was little sympathy for the local alcoholic who had besmirched the sanctity of the church, the dishevelled little woman, an embarrassment to the establishment. Straight-faced parishioners filed past her with an unsympathetic shake of the head.

'Look at the state of her now,' muttered one. 'Always was a loose 'un, that one, even in her younger days.'

'A disgrace,' said another. 'What that poor man must be going through...'

'She's as rough as a bear's arse – allus has been,' said yet another with a sniff as the crowd lingered outside the porch awaiting the customary handshake and niceties from Father Venables.

George looked a crushed man as he attempted to take stock of the embarrassing situation he'd been placed in because of his wife. His face was crimson and there was hurt in his eyes as he anxiously planned his exit. His one and only mission now was to get home, as fast as possible.

One onlooker, however, a well-nourished forty-one-year-old widow with large, open eyes and a soft, well-cared for complexion didn't show any empathy towards George. With a tight auburn perm and wearing a black and white checked woollen coat, she silently surveyed the state of affairs. She watched as Father Venables led a trembling Stella out of the church and delivered her back into the hands of her husband. She heard him offer words of comfort and George's muted reply of, 'Right y'are, Father.' She witnessed the vicar as he swiftly and efficiently shed his hands of the matter before attending to the rest of his flock, leaving an overly stressed Mr Betts to clear up the mess inside the church. She quietly observed as Stella faltered her way up Pontefract Lane with her skeletal frame and stooping gait struggling to keep pace with the strong, lumbering stride of George who walked two yards ahead of her. The recently widowed Peggy Bowden, with her tight auburn perm and checked woollen coat, kept her own counsel.

*

It was two days later when Peggy tweaked her net curtains to see George, dressed in work boots, boiler suit and donkey jacket, quietly close his front door behind him and make his way towards East Moor Drive to catch the number 62 circular into town. It was seven a.m. as he shuffled over the road with a duffle bag slung over his shoulder containing a flask of tea and a simple lunch of potted meat sandwiches and a lump of cheddar cheese, both wrapped in toilet tissue. He walked with his usual slow, lumbering gait and wore his usual blank expression.

Once he'd passed her front window, Peggy opened the nets more fully in order to check on the weather. It was her day to use the communal block and pulley washing line, which was strung between the two rows of back-to-backs and shared between four households, one of them being the Wilsons, George and Stella, who lived directly opposite. It was a good drying day with clear skies and a vibrant breeze. She peered into the Wilsons' living room window and saw the hunched figure of Stella ghost past into the kitchen area.

An hour later and Peggy was stood outside her neatly painted house hoisting up the washing line which was fully pegged out with freshly washed linen and towels. She wore a burgundy dressing gown over various layers of undergarments of the type worn by middle-aged women, along with matching slippers – or house shoes, as she referred to them. Her head was festooned in plastic rollers lined up with strict military precision and subsequently covered in a headscarf fastened under her double chin. The boisterous winds animated the spotless white laundry under the crisp East Leeds skies, injecting life and character into the little street of back-to-backs. Terry performed a U-turn at the railway end of the street as he manoeuvred his handheld milk cart with expert ease. He'd now completed his deliveries and was making his way back out towards East Moor Drive. The familiar low hum of the electric motor reverberated around the tiny cul-de-sac as he guided the cart over the cobbled road. The crates and bottles rattled in unison like a troupe of Irish folk dancers.

Peggy tied the line onto the metal cleat and once again looked over to number 10. All was quiet with no discernible activity. She hesitated before resolving to cross the road amidst the gentle flapping of the washing. 'Morning, Terry,' she said as he passed in front of her.

'Good morning, Peggy, my darling,' chirped back the affable milkman, cocking his head to one side and aiming a mischievous wink without breaking stride. 'What an absolutely beautiful day to be out and about.'

Peggy smiled back and nodded. 'Aye, it is,' she said, 'for some, anyway.'

'See ya later, me little beauty,' he replied, grabbing his cap and holding it aloft as he continued on his way.

'Aye, see ya.' She chuckled and held up her arm as she crossed the road to number 10. She hesitated before softly knocking on the tired panelled door and listened for any trace of audible activity from within the house. All was silent. She knocked again, this time a little harder. Then, with folded arms, she took a couple of steps backwards onto the road in order to check out the first-floor windows. Nothing. She gave it one last go, this time hammering on the door with much more gusto. She bent

1 - 9798629989639 - page 84

down and opened the letterbox. 'Stella, it's me, Peggy. Are you in, love?' she bellowed.

After two or three seconds there was a scrambled commotion, accompanied by disgruntled mumblings. She eventually heard the sound of the key being turned, followed by the door opening just wide enough for Stella to peek her head through the gap.

She looked at Peggy narrow-eyed and full of suspicion. 'What's up? What do *you* want?' she croaked, causing Peggy to catch an immediate waft of alcohol in addition to the less than fresh odour that radiated from within the house.

'There's nowt wrong, love. I'm just checking to see if you're all right, that's all.'

'Aye, I'm all right… I'm allus all right… Why shunt I be?'

'Well, I saw what happened on Sunday – you know, at church – and just wondered if everything's all right and if there's owt I can do.'

'I'm all right, but it's nowt to do wi' you or anyone else, is it?' replied Stella. The prospect of a confrontation seemed to energise and sharpen her caustic demeanour.

'No, I know, love. I'm not prying or owt, but…'

'I'd upset stomach, if ya must know,' she said. 'It's them Chinese curries he gets us at 'weekend. Anyroad, I heard y'all carping and—'

'No, love, I didn't—'

'Carping and going on about me. I'm not thick, y'know. I've got ears – I can hear.'

'I know, love, but…I'm just making sure everything's all right, that's all. If there's owt ya need, I'm only over 'road,' said Peggy as she stared deep into her neighbour's eyes. She saw a frightened, hopeless soul, confused and empty.

The momentary intimacy of eye-to-eye contact struck a chord within Stella. Detecting just a sliver of compassion from her neighbour, she pared back on her vitriolic defensive mode. 'Well, I'm all right...but ta for asking. It's not all my fault, y'know...'

'I know, love, I know...don't you think I don't. But locking yourself in the house all day isn't gonna help, is it? Why don't you nip over later for a cup o' tea? If you get time?'

'If I get time, I will...if I get time... All right, thanks... I've gotta go now... Ta-ra.' Stella slammed the door shut leaving Peggy standing alone, looking and feeling a little foolish.

She looked around, but there were no witnesses to the brief encounter with her troubled neighbour. The street was empty. Trudging back over the cobbles and deep in thought, she stalled and briefly looked over her shoulder at the house opposite. She then continued and disappeared into her comfortable little back-to-back.

CHAPTER 5

October 2016

I t had been over a month since Phil had ripped open the back wall of the tiny kitchen to reveal the entrance to a secret cellar. His vision to convert the musty little room into a modern underground playroom had remained just that – a vision.

Work was flying in for Phil, so there'd been no progress on the conversion whatsoever. In fact, he'd only descended the stone steps a handful more times since the discovery. Sophia had taken one cursory peek and decided that she didn't like it, preferring to spend time in the attic bedroom with Princess, her parents having relented in allowing him to share the room after all. Even Princess was apprehensive in and about the kitchen, never venturing anywhere near the cellar-head. Zoe flatly refused to discuss the matter until the work was fully completed, although she had doubts as to whether that would ever happen. She hated the kitchen, forever conscious of the hole in the wall and the cellar beneath, only feeling comfortable in the house when the bifolding door was firmly closed.

Since the episode of the secret cellar had been thrust upon her, there had been a gradual deterioration in Zoe's already temperamental and unpredictable state of mind. She'd striven hard since the move to buy into the vision that Phil had laid out for their family. For his sake, and for that of their daughter, she'd pushed herself, forced herself, to accept her lot and attempt to make the best of things. This last month, however, had seen a marked decline in her mental health.

'You don't look well, love... You all right?' asked Phil whilst peering over the top of his newspaper as he lolled on the sofa.

Zoe was sat in the armchair next to the living room window staring at the blank TV screen continuously playing with the zip on her long-sleeved hoodie. 'Yeah, I'm all right,' she answered after a short pause.

'You sure, love?' persisted Phil. 'You haven't seemed your usual self this last couple o' weeks.'

'Yeah, I'm fine,' she said after another brief pause, continuing to fumble with her zip.

'Why don't you go see the doctor?'

'What do I need to see the doctor for?'

'Well...I'm just saying...y'know.'

Zoe maintained her stare at the TV screen, obliviously pulling her zipper with increasing vigour.

'If you're gonna stare at the telly, love, then we might as well have it on.' He reached over to the coffee table, picked up the remote and pressed the on button. 'And for God's sake stop messing about with that bleedin' zip, will ya? It's driving me mad.'

This brokered a reaction from Zoe, a fleeting cursory glance, but no hint of any expansion on the current interaction.

'I'm just worried, love,' pressed Phil. 'I don't want you ending up...in the same place you were before, that's all.'

This time Zoe reacted more robustly as she turned to face him square on and looked him straight in the eye. This time she gave him her maximum attention. This time the fidgeting with the zip ceased. 'Don't even go there,' she ordered.

'I'm not, love, I'm just concer—'

'Don't!' came the razor-sharp riposte, delivered with the ferocity and accuracy of a sharp, piercing arrow straight into his heart.

Phil's simple, matter-of-fact demeanour and outlook on life was no match for the complex, multifaceted and sometimes hostile psyche of Zoe, but he knew the procedure to follow when those menacing eyes flashed in his direction. That procedure was to keep quiet. He kept calm, but silent, musing over the situation, rubbing his black whiskers and not daring to look Zoe directly in the eye.

She eventually broke the ice-cold silence. 'You out again tonight?'

'Only for a couple.'

'A couple? Huh, you must have had more than a couple last night.'

'Why? I didn't have that many.'

'Mitt prints again – bloody sauce or summat all up the banister and daubed all over the kitchen wall. I got up for a drink and thought you'd been in an accident, and then I saw the kebab carton in the bin,' she said, shaking her head and shooting a sideways glance.

'I don't think I had any sauce or owt—'

'You don't think? You don't know, do you? Cos you were that pissed up, you've no fuckin' idea. You can't even control yourself.'

'I honestly don't know what you're on about, love. Yeah, I remember the kebab, but I didn't have any sauce —'

'Oh, don't bleedin' lie, Phil. You know exactly what

I'm on about because you cleaned it up before you went to work.'

'Eh? What?' he said, half chuckling. 'I haven't cleaned owt up...'

'Well, I didn't clean it up, so you must have.'

'Well, I didn't—'

'You bleedin' well did!'

'I didn't, love, honest,' replied Phil, now in full chuckle mode.

'Ah, I get it. It's all in me head, is it? Like the bloody music that you never hear – that's all in me head, is it? Like you coming in at one in the morning and making a racket dragging your arse all around the house in your pissed-up state – that's all in me head, is it? Like you farting and snoring like a fat, sweating pig every night, keeping me awake – that's all in me head, is it? You need to take a good look at yerself, love, before you start questioning what's going on in my head. If anyone's got a problem in this house, it's you. It's about time you opened your bloody eyes and smelt the shit! *You* go and see the bleedin' doctor.'

Phil sighed and quietly shook his head. He pointed the remote at the TV and pressed the off button. 'Right, just listen, love,' he said. 'You're right, I can hear summat, only faintly, but it's there, can you—'

'Oh, stop taking the piss, Phil. It's Sky bleedin' News from next door. Don't try to be funny.'

'Well, if we can only just hear that and we know it's one of the neighbours with the telly on, then why can't this music you're hearing just be the telly, or the radio, or someone just playing some music at odd hours in the middle of the night?'

'I'm not going over it all again. You're just taking the

piss, as usual. Just forget it and stop trying to be a smart-arse... Anyway, when you gonna sort that cellar out? It's been stood there now for over a month, and it's getting on me friggin' nerves!'

'Well, you know I'm working in Cornwall this weekend, and then I've got two weekends free, so I promise I'll spend them working on the cellar...I promise.'

'Huh, I'll believe it when I see it... You were out last night, you're out tonight, then you're working away all weekend, and I'm stuck here in this hellhole on me own, and you wonder why I go on...'

'Listen, love, I promise... I've got to go out tonight cos it's Andy's birthday—'

'Andy piss flaps! I'm sick of hearing about bleedin' Andy! Last week it were his brother's engagement piss-up, the week before you were out on the piss cos his cat got run over. You'll be out boozing if he changes his knickers next, so don't be giving me Andy's bleedin' birthday. You're pathetic, you really are!'

'Well, it's his thirtieth, love, all the lads are gonna be there.' Phil grinned with the enthusiasm of an excitable teenager. 'We're watching the match, and then we've ordered a kissogram for him in the pool room, but what he doesn't know is that... Listen to this... It's gonna be an old granny!' Phil cackled with delight. 'It's gonna be great. I'm buzzin'...'

'Buzzin'! What are ya, a fuckin' wasp? Shut the fuck up, Phil, and act your bloody age. Buzzin' my arse.'

'Well, all I can say, love, is that once this weekend's out of the way, I'll be making a start on the cellar. Promise. And, wait for this, Andy's gonna give me a hand with the tanking out, so you'll be able to thank him from the bottom of your heart,' replied Phil with a grin.

'I'll thank him fuck all. Don't be bringing that fat drunken bastard home here – I'm telling you now,' replied Zoe. 'Anyway, if you're disappearing out again, I'm off to Sally's for some lager. You can do what you bleedin' want. I couldn't care less.'

'Don't be like that, love,' protested Phil.

But Zoe *was* being like that as she threw on her leather jacket, wrapped a scarf around her neck and stormed out of the house, slamming the door behind her.

Zoe didn't go straight to Sally's. Instead, she took a march down towards the dark and desolate East Moor Park, just a short walk from the house. She paced past the huge angular gable ends of the back-to-backs and then dodged the traffic to cross East Moor Road. The park was empty – no dog walkers, no bored gangs of youths, no loitering weirdos – just her.

Wandering around the deserted playground, she kicked sporadic empty cans and beer bottles as she contemplated her current existence. Slouching on the skewed seat of the solitary swing, she scrutinised a nest of spent needles lying in a hole in the tarmac which had been used as a makeshift fire pit at some stage.

She surveyed the silhouetted terraced housing across the road that loomed up in front of her – one of which now served as her home. The dim illumination given off by the street lights seemed less bright than the lamp posts in Seacroft, the posts themselves less populous. She lamented at how far her life had nosedived since the move.

Zoe had been content living at her mother's. Things hadn't been perfect, but they were preposterously better than her current state of affairs. She didn't like the house, she didn't like the area, she didn't like her neighbours –

and she'd had no input in the choosing of any. Her partner worked almost every day and pissed it up with his mates on an evening whilst the quality of *her* existence deteriorated on a daily basis. These secretive night-time visits to the squalid little park served as her only outlet which, she believed, summed up her whole miserable existence.

*

Back at number 10, Sophia had descended the two staircases from her lofty bedroom to join her father in the living room. Dressed in pink pyjamas and matching dressing gown, she sat on Phil's knee quizzing him with pertinent questions as typical six-year-olds do. Princess completed the snug little trio by curling up on Sophia's lap.

'Daddy?'

'What, love?' replied Phil with one arm around his young daughter but with both eyes fixed firmly on the sports news channel.

'Why is Mum always shouting?'

'Well, sweetheart, she's not well at the moment, and she's just getting used to the new house. Don't you worry your little cotton socks off, love. She'll be OK. We'll all be OK. You, me and your mum…and Princess, o' course.'

'Daddy?'

'What, love?'

'Is it about the cellar room?'

'Well, I don't think she's too happy about that, sweetheart, but I'm starting work on it next week with my friend Andy, so it'll all be good in a few weeks' time, and then she'll be OK.'

'Daddy?'

'What, love?'

'Why does Mum cry at night-time?'

'She'll be all right, love. She's just tired, that's all. Don't worry, we'll sort her out.'

'Is it because you go to the pub with your friends and wake her up when you go to bed when you're drunk?'

'Er...no, love. I'm very quiet when I come home,' answered Phil, glancing down at his daughter. 'And it's not every night I go out with my friends...and I don't always get drunk.'

'Well, I can sometimes hear you banging about at night-time. Sometimes you wake me up as well.'

'OK...well, I'm sorry about that, sweetheart, but I'll try my best to be quiet in future. What else do you hear when I come home on a night?'

'Well, sometimes I hear Princess barking...and you messing about and making a noise.'

'Well, I'll try to be extra quiet from now on.'

'Daddy?'

'What?'

'Who's the old lady that sometimes stands next to my bed?'

Phil stiffened up and stared at his daughter. An ice-cold chill surged the length of his spine. He didn't answer. He just stared at his daughter and tried to look calm. He couldn't answer; he had no answer. Eventually, he fudged the issue. 'You'll just be dreaming, love,' he said in a slightly wavering tone. 'There's no old lady in here.'

'Oh, there is, Daddy. I'm not dreaming. She's nice and she smiles at me,' replied Sophia in her innocent matter-of-fact manner gazing directly into her father's eyes. 'Daddy?'

'What?' he replied sharply.

'Why does Mum call Princess "Jimmy"?'

*

'That'll be nineteen pounds twenty-five, love,' said Sally as he placed a four-pack of lager and two bottles of Chilean Merlot into a plastic carrier bag. 'Everything OK, me sweetheart?' he continued, exercising his best and most sincere bushy-whiskered grin.

Zoe handed over the cash and tendered a weak smile and a slight nod in return, not having the energy to muster up small talk – which, in any case, she reasoned, might develop into a fully fledged conversation. As she waited for the change, the cumbersome Mrs Patel squeezed through the back room door and stood behind the counter facing Zoe. Aw fuck, thought Zoe, this is all I fuckin' need.

'Hello, missus,' said Mrs Patel smiling and firmly locking eyes directly with those of her vulnerable customer. 'Have you settled in, then? Husband tell us about the underground cellar room and how he do it up. He clever man, your husband.'

'Well, he's not that clever cos he's out on the piss again tonight with his scaly mates, in't he?'

'Oh, don't be like that, missus. Your husband is good man—'

'Says who?' fired back Zoe. 'And while we're at it, why don't you keep your fucking nose out o' my fucking business, you interfering old fucking cow? I don't know how he puts up with you, ya silly old bitch,' she snarled, nodding towards Sally. Dumbfounded, Mrs Patel stood silent as Zoe stormed towards the door tapping the side of her nose. 'Fuckin' keep this out, missus!' She exited the shop and slammed the door behind her with such force that the traditional doorbell flew off its bearings and landed on the countertop, just in front of Sally, making him flinch.

He stared at his wife. 'Why can't you keep your mouth shut?' he demanded as he carefully placed the unclaimed change back into the open till.

'Why don't you keep your own mouth shut, mister? And she can pay for damage... She lunatic!'

'I say what goes on in this shop, missus, and I'm telling you to keep your nose out. It's my business. I'm the man of the house, not—'

'Man! Man, you say? Ha, ha, don't make me laugh, mister. I see bigger dick on lollipop stick! Never mind man of house,' retorted Mrs Patel as she turned away and squeezed back through the door into the living quarters beyond. 'Ha, ha... Man, he say...'

Sally looked down at the counter and picked up the damaged shop-door bell. He stayed silent for a brief period of self-reflection before raising his eyebrows. He proceeded to tidy up and reorganise the penny sweet tray.

Having slammed a door behind her for the second time within the hour, an angry Zoe seethed at how that wretched woman could possess the barefaced audacity to interrogate her on such a sensitive and raw issue. 'Silly old bitch,' she chuntered. With head down, she stormed towards home, a tempest brewing within her troubled psyche.

She didn't get far, as within half a dozen steps she'd bundled into an individual, a woman, almost knocking her to the ground.

'Watch where you're going!' she snapped before looking up and receiving a shock that immediately sobered her pent-up anger. Her heart thumped and her face turned ash white.

Within six inches of her stood a shaken but staunch bulbous-eyed, white-haired old woman. *The* bulbous-eyed, white-haired old woman. Eye to eye. Face to face.

With a shock of frizzled white hair and huge globular eyeballs, the neighbour stood firm and delivered an ominous stare.

Zoe's legs trembled as the bravado that had been fuelled by anger and frustration just a few seconds previously had now evaporated. It had been replaced by uncertainty and fear. 'Er...I'm sorry,' said Zoe as she stood aside, maintaining fixed eye contact.

Unflinching and with eyes almost popping out of her darkened eye sockets, the old woman stood silent and glared long and hard into Zoe's eyes. She then waved her arm and brushed her way past before waddling towards the shop entrance and disappearing inside to the dull sound of the shop door banging closed.

Zoe was shaken. Her emotions raged. With head bowed, she quietly and slowly walked the last few yards to what she perceived to be her cold, unwelcoming home.

*

Zoe had been experiencing sleep paralysis at a rate of two or three occurrences per year since she was a teenager. She knew that such encounters were more prevalent when she was run-down, when her resistance was low and when her mind was in turmoil. However, this unnerving experience had begun to occur much more frequently since her move into the house.

They would start with a buzzing sensation from deep inside her head as she began to drift off to sleep. Burning sounds of crackling fire, and metal chains scraping and clanking would follow...and then the whispering would start. It was evil and wicked. She knew this instinctively, deriving from deep inside her ear canal, yet she would feel the sensation of hot breath on her neck and ear. The only word she could ever clearly make out was that of her own name, spoken softly and mocking: *Zoe...Zoe... Zoe...* A shrunken, fully bearded head of an entity would smirk and ridicule in the most intense and personal manner from behind her right ear, like a cruel parrot clinging onto her shoulder, whispering obscenities, laughing and cackling.

She'd lie on her back whilst the constant buzzing rendered her physically paralysed, although her conscience remained lucid, her senses intact. She remained aware of the world around her, of the outside traffic, of the lavender air-freshener, of the movements of others within the house.

At times, she'd struggle to breathe under the pressure exerted by the malevolent force, straddling her, forcing her down into the mattress, assigned with purposeful sexual intent. She was conscious, but physically paralysed. Her heart would thump, and even though her eyes were tightly closed, not daring to risk a face-to-face confrontation, the lingering image of the mocking, smirking head was branded into her mind with harrowing pitch-perfect clarity.

After each encounter, Zoe felt weak, drained and, above all, scared shitless. She accepted that these experiences were a natural and common phenomena, that it was all in her head. But, nonetheless, she didn't like them and sought to avoid them, at all costs.

*

With her emotions running ragged on this early autumn evening, her options had been to either spend the evening watching mundane reality TV in the futile hope that her negative mood and energies could be dispelled, just for the night at least, or alternatively she could consume enough alcohol in order to get smashed into oblivion. She'd chosen the latter. Left unattended, she knew her negative mindset would eat away at her mental stability, possibly triggering the onset of yet another harrowing sleep experience, not to mention the weird events she was experiencing in the house. The decision had been an easy one to make.

It was nine o'clock as Zoe sat on the sofa opposite the living-flame gas fire. The TV was on, but she wasn't aware of the programme being aired. That there was activity and noise within the room offered some minimal comfort. Sophia, minus Princess, lay fast asleep two floors above, unaware of the mental torment her mother was suffering.

On the sofa next to Zoe lay a fake crocodile-skin handbag, a magazine and a slice of ham carefully wrapped in tissue paper. The four-pack of lager had been reduced by two. The unopened bottles of Merlot and an empty wine glass stood close by on the coffee table, within easy reach. She looked at the laminate flooring, to the area directly below the window, and envisaged the armchair just a few feet below. She looked to her left at the firmly closed kitchen door. *He's out enjoying himself*, she thought, *partying with his mates. Bastard!*

She'd already decided that the services of a buddy would help ease her through the night. 'Hey, Jimmy! Come on over here, ya little bastard,' she commanded.

Princess, curled up in his basket, looked up less than

enthusiastic at the tone of Zoe's stark instruction.

'Come on, get over here, ya little shit.' Any love or affinity she may have initially harboured for the puppy had disappeared down a sinkhole during his fateful debut in the house when he'd attempted to rodger the ankles off of her six-year-old daughter. She now spoke down to him; he could sense he wasn't her favourite. 'Come on, here,' she said as she opened the tissue paper and waved the floppy piece of ham in the air. 'Here, ya little dope... food.'

Princess's fickle resistance lasted less than a second once his eyes and nose combined to inform him that there was food on offer. He yelped, jumped out of the basket and raced over to the sofa where he scrambled up and onto Zoe's knee and proceeded to gulp down the ham.

Zoe despised the animal but was prepared to use him in any way she needed – anything to help get her through the night, no matter how much ham and false affection it would take.

*

She never managed to finish the Merlot. She gave it a good go, demolishing all the lager and the first bottle of wine with no problem, but, after just a glassful from the second, she dozed off. By the time she regained consciousness she'd had enough. She decided to call it a day, being sufficiently pissed not to give a fiddler's fuck about the house, Phil or anything else. She looked at the clock; it was twenty past midnight. *It won't be long before silly bollocks is back.*

Princess was fast asleep on the sofa next to her, still with lead attached, which Zoe had used to ensure he accompany her on visits to the bathroom on the first floor.

She turned off the TV and listened intently. The alcohol had induced both Dutch courage and tiredness. Zoe could hear nothing.

She decided to ditch her buddy, poking him awake with the rolled-up magazine and unleashing the lead. 'Go on...fuck off upstairs,' she said quietly as she stood up and opened the stairway door.

Princess obeyed and duly scampered up the stairs to his little mistress in the attic.

With her hand on the stair door handle, Zoe glanced over her shoulder, her senses dumbed down, her mental processes sluggish. The room, the house and the street were silent, apart from the morbid, incessant tick-tock-ing of the digital clock.

She staggered up the steep staircase and turned the winding corner at the top before lurching down the short landing area and almost falling into the main bedroom, having already decided to 'fuck the ablutions'. After switching on the bedside lamp, she climbed into bed and within two minutes she'd sank into a deep slumber, with no signs of sleep paralysis, chains or demons, and no distant banging sounds or music. In fact, just for a short while, the little house at number 10 was a sanctuary of peace and tranquillity.

*

Phil had returned home and his drunken, clumsy movements had once again awoken Zoe. She didn't open her eyes or move. In one way, she was relieved that she was no longer alone in the house; but in another way, she was perturbed that, once again, his intoxicated behaviour had disturbed her sleep.

As the banging and clattering continued, she decided

to ride it out and leave him to sort himself out. She tossed and turned and cursed and grumbled, but the banging and clumping continued. *What's the silly fucker doing?*

She began to ruminate as she gently eased out of drowsy mode, becoming more lucid by the second and eventually opened her sleepy eyes. It was dark. She looked at the bedside table. The lamp was turned off. As the banging and clattering continued, it gradually became coupled with the faint sound of music.

Zoe sat up and surveyed the situation. *Pitch twatting black, silly bollocks downstairs playing music... Has he brought his mates back? He'd better not 'ave brought that slack bastard Andy home!*

Just as she was attempting to make sense of the situation and without any prior warning, there came the sound of heavy breathing followed by a snorting, guttural grunt. She stiffened, her awareness intensified. *That isn't from downstairs... That's in this fucking room!*

'What the fuck?' She turned on her side and fumbled to switch on the bedside lamp. With the room illuminated, she looked to her side and everything fell into place, leaving her feeling just a little awkward. There, lying on his side in a hulking, drunken stupor, was her partner, totally spent.

'What a twat,' Zoe mumbled as she realised that she was now wide awake and rational, the earlier effect of the alcohol having seemingly left her. She reached over and shook him by the shoulder. 'Wake up, ya drunken get,' she demanded. 'You've left the bleedin' telly on.'

Phil didn't respond. Both the bedroom door and the door at the bottom of the stairs had been left open as she could now see chinks of moving light from the TV flashing on the landing wall at the top of the steps.

'Wake up, Phil, you've left the telly on,' she continued as she shook him again, this time more aggressively.

'Wha... Whazit?' he burbled before further utterances of indiscernible grunting and groaning.

There was no way she was going to rouse him. She sat up, wide awake. She dug her elbow into his back. 'Shut the fuck up, will you?' she fumed.

But Phil was in a different universe, in an alternative realm, boozing and buzzin' with the hellraising football angels in the glorious heavens above.

With the grunting from Phil on one side and the blaring light show from downstairs, Zoe was resigned to removing her backside from the comfort of the bed in order to switch off the TV herself. She wasn't happy.

She shook her head and tutted as she threw back the duvet, jumped out of the bed and rammed her dainty feet into her slip-ons before throwing on her nightgown. She looked down at her partner and slowly shook her head. 'Wanker!'

She approached the open bedroom door and clearly saw streams of light flashing and shining through the opening of the downstairs door which, she assumed, had been left ajar.

By the time she'd walked onto the landing, flowing music accompanied by the clinking of glasses and indiscernible mutterings could be heard. She got the impression of a 1940s or '50s musical film being aired. *What's the silly get been watching?*

She crossed the short corridor, but as she turned the winding corner, she became unnerved. 'Phil,' she called out as she stopped in her tracks and looked back over her shoulder. 'Phil!' she repeated, but she knew her attempts at rousing him were in vain. She steeled herself to complete the duties which, in her view, were those the man of the house should be performing, but the man of the house was unavailable. According to Zoe, the man of the house was a pissed-up drunken twat. It was down to her, and her alone.

She slowly edged her way around the winders. As she saw the bottom of the staircase, it confirmed her suspicion that Phil had left the bottom door ajar. Grabbing onto the banister, she took another step down and stopped. She listened. She looked. She was unsure as to what state Phil had left the room in. Seeds of doubt developed. Another step and then another. The music and shafts of light and shadow became more intense, more defined and more puzzling.

By the time she'd reached halfway down the stairs, the music had morphed into the now recognisable melody which was slowly increasing in volume with each step taken. *It's that Mantrovardi bloke and his bleedin' band... I bet the idiot's been playing them records when I told him to sling'em.*

But it wasn't as simple as that. She sensed a peculiar, odd ambience playing out in the downstairs room. The lighting and shadows didn't seem natural. It didn't seem, to Zoe, to be consistent with the light that the TV would give off. The room appeared to be lit, not by the main central light, but by a less harsh and more subtle light, more of a glow. The standard lamp was at the other side of the room compared to where the glowing light appeared to be deriving from.

Zoe took another step down. Her heart thumped hard; her breathing was laboured as the tone of light and shadow danced in the room below. Confused and apprehensive, she knew she had to confront whatever, or who, it was playing out the scene on the other side of the door. And she had to do it alone.

She reached a position far enough down the stairs to grab hold of the door handle with her left hand whilst tightly gripping the banister with her right. She realised that whatever it was in her front room, it wasn't from any entertainment system – be it the TV, the PlayStation or anything else that may have been abandoned by Phil. There was someone in the house, of that she was sure.

The subtle racket and clamour was consistent with the movements, the fleeting movements, of a person. The music became louder, and the light and shadow became more erratic. She stood transfixed, standing behind the door, where, just a few inches away, a performance, of a type beyond her comprehension, was being played out.

She stood still and held her breath. She detected the low murmurings of a person. She sensed a humming, loosely in tune with the music. Not quite singing, but humming, as one would do in one's own company, but clearly a voice. Her brain became overloaded. She attempted to make sense of the information being transmitted – there was no sense to make.

Zoe was only of slight build. Her mind was in turmoil, and she was dressed in soft slippers and dressing gown. But one thing she wasn't short of was spirit, a determined spirit, and she rarely backed down from any situation, from any confrontation. She knew she had to open the door, so she braced herself to do just that.

She removed her hand from the door handle and strengthened her grip on the banister. She hesitated. As she did so, the music, humming and light flashes became even more intense, as if the whole scene was being relocated from the living room directly into her head.

'Fuck you!' she screamed as she leant back and kicked open the door with the heel of her right foot with such force it slammed into the back wall and almost sprang back closed before slowly recoiling into a wide open position. The sight that befell her made no logic as she stood open-mouthed.

With the door now fully opened, she was unable to believe what she was seeing. There was no reaction; she was emotionally inert. She looked down into a totally darkened room that just a second ago had been subject to what had seemed a dazzling light show with dancing shadows and pulsating light to the nauseating rendition of 'Lonely Ballerina' by Mantovani and his orchestra. The only audible sound now was the continuous tick-tocking of the designer wall clock directly above the fireplace. All was silent. No music. No bumping. No humming. Just a dark, tick-tocking silence.

Zoe stood frozen, unable to move, in physical lock-down, her psychological faculties muted. She stared into the black, empty space without comprehension and without a plan.

Her mind slowly scrambled the information her senses were collating, but there was still no sense to it all. As the initial shock began to dissipate, she began to evaluate the situation. *It's dark, so the light must be switched off. Turn the light on. Where's the bleedin' switch?*

She pondered as to the location of the light switch and concluded that it was positioned on the living room wall at the side of the door. She could just about reach it from where she was.

Continuing to grasp hold of the banister with her right hand, she stretched and reached around the door opening with her left and fumbled before locating the switch. She flicked it down, the sharp click distinct against the unremitting silence. But the darkness remained and hung over the room like a black velvet shroud. She tried again, toggling the switch repeatedly, but nothing.

She knew that one certain way to test for false awakenings during sleep paralysis was to switch a light on – any light, the main light, a table lamp, anything. If light failed to materialise, it was almost certain that one remained incarcerated within the sleep paralysis cycle. But this felt way different from any sleep experiences she'd endured in the past.

Deciding to conduct her own test, she brought her slim hands together and dug her right thumbnail into the top of her left hand, hard. Not only did she dig it in, breaking the skin, but she gouged it, causing as much pain as she could bear.

'Ow…bastard!' she whispered. Although she couldn't see, she could feel the warm sticky liquid as it slowly oozed out of the small wound. She wiped the blood with her right hand, and then wiped both hands on her dressing gown.

She noticed that it was now quite cold, her grey breath visible against the dark room set before her. As her sight became accustomed to the conditions, she could just about pick up a small red light over in the far corner of the room, which she assumed was the standby light of the TV. The shadowy, indiscernible shapes of furniture, lifeless, silent witnesses, loomed in the dark.

The drop in temperature became more evident as she realised the end of her nose was now ice-cold. She shivered as the sound of the ticking clock grew quieter and softer as if drawing back into an alternative dimension. Then the ticking ceased altogether and the temperature continued to fall.

The skin and hair on the back of Zoe's head and neck produced a prickly, tingling sensation. Her brave front was beginning to wear thin as negative thoughts bundled through her head, knocking aside the bolshiness that had carried her this far.

Shuffling sounds began to materialise. She cocked her head. The sounds intensified. An umbrella being shaken, a hard flutter. The noise appeared to derive from an airborne entity from inside the room.

As she narrowed her eyes, she could see a black form, blacker and darker than the blackness in front of her. She could barely determine the outline of the object that was now flitting around the room erratically. Flapping, hard flapping. She sensed the object getting nearer and nearer as if it was homing in, targeting her, ready to pounce. It flew so close that the vigour of the motion dispersed her exhaled breath as she flinched backwards. Swishing, flapping, louder, sinister, pandemonium!

From the far corner of the room, the entity launched itself straight for Zoe as it zoomed in on her, fuelled with malicious intent. She screamed and fell back onto the stairs, automatically throwing her arms up to protect her face. Confused and terrified, she began to shake.

'What the fuck!' Panic invaded every cell of her body as the entity's flapping became increasingly erratic, more resolute and more determined. She peeked through her arms and fingers to see two piercing blood-red, pinprick eyes glower directly into her vulnerable soul like malevolent laser beams.

The creature released a series of deafening chacking cries and, amidst a mass of confusion, a gnarled beak pecked and poked at her arms, hands and face. With her eyes clenched tightly closed, she yelled and screamed with all the strength she could muster, 'Fuck off! Ya bastard!' She lashed out with her arms flailing wildly. 'Fuck off!'

The flapping entity fucked off. Within an instant, all was silent. No flapping, no blood-red eyes, no hacking beak.

Breathing heavily, her whole body shook as she struggled to raise herself upright. No amount of bravery would allow her to overstep the threshold and enter the room. Her senses were now on high alert with widened eyes, flaying nostrils and ears poised like satellite dishes.

Once again, she watched her breath continually expel into the cold air, but this time at a faster rate. She tried the light switch again – nothing; she listened for the sound of the tick-tocking of the designer clock – nothing. All appeared to be calm once again, but the tension remained, the negative ambience hung in the ice-cold atmosphere. She questioned herself as to whether this was real life or a figment, an encounter, within her mystified head, but she didn't have much time to think.

There was now a small scratching, scraping sound. Zoe zoned in. The noise was repeated, but this time louder with more substance. And again, bumping and banging close by. A heavy object was being dragged slowly and in intermittent stages. But this time it was not in the living room. This time it originated from the kitchen, behind the wall to her left. The sounds became more laboured, as if a great energy was being mustered in shifting, dragging some heavy, dead weight. Suddenly, there was the creaking of a door. Zoe stood spellbound.

Fuck you, Phil... This is happening in OUR house – not

the fucking neighbours'. This is in here, you drunken fuck! Where are you? Where are you when I need you? You drunken bastard.

The muffled, dragging and scraping noises continued for a short while before gradually diminishing. Zoe stood mesmerised. She surveyed the dark room as the dragging sounds petered out giving way to a distant bumping noise, which, she felt, came from the depths of the cellar, directly beneath where she stood.

Zoe was confused, physically shattered and mentally drained. She'd had enough. She reached forward, took hold of the handle and gently closed the door, pulling it towards her, shutting away the scene, closing it off, out of sight.

She slowly ascended the stairs backwards, methodically retracing her steps all the way to the bedroom, facing forwards and walking backwards, not daring to look away. She backed into the bedroom, closed the door in front of her and walked backwards to her side of the bed. She eased her listless body under the duvet, dragging it completely over her head, and wrapped her arms around the steaming, sweating hulk of the drunken partner she'd spent the whole day and night blaspheming about. She closed her eyes and cried herself to sleep. Phil remained in his deep alcohol-induced sleep.

*

Zoe opened her eyes. She was still under the duvet, but now all alone, Phil having already left the house for work. Her mind immediately returned to the events of the early hours. The sentiment of dread saturated her heavy heart. The dried blood daubed over the bed sheet and duvet convinced her that the experience had not been a sleep paralysis encounter.

CHAPTER 6

May 1975

'What we having for tea?' asked George, eyeing up the mantelpiece clock as he lounged in a tired armchair, part of an orange three-piece suite with chocolate brown seat cushions. There were two armchairs set against the party wall, where the property abutted its back-to-back counterpart, and a three-seater settee against the kitchen wall behind a small, cluttered coffee table.

'You'll 'ave what you're given,' came the curt reply from behind the dark curtain which hung in the kitchen doorway, separating the two rooms.

'I know I'll 'ave what I'm given, love. I was just asking what it is, that's all.'

'Liver 'n' onions, wi' mash an' gravy. Like it or lump it. Why, what's the rush?'

'There is no rush – I'm just asking.'

'Humph...never mind just asking.' She pulled the curtain back and looked at the clock. 'Ah, I see, you're getting edgy, are ya? Club night, in't it?'

'No, love, I just wanted to know what—'

'I can read you like a book, lad,' she mocked as she tottered out of the kitchen with a plate of hot food at arm's length. 'Here,' she said, planting the dish onto George's lap and then brusquely handing him a knife and fork.

'Right y'are, love,' he replied.

Stella retrieved her own paltry serving and sat down on the settee. She picked at the food, grimacing at the thought of actually having to consume any of it. 'And don't be swanning off to your bloody club before you see your granddaughter,' she said. 'Y'ardly ever see her... You're allus flitting off somewhere, or messin' about in the bloody cellar wi' your flea-bitten animals. God knows what you get up to down there.'

'I'll see her in 'morning if I don't see her tonight.'

'Never mind seeing her in 'morning. You can bloody well wait till she gets here tonight. That's what you can do... D'y'ear? I said, d'y'ear?' demanded Stella, tapping her fingernail into fresh air.

'What time's she dropping her off?'

'Same time as she allus drops her off. It's 'only time our Susan gets a bit o' peace, and it's 'only time we get to see us granddaughter, so you can put yerself out for once.'

George gave up trying to reason with his wife. Instead, he concentrated on guzzling down his liver and onions, with mash and gravy.

The couple ate in silence as canned laughter echoed around the room from the black and white television set in the far corner of the room.

'Did I tell you I'm off to 'club a week o' Wednesday to watch Leeds?' said George, suddenly breaking the taut atmosphere.

Stella looked up. 'You can go where you want. It dun't bother me. What you going there for on a Wednesday, anyroad?'

'Me and me pals, we're watching United in 'European Cup final. It's bein' played in Paris—'

'Pals? You an't got any pals, you. What pals have you

got?' said Stella with suspicion etched over her wrinkled face.

'The lads, from 'club...'

'Lads? You mean them simpletons you sit wi' in 'telly room? I've seen more life in a tin o' pilchards than that lot! They're all from 'Sally Army hostel, aren't they? Lads? Don't make me laugh. There's that 'un who cries if ya look at 'im, and that silly bleeder wi' 'dicky bow who looks like Blakey from *On the Buses*. Then there's 'bald feller wi' 'glasses who gets dressed up in a suit and thinks he's James Bond – an' when he opens his mouth, he an't got a bloody tooth in his head... Ha, pals?'

'They're decent lads...'

'Decent lads? They're a right set of oddballs, they are. You fit right in wi' that lot, you do. Yer never even talk t'each other, anyroad. You go in, nod yer 'eads, sup yer four pints o' mild, watch a bit o' telly an' then go home. And that's it... Oh aye, and what about that silly old bugger who pissed hissen in 'corner that time?'

George turned and shot Stella a stare before thinking better of it and looking away sharpish. 'That were Jacko. He didn't piss hisself – he dropped his beer, that's all.'

'Jacko my arse! He pissed hisself and got booted out... I saw 'em carry 'im out... I were there, remember? Anyroad, you won't get me back in that place. I'm not spending another Sat'day night wi' that group of senile old buggers.'

'Well, love, you haven't been invited back, have you? And it's just as well in't it cos you're still scratched (barred).' George clammed up immediately. 'They're playing Bayern Munich,' he said, eager to change direction.

After a short pause, she replied. 'Who are?'

'Leeds United, in 'final o' 'European Cup.'

'Huh! Don't mention Leeds United to me,' she said, dismissing out of hand any gravity George was attempting to place on the event.

'It's the European Cup final—'

'I'm not bothered if it's 'Eurovision Song Contest final! They're all bloody hooligans, anyroad... And them footballers – they're like schoolgirls the way they fall about, an' roll on 'floor, bloody kissin' an' cuddling each other like a group o' pufters just cos they kick a bit o' leather into a net. Me dad played scrum half for 'Unslet. Rugby league. A proper game. Played by proper men. If they got carried off, you knew it were serious. No one ever walked off. Me dad used to say, "If yer could walk, yer could bloody well carry on playing." Not like these footballers today, wi' their long hair and fancy cars. They wun't last five minutes in rugby league. I'd a' liked to see you play rugby league... You wun't have lasted five minutes.'

'Anyway, I got you some Mackesons. You know what they say, love... It looks good, it tastes good and, by golly, it does you good.' George smiled weakly and paused for a second to gauge any reaction from Stella at his tame attempt of humour. He had wasted his time: there was no reaction. So, he continued, 'There's four bottles in the carrier bag under the window, with half a bottle of vodka.'

'I know. I saw you bring it in, din't I?' snapped Stella shaking her head and reacting to his insubordination by shooting him yet another cutting sideways glance.

'Do you want me to bring you a couple o' miniatures in from 'club?'

'You can please yerself what you do. I'm not fussed.'

The remainder of the meal was consumed in silence as

George eagerly anticipated his weekly trip to the club, convening with his Salvation Army hostel comrades in the dingy TV room of East Moor Park Workingmen's Club. Stella faced an evening in front of her own TV with her granddaughter, and the prospect of a sherbet or two thereafter.

*

It was around eleven o'clock by the time Stella heard George insert his key into the lock and enter the house. By this time her head was hazy, her movements sluggish and her speech unhurried. 'You're back, then?'

'Aye, love. Everything all right? I've got you a few Bell's, and yer chips an' curry from 'Chinky.' He relieved his trouser pockets of six miniature bottles of Bell's Scotch whisky and placed them onto the coffee table.

Stella was slouched on the settee listening to her collection of 1950s records. Her grinning teeth lay dehydrated on the chocolate brown cushion next to her. The combination of music and alcohol had liberated Stella of the weight of everyday life, of the station dealt her by the lottery of existence. The Mackeson and vodka had disappeared – and with them the sharp, prickly edge to Stella's disposition. The upshot of which was a much calmer, albeit inebriated, state of mind.

With the soothing tones of Slim Whitman's 'Rose Marie' resonating around the room, George came out of the kitchen with two plates of chips and curry, carefully placing one onto Stella's lap. He retreated onto the alcove armchair, next to the fire, and set about his own insalubrious supper.

'Thanksh,' said Stella after searching her fuzzled mind for the correct response. Her fork quivered over the food before taking the plunge, attacking the chips like a peregrine falcon diving for the kill. Through more good fortune than judgement, the sortie was successful, as a large, fat chip, dripping in a dirty brown gravy–curry coagulation, emerged from the pile of prey firmly impaled on the fork before being transferred to the mouth for consumption. 'Did y'ave a nishe time at 'club?' she asked, her head bobbing around like a nodding dog on a car dashboard.

'Aye, it were all right,' replied George. 'What about you two?'

'Yeah...we watched *Morecombe an' Wise*... It were 'film, y'know...film... An' then Mike Yarwood... An' then she went to bed with her comics... Ha, ha... An' the resht, as they shay, is...'ishtry...'

'Is she all right?'

'Aye,' said Stella, attempting to dock another curry-laden chip into her mouth. 'Aye...tucked in an'...fasht asleep.'

The couple continued with the small talk. George with his simple questioning and single-syllable answers in his peculiar high-pitched monotone. Stella conversing with her throaty, slurring voice as she continued to glug the whisky whilst listening to Whitman.

She had a tendency to play the same record over and over again, hour after hour, before progressing to another from her modest library of half a dozen. It was a very regimented routine, and one with which George was very familiar.

By the third miniature, she'd abandoned the use of a drinking receptacle altogether and instead swigged directly from the bottle as her demeanour continued to lighten and her physical dexterity and slurring speech continued to deteriorate.

'Lessh put on me favourite...' she said, attempting to reach over to the table where the portable record player was positioned.

'Let me do that,' said George. 'You'll have the bloody thing over. Which one d'ya want on?'

'Which...d'ya think?' she drawled, smiling at him.

'I've no idea, love, which?'

'*You* know...lover,' replied Stella with a mischievous wink.

George straightened up. 'You want Mantovani on? The one you like to dance to?'

'Thash the one,' she said with a huge crooked smile now emblazoned across her face.

George removed the Slim Whitman disc, placing it onto the coffee table, before carefully easing out the Mantovani record from the worn sleeve. He gently dropped it onto the revolving turntable and positioned the stylus.

'Will you danshe with me...my lover?' blurted out Stella.

George's cheek twitched. He scratched his clammy forehead. 'I'm 'aving me chips, love, an' then I'm off to bed,' he replied.

'Oh, danshe with me, George... Pleashe, love...danshe with me...'

'I'm dancing wi' no one... I've got a bad back...'

'Pleashe, my love...danshe with me...' Stella's pleading for an intimate altercation with her husband, to the tones of Mantovani and his orchestra's rendition of 'Lonely Ballerina', forced George to cram the last few chips into his mouth and gulp the remaining curry direct from the plate. The greasy liquid dribbled onto his white, crumpled shirt. He wiped it with the outside his hand,

and then subsequently wiped his hand on his trousers.

Stella rose unsteadily from her drunken bolthole and began to flail her arms about in a flamboyant manner, to what she perceived to be in tune with the music. She had been quite an accomplished ballerina in her distant youth, but her working-class background had dictated that she abandon that particular career prospect, and she ended up working at the huge Montague Burton tailoring business in the Harehills district of Leeds. Even though Stella was blind drunk, she clearly remembered some of the technical moves and routines, but age and alcohol now yielded her attempts at the gracious art of ballet to something akin a three-legged hippo, living it large, up on a high wire.

Having returned his licked-clean plate into the kitchen and quietly placed it into the sink, George watched, with a careful eye, the antics of his wife. From behind the partition curtain, he observed. He observed her throwing her arms around in dramatic fashion. He scrutinised the bizarre angles her toes were being pointed. He listened to her humming, out of tune. He surveyed the whole scene through narrowed eyes. He knew that once the dancing commenced, she would be beyond the point of return – that she was done for the night.

'Come and danshe with me, lover boy,' she cried as she swirled her arms aloft, looking more like a desperate crab in a pot of boiling water than a woman of poise, grace and class.

'Dance wi' yourself, love, I'm off to bed,' replied George as he strode out of the kitchen towards the stairway.

'Love me, George,' cried Stella as he opened the bottom door. 'Danshe with me, George, my love... George... Love me...'

'I'm off... Ta-ra.' With that amorous parting shot, he began his slow, laboured lumber up the staircase. The dull thud of his leather brogues resonated against the threadbare-carpeted stairs, half drowned against the poignant orchestral masterpiece of Mantovani. He lunged his bulking frame up the stairs, using the banister to steady himself, slow and heavy, methodical, around the bend at the top and out of sight.

'George!' cried Stella, but her demands for romance were futile. She was alone, left to float on the stage of clouds, with her music and booze, in a counterfeit sanctuary, a temporary sanctuary, her only sanctuary.

On this stage she could relive her vivacious youth; she could invent the life that had been cruelly denied her. She hummed and crooned nonsensical mutterings as she twisted and gestured, arching her neck and back as gracefully as her arthritic joints and saturated brain would allow.

Alone, in the artificial light of the single ceiling rose bulb, she danced around the coffee table and the orange three-piece suite with the chocolate brown cushions. She skipped across the foam-backed carpet against the backdrop of the dark curtains and floral wallpaper. Alone, to Mantovani's composition of the 'Lonely Ballerina', she was in paradise.

*

It was almost ten thirty when Stella finally stumbled downstairs the following morning. She usually slept downstairs on the settee during her heavy Saturday night sessions, drunk and incapable, but on this occasion she'd somehow managed to make it up to bed. She couldn't recollect how she got there. The last thing

she could remember was George spilling curry down his shirt – after that, it was just a hazy blur.

She slinked down on the settee as George planted a teapot on the coffee table with milk, mugs and sugar bowl. It was an unusually cold, grim morning for May. The gas fire fizzed away creating a warm and cosy setting. Stella grabbed Woodbines and a lighter from the table. The soothing combination of nicotine and freshly mashed tea gradually steadied her nerves, the shaking becoming less erratic.

'Has she been?'

'Who?' answered George, sitting in the alcove armchair reading the sports section of the Sunday newspaper.

'Our Susan, who do you think?' replied Stella, her croaky voice wavering.

'Been and gone.'

'Why didn't you wake me?'

'I tried.'

'You didn't try hard enough then, did ya? Were they all right? Did she say owt?'

'No.'

'Did you make her a cup o' tea?'

'Didn't want one... Said she'd see you next week.'

Stella shook her head. She looked out of the window. It was a dull day. A gloomy day. The terraces were so close that on their side of the street, being north facing, they only received a fleeting glimpse of the setting sun during high summer. The only other time the sun's rays penetrated their windows was at the break of dawn. They had to rely solely on the light cast onto the opposite row of terraces to get any feel of light or warmth. But on this day, a thick range of grey cloud hung over East Moor Park, prohibiting any shaft of sunlight from striking any brick, slate or window in the little cul-de-sac.

'How you feeling today?' asked George, still engrossed in the newspaper.

'How do *you* think?' she replied.

'Did you take your tablets yesterday?'

'I've told you before to keep your nose out of my affairs wi' them there tablets, an't I? It's nowt to do wi' you whether I've taken 'em or not. You're allus sticking your nose into my business.'

'You know the doctor said you shouldn't take 'em wi' drink.'

'It dun't stop you buying me it, though, does it?'

George peeked at her over the newspaper.

'You can look! You 'ad your booze last night, din't ya? So don't go and try making me feel guilty about 'aving a few drinks in me own 'ouse... I'll buy me own in future.'

'Well, when I don't get you owt I'm in the wrong, and when I do get you summat I'm in the wrong. I can't win, can I?'

'No, ya can't, so just shut it and keep quiet.'

'What you doing today, then?'

'What am I doing today?' she answered with a look of incredulity. 'What am I doing today? I'm off camping with the bleedin' milkman! What d'ya think I'm doing today, ya gormless get?'

'Well, if you're gonna be like that, I'm off downstairs to get a bit a peace and quiet,' he said standing up, folding the paper and brusquely surrendering it to her.

'Aye, you do that... You'll get more sense out o' that there ferret than I get from you... Go on...go to ya little hidey-hole, wi' ya silly radio on... Go on...'

'I'm going...right y'are.' And go he did, leaving his wife

to jabber on, laying low, smoking Woodbines and sipping tea whilst her frail body, once again, struggled with the slow process of recovery after the exertions of yet another shocking bout of alcohol abuse.

'Tablets,' muttered Stella. 'I'll bloody tablets 'im.' She knew to her cost the consequences of the combination of her prescription drugs and alcohol. It was one or the other, and she'd made the decision to take her chances with the alcohol. She'd been stockpiling the antidepressants for months. *He doesn't know, and what he doesn't know can't harm him. Bleedin' middin bin, he is!'*

George, armed with his mug of lukewarm tea, descended the dark stone steps to the basement, the cellarhead door closed firmly behind him. He grabbed his grubby donkey jacket hanging from a nail in the wall and slipped it on. The central light bulb did little to illuminate the dark space, so he lit two candles which he placed on saucers on either end of timber shelving, at the furthest side of the room, directly under where the fireplace was positioned on the floor above.

The earthen flooring at one corner of the party wall had collapsed and was now covered with timber planking. During heavy rain, the water would rise through the fault and flood the cellar with a black, silty liquid. Hence, George had built some of the cages and coops on stilts to counter the possibility of harm coming to his beloved animals.

His favourite was a ferret purchased from one of his pals at the club who worked at Leeds Kirkgate Market. He'd got it on the cheap due to a slight deformity to one of the front feet, but it hadn't seemed to affect the health and vitality of the animal. Apart from the ferret, he cared for two rabbits and an injured magpie he'd found in the street. He didn't really know anything about animals, but he enjoyed spending time in their company, holding, caressing and fondling them. It was his escape from the ravages of his wife's tongue.

He opened the front hatch of a crudely fashioned coop with a chicken wire mesh and front which stood behind a centrally positioned stone-slabbed table. He carefully slid his hand into the end compartment and felt around the damp sawdust. He located, grabbed and pulled out a fine black-eyed white ferret with a firm grip on the long, slender body.

Samson was about a year old and had subsisted in this subterranean compound for most of his life. He stank of stale piss. George raised the animal with both hands to eye level and caressed the muscular, tight and lithe body. He stared into the tiny ink-black eyes, kissed him on the crown of his head and then turned him loose onto the dirty earthen floor before checking on the welfare of the rabbits, Stan and Hilda.

He stuffed a handful of crisp lettuce through the top hatch. They were fine, apart from the damp sawdust bedding, which hadn't been changed for a week, the strong smell of urine saturating the already dank air. The unpleasant odour had percolated into the kitchen above, much to the displeasure of Stella, but he'd promised to pick up a sack of fresh sawdust from Jackson's sawmill on his way home from work the next day. For now, though, there was nothing he could do. In any case, he was used to it. It didn't bother him. It didn't bother him that his dirty work clothes, hanging behind the cellar door, also reeked of piss. This was his world, his domain, his bolthole. If others didn't like it, then that was their lookout.

He opened the front of a large upright cage purposely

fabricated, by himself, for the housing of birds. It had been mostly pigeons and an occasional blackbird that had lodged here in the past; however, the only resident at this time was a striking magpie. He'd found it injured on East Moor Drive some weeks previous and had intended to coax it back to health. Although he'd succeeded to some extent, the creature couldn't, and wouldn't, ever fly again, so he'd decided to keep it.

He'd assigned the bird the name of Maggie but had no idea of whether she was actually female. He reached in and, after a burst of frantic flapping, managed to pull her out of the cage. He held her aloft with both hands and stared into her dark eyes. He was captivated with the eyes of animals and birds – the blacker the better – the malevolence they suggested, the intent, but also the silence, the deathly silence.

With Maggie now in tow, he retreated to the oversized, battered armchair positioned directly under the cellar window. The window extended only twelve inches or so above the level of the external pavement and was closed off with cast-iron grating. However, internally it extended to well below road level, creating the odd situation of having a full-sized window built into the building but with only the top few inches allowing the passage of light.

Wooden beer crates were stacked either side of the armchair. One tower was used as a platform for tea, food and newspapers. The other accommodated an old transistor radio through which he spent countless hours listening to classical music, or occasionally live football on BBC Radio Leeds. In front of the chair was a small gas heater. Although not much use during the raw bowels of a cold winter's day, it would generally generate sufficient heat to make George comfortable during the spring and autumn months.

He continued to gaze into the dark abyss of the magpie's eyes, the inky silence, the total control. He stroked and caressed the striking plumage, the iridescent blue and green tail and wing feathers. He stroked her soft throat with his thumb over and over and over again while staring into her tiny eyes. Maggie blinked, oblivious. He threw her in the air and after a frantic display of flapping, she once again resigned herself to life on terra firma, on the dirty floor of the cellar.

George slid out a small tobacco tin from the inside of his coat and opened it. He flicked a handful of succulent pink earthworms onto the floor, which he'd dug up from the allotment the previous day. Maggie hopped and ran, almost skipped over, and commenced her Sunday lunch, devouring the juicy worms with gusto.

Samson, picking up on the flurry of activity, moseyed over. However, George had a special treat for Samson, who was by far his favourite. He whipped out a bag from his coat and flicked at the paper whilst producing a 'kek' sound using the suction of his tongue against the roof of his barren gum line.

Samson, recognising the rustling and the call, reacted by slinking towards him, running up his leg and onto his knees. He was clearly excited as he circled around on his master's lap squeaking and producing a chucking sound, not too dissimilar from the louder chacking noise from an agitated Maggie.

George opened the bag of raw steak mincemeat and watched Samson gulp down the food direct from his hand. He listened carefully as the ravenous ferret masticated the food with his tiny, razor-sharp teeth.

Once the meal was finished, George held up the animal and looked deep into his glistening black eyes. He gently squeezed the warm, firm torso, gradually increasing the pressure, to the point where the animal was forced to resist. The ferret struggled to break free, squealing in desperation, but George held firm. His grip would be released on his terms, not before. He stroked and caressed the animal, exerting ironclad control, before kissing him once again on the crown of his head and gently releasing him back onto the cellar floor.

George had spent many hours alone with his animals, listening to the radio, sometimes by candlelight and other times by the dimmed light from the naked ceiling bulb. This dark, cramped den was where he was in charge, where he controlled matters, where he could command respect.

It was exactly how he liked it. Intimate, uncomplicated and free from the constant interference and admonishment meted out by his vengeful wife. The cellar had other uses, too. With the light switched off, and in the darkened silence, he could watch the outside world go by, anonymously, in secret. There was no sunshine radiating through this tiny section of window; it was constantly in the dark, murky shade.

Not only could he see out of the window, he could observe from below pavement level, from his low and inconspicuous vantage point. He could silently monitor the comings and goings of neighbours and visitors going about out their daily business.

He was specifically interested in females, females of any description, but especially those wearing short skirts. Knowing which weekends Peggy Bowden had use of the washing line, George would sit in wait, hoping for a gentle breeze to whip up. He'd silently observe as she stretched and strained in a manner that accentuated the form and robustness of her ample, voluptuous breasts. He'd scrutinise her intimacy as the wind meandered and swirled around her thick ankles, lifting her skirt to reveal her fleshy thighs and full-bodied, sensible undergarments.

As his blood pressure increased and perspiration oozed from his potholed forehead, his heart would race and his hands would tremble as he fumbled to release his pent-up sexual urges. Peggy Bowden was unaware of the unassuming, oddball George Wilson, her quiet neighbour from across the road, frantically jacking himself off, just a few feet away from her, as she went about her daily chores. His contorted features would play out to an audience of a ferret, a magpie and two rabbits, and to Pachelbel's 'Canon in D Major', in the shadows of the dark cellar, on his terms. This was his world.

CHAPTER 7

October 2016

She begged Phil not to go whilst clinging onto him like a cluster of sticky buds matted to the arse cheeks of a grizzly bear. He stood in the doorway with an Adidas sports bag hanging from his shoulder and held her tightly. The bag was packed for a two-night stay in Torpoint, the gateway to Cornwall, on the south coast. His plan was to travel down on the Friday evening, work throughout the full day on Saturday, and then return home at first light Sunday. It was a tight schedule but essential as part of the rolling contract he'd signed up to and, more importantly, it was a very lucrative field of work. Cancellation was out of the question, he'd tried to explain. He was doing it for them, her and Sophia, the family. It was their ticket to financial security, a comfortable life, better than either of them had ever known or been used to.

'You'll be fine, love. I'll be back before dinnertime on Sunday, and then I'm not due to work another weekend for a month. Stick in there, love,' he said. 'Stick by me and trust me…for our sake and Sophia's. It won't be forever.'

Zoe was having none of it as she sobbed and tried to reason with him, but she knew her pleas were in vain. It wasn't her style to let her guard down. She felt uncomfortable exposing the soft, vulnerable side of her nature. Eventually, even in such desperation, she had to steel herself and let him go. *Go then, you selfish bastard... It's only two nights alone in the house... I can do it, I don't need you... Go if you want to.*

*

It was Saturday morning. Friday evening had been uneventful. Zoe had stayed up late with Sophia and Princess watching Disney films, which had left her feeling tired and weary. Even so, she hadn't slept well, as her finely tuned senses had detected every minute, discernible sound, smell, sight and sensation, with her overworked brain setting about to meticulously analyse each.

She never made it upstairs to bed as she eventually sparked out on the sofa. This had been part of the master plan. However, the effects of the alcohol had also hampered any chance of a smooth and lasting sleep. A commotion outside in the street had woken her up in the early hours, and she'd fazed in and out of consciousness ever since.

And so, here she was, the morning after, laid out, shattered with baggy eyes and little energy. She looked at the digital wall clock. Ten thirty. *This time tomorrow he might be back... Twenty-four hours. One night down and one to go. Last night was fine; maybe tonight will be the same. Just one more night to get through. You can do it, girl.* She lay on the sofa wrapped in a fake fur blanket and stared out of the window. It was grey, drizzling and devoid of inspiration.

Sophia opened the bottom stair door and descended into the room still in pyjamas and clutching a Nintendo 3DS. She yawned. 'What's for breakfast, Mum?'

'Get some cereal,' murmured her mother without moving and with her eyes now closed.

'Princess wants his breakfast as well, Mum.'

'Get him some biscuits.'

'Do you want some breakfast, Mum?'

'No.'

'Are you OK, Mum? What are we doing today?'

'Don't know.'

'When's Daddy back, Mum?'

'Tomorrow.'

'Can we take Princess for a walk later?'

'For God's sake, Sophia, give it a bloody rest, will ya?' snapped Zoe. 'Just go and get some friggin' cereal and give me head some bleedin' peace!'

'Sorry, Mum,' the little girl replied meekly. She entered the kitchen and prepared herself milk and cereal, and then climbed onto the worktop via an upturned wash basket in order to reach the dog biscuits. With a bowl of food in each hand, she rejoined Princess on the fireside rug and turned on the TV, expertly employing the remote control and surfing the channels until she found *SpongeBob SquarePants*.

She crunched her Crunchy Nut Cornflakes whilst Princess munched on his dried food. Side by side, they watched the high drama and comic antics of SpongeBob, Squidward and Patrick, although there was no laughter.

Sophia looked over her shoulder at her mother, who was by now fast asleep and curled up on the sofa, like a modern-day Bagpuss. The little girl intermittently stroked Princess whilst keeping an eye on the cartoons.

On finishing her breakfast, she carried her dish back into the kitchen. Reaching up and over, she struggled to place it quietly into the sink. After re-entering the living room, she again gazed over at Zoe. She surveyed the state of the room, the clutter, the chaos, the confusion. Her innocent mindset told her there was something wrong, that things weren't quite as they should be.

She decided that with her mother incapacitated, she'd best step up to help the situation and promptly set about collecting the empty lager cans littered on and around the sofa and coffee table. Carefully ferrying the first batch of three to the waste bin, she gently placed them inside without making a sound. However, the second batch of four was too much for her awkward little grip. The cans soon spilled out of control and crashed onto the kitchen floor. The little girl grimaced.

'What? What's going on?' shrieked Zoe, flinching at the sudden clatter. 'What the hell are you doing, Sophia?'

'I'm sorry, Mum. I'm just tidying up for you.'

'Well, be quiet about it and turn the bleedin' telly down. It's blaring out too loud... It's giving me a right headache.'

'Sorry, Mum,' whispered Sophia as she hurried to grab the remote. She turned the television off completely, taking no chances.

Princess, sensing the tension, started to yelp.

'Bloody SpongeBob... An' shut that twatting dog up, will you?' screeched Zoe with a fiery injection of venom. 'Fucking thing!'

Sophia's heart pounded as she jumped down to hold Princess's mouth closed with her small, stubby fingers. 'Shhh,' she demanded as she crouched over the little canine, holding his mouth with one hand while the index finger of the other stood upright against her lips. 'Please be quiet, Princess...pleease.'

With the excitable puppy reassured, Sophia stood up on her tiptoes and looked around the room. A cluster of empty cans remained at large by the sofa, but there she left them. The coffee table was littered with junk. Magazines, dirty cups, glasses, letters, and remnants of food and snacks. Sophia examined the scene. She hadn't been used to this kind of chaos, certainly not when her father was at home.

Even with a mouth as putrid as a stinking cesspit, her nanna had kept a spotlessly clean and orderly house back in Seacroft. She missed her nanna. She missed the fun and laughter and the love bestowed upon her; she missed the garden and Tosh the cat. She missed the iron-fisted security and the home-baked cakes and pies. She missed Seacroft. For now, though, she stared at the woman on the sofa, curled up asleep.

She tiptoed over and lowered her face towards her mother's, closely inspecting the wrinkles that had surfaced around her forehead. She examined the grey skin, the baggy eyes and the vein-ridden hands, clasped together as if in prayer, tucked under her chin. She yearned to reach over and kiss her, but was hesitant, eventually declining the thought altogether, not wishing to provoke any further outburst.

She silently surveyed the contents on the table and lowered herself to inspect more closely a slim hypodermic needle lying amongst the disorderly mess. She stared again at her mother, incapable, unresponsive and unstable, at 11 o'clock in the morning. A tear meandered down the cheek of the little girl as she picked up her Game Boy and gestured to her dependable little buddy to quietly follow her up the two winding staircases to the orderly haven of her top-floor attic bedroom.

*

Zoe sat up with a start and looked at the clock. It was ten past five, and it was pissing it down. *Another eight-*

een hours. One more night. Although the sun wasn't due to set for another forty minutes, the black clouds ensured that it was already dark outside. Not that the sun had shone its righteous rays on East Moor Park at all on this day – and even if it had, they wouldn't have shimmered through the windows of number 10 Reginald Street. The light showers from the early morning had now developed into heavy, persistent rain. A restless, squally wind had sprung up and fired intermittent spears of stinging rainwater against the facade of the beleaguered little house.

Zoe laid her head back down and watched the rain hammer against the transom window above the front door in sharp bursts. She became mesmerised by the stormy conditions prevailing outside before it dawned on her that she was responsible for the welfare of her six-year-old daughter, whom she hadn't seen or heard of since the morning.

She looked around the room and rubbed her eyes. The kitchen bifolding door was closed, exactly how she liked it. The TV was turned off, and the space around her was dark and moody. She looked at the mantelpiece and the papier mâché model of a witch on a broomstick, with a crudely fashioned cardboard black cat, which sat erect on the rear brush. The absurd grin of the cat contrasted starkly with the evil, crooked countenance of the hideous witch. It was almost Halloween, and the arts and craft staff had devised the children to make fun Halloween models to take home. *Fun? Fuck me O'Reilly!* Sophia was immensely proud of her efforts, as was her father, who insisted the effigy take pride of place above the fire on the mantelpiece, but Zoe hated it, mustering up only begrudging praise. As she stared at the work of art, the dim, low lighting momentarily tricked her negative mindset into animating the figure, the head appearing to turn towards her, the evil eyes zoning in on hers.

She snapped out of the spell and sat up rubbing her cheeks before once again glancing up at the clock. She resigned herself to shifting her thin frame and attending to her daughter, who, she assumed, had been entertaining herself all day, alongside, of course, the lively little half-breed Yorkie.

A sudden double bolt of silver-white lightning pierced the street and illuminated the whole room before instantly retracting and thrusting the scene back into an even darker blackness. *Shite, that's all I need, thunder an' bastard lightning.*

She threw off the blanket, lunged her body from the sofa and staggered over to close the curtains as the distant holler of thunder echoed and rumbled in stereo over the stormy Leeds skies. As she pulled the curtains together, she heard distinct scratching, a click and a swishing sound before sensing something land near her feet. She stiffened up and looked around. She realised that the room was now in almost total darkness with the curtains closed. She panicked and reached over to turn on the light switch.

Now brightly lit, she surveyed the room. At first there seemed nothing untoward until her gaze hit the mantelpiece. She then stared down at her feet to the sight of the papier mâché witch, now lying motionless, staring up at her, with bulbous eyes and a crooked, evil smile. Zoe's stare returned to the mantelpiece and then back at the witch lying on the carpet by her feet. She closed her eyes and stood motionless, blank, heart thumping, stunned. *It's starting. It's here. Prepare yoursen, girl. It's gonna happen;*

the bastards are out to get you.

She opened her eyes and, after a brief moment of deliberation, stamped on the macabre effigy and picked it up with forefinger and thumb. She unlocked the front door and launched it through the security grill out onto the exposed, rain-lashed street. *Fuck off!* She wasn't messing about. *I need to get out of this fucking place.*

*

'Where are we going, Mum?' asked Sophia as Zoe pulled down a bobble hat over her daughter's blonde hair, zipped up her coat and pulled the hood up.

'Out,' she replied.

'But it's raining, Mum, we'll get wet.'

Zoe ignored her as she pulled on her own coat and grabbed an umbrella from the side of the chair.

'Can Princess come?'

'No.'

'Why?'

'Cos I said so, that's why... Now, be quiet and come on.'

Sophia bowed her head and kept silent as instructed.

Zoe checked the clock. *A quarter to six.* 'C'mon,' she ordered, with the storm lashing against the tiny back-to-back. As she turned to unlock the front door, there came a thundering crash from upstairs.

'What's that, Mum?' shrieked Sophia.

Zoe was horrified but had to think quickly for the sake of her daughter. It had sounded like a door being violently slammed. With a thumping heart, she attempted to compute what was going on around her. 'It's the wind!' she blurted out. 'I must've left the bedroom window open. Now come on – we're going out.'

'I don't like it, Mum,' said Sophia now in tears. 'Can we

go to Nanna's, Mum? I want to go to Nanna's, Mum,' she sobbed. 'Can we?'

'No,' replied a stony-faced Zoe. 'Now, come on...out!' She opened the door and grabbed Sophia by the arm, almost dragging her across the threshold into the raging, outside world. It was total chaos as she locked the door and security gate behind her and then attempted to engage the umbrella. The brolly subsequently collapsed in the squall whilst the sharp-eyed Sophia quickly detected the ruined witch model lying on the rain-sodden pavement.

'Mum, look.' She pointed towards it.

Zoe grappled with the upturned umbrella as the rain pelted down. Her veil of patience threatened to explode as she struggled with the multitasking of battling the umbrella, listening to Sophia's desperate pleading and contending with the rain pummelling her face like a thousand darts. 'Bollocks!' she cried as she threw the umbrella to the ground. 'Shut the fuck up, Sophia! Come on, we're going to the friggin' park!'

'But, Mum, look,' she protested, pointing at her crushed and saturated masterpiece.

'C'mon, I said,' replied Zoe as she yanked her daughter's arm to her and stormed towards East Moor Drive en route to the dark, wet and desolate East Moor Park.

After spending twenty minutes walking along pitch-black, muddied footpaths and weaving in and around the rain-lashed playground, they eventually sought temporary refuge under the bus shelter on East Moor Road. It was just a basic overhead rain shelter which did little to protect them from the lateral trajectory of the chaotic, monsoon-like rainfall.

As the thunder and lightning inflicted its vitriol upon

the sorry little scene, Sophia's grip on her mother's hand tightened, little by little. The tears that ran down her cold cheeks were drowned within the copious rivulets of rainwater that also diluted the watery mucus trickling from her numbed button nose. She closed her eyes. 'I wish Daddy was here,' she whispered.

Zoe contemplated her next move. There was nowhere else for them to go as the storm showed no signs of abating. The cold, saturated conditions helped her to refocus on the situation she'd fabricated herself. She was thinking a little more rationally. She realised that dragging her young daughter out in such atrocious weather, with the lightning being especially prevalent, was irresponsible. She hadn't been thinking straight.

She didn't want to go back to the house, but she began to question whether her fears were unfounded. Last night had been incident free. She loved her daughter dearly and had responsibilities towards her, but she couldn't go back to Seacroft. *If only me mother was as gullible as Phil. We'll have to go back to the house...but what about the witch doll? It might have fallen accidentally... The crash...? Maybe I did leave a window open... What about the music...? Is it all in me friggin' head? The other night with the flapping...the dragging...the blood on the sheets.*

Confusion and uncertainty raged through her headspace, and she, too, had tears diluted by the rainwater streaming down her face. She was trapped, backed into a corner; but when Zoe was backed into a corner, she was at her most belligerent. She was a fighter, and she never, ever backed down. *Come on, you silly little bitch. Let's 'ave it...bring it on!*

She would face up to another night in the house, she had to, but she'd utilise the old chestnuts of alcohol and drugs to help her through it. She'd up the ante in order to maximise the effect – not to ease the mental anguish, but to fucking obliterate it. *Obliteration, that's it. That'll sort it, total fucking obliteration. Just for tonight. Just a one off.*

'Come on, love,' she said with a sigh. 'Let's go get you some sweets, and then we'll go home and get you warm and dry.'

*

'Bloody hell, you're both drenched,' said Sally. 'What you been up to? Haven't you got a brolly or summat? You shouldn't be out on a night like this. Is there owt up, love?'

Zoe shook her head as Mrs Patel, who was already standing sentinel behind the counter, looked on in astonishment at the state of her dishevelled customers. Zoe's wet and wizened features painted a clear picture: bedraggled, soaking hair and red-rimmed, dark-bagged eyes.

She wouldn't look Sally in the eye as she banged two 4-packs of Stella lager onto the counter. 'And a bottle of Grants,' she mumbled, before indicating for Sophia to choose crisps from the half a dozen flavours stacked behind them in opened cardboard boxes. She grabbed two bags from the nearest box.

'Are you all right, love?' repeated a concerned Sally with a sincere frown carved into his forehead. He reached behind him and plucked a bottle of whisky from the highest shelf.

Zoe nodded, again without making eye contact, and then ushered Sophia to choose a chocolate bar from the front display cabinet. She turned to see Sally about to drop the whisky into a carrier bag and held her hand up. She shook her head. 'No, a big one.'

'Ah, a full bottle,' replied Sally, rolling his eyes as he turned away from her.

Zoe nodded. 'Yeah...a full bottle.'

Mrs Patel looked on in silence.

Sally replaced the small bottle of whisky and took down a larger 70cl bottle and carefully placed it into the bag. He looked down at the impoverished little girl who now stood in a small pool of rainwater, shivering as the cold and wet clothing clung to her pale skin. 'And how are you today, me lovely?' he said. 'Are you OK?'

The little girl nodded.

'You're soaking wet, aren't you, luvvie? Come 'ere, give us your sweets,' he said as he reached down for the crisps and chocolate and placed them into the carrier bag.

Zoe handed over two twenty-pound notes.

'Hey, d'ya know summat?' said Sally as he nodded towards Sophia.

She replied with a timid shake of her head.

'Did you know I used to be a boxer?' He looked down at her with widened eyes. 'Oh aye, I were a boxer, me. I bet you din't know that, did ya?'

A bewildered Sophia stared intently and shook her head again.

'Oh aye,' he said. 'I worked at Smiths Crisps for over a year!' He immediately collapsed in laughter as he realised his punchline and slapped the countertop with the palm of his hand. His eyes streamed with tears of unadulterated mirth; he couldn't contain himself. His gesture of trying to put a smile on the little girl's face was blown away by his own uncontrollable reaction to his shallow dad joke. 'D'ya get it?' he said through cries of laughter. He indicated the shape of a box with his hands to Zoe and then imitated placing bags of crisps into the imaginary box. 'Boxing the crisps... Putting 'em into 'box? A boxer... Smiths Crisps!' He turned away and again slapped the counter, this time twice in quick succession. He crouched over. 'Boxer... Smiths Crisps...'

The blank looks on the faces of his bewildered customers only served to crank up the intensity of his hilarity.

He eventually composed himself and straightened up as he retrieved Zoe's change from the till, but he continued to chuckle, barely able to see through his welled up eyes.

There was no other sound from inside the shop, no reaction, no movement. Sophia stood silent and befuddled, while the joke completely flew over Zoe's head.

Mrs Patel stood in muted disgust. Sally's genuine attempt to inject humour into a sensitive, highly charged and emotional situation had failed miserably, although he didn't comprehend it that way.

His shoulders were still rocking as he handed the change to Zoe and passed her the bag whilst shaking his head. This time it was Sally who avoided looking her in the eye. 'Smiths Crisps,' he muttered again, 'it's a belter.' He continued to chuckle at his one-man variety show.

Zoe took the bag and grabbed hold of Sophia by the arm. 'Come on, love, let's get home.' Drenched and confused, they stumbled towards the door.

'Hey, missus,' cried out Mrs Patel.

Zoe stopped in her tracks.

'Look at me,' she said. 'Come here, look at me in eye.'

Zoe turned her head slowly until eye contact was made with the interfering Indian woman whom she so despised. They looked deep into each other's eyes.

'I know husband is away this weekend. He told us. I know things not good for you,' said Mrs Patel as she continued to lean over the counter glaring directly into Zoe's sorrowful eyes. 'I let you know, missus...if you need anything...anything, you come here and see me, Mrs Patel. I only at end of street, and if you or little one need anything, or anyone...you come see me...OK? You get that? You understand?'

Tears were now streaming down Zoe's cheeks as she nodded.

'You don't forget now,' added Mrs Patel, nodding and pointing at her as she turned and carried on towards the exit.

'Thank you,' whispered Zoe. She opened the door to the sound of a digital doorbell and disappeared into the wild, dark night.

Mrs Patel tuned her attention to Sally, who was still giggling and shaking his head at his masterful performance and impeccable timing in delivering his punchline. According to him, he'd smashed it, even though his intended audience of one, a six-year-old, hadn't appreciated it. He'd smashed it, and he'd smashed it big time.

'I should've been on 'bloody stage, me. I missed out somewhere,' he mumbled to himself, unaware of his wife's utter contempt for him.

'Stage my arse,' she muttered as she squeezed her ample torso through the half-opened door and into the back room. 'You miss out big time on fucking brain. Dickhead!'

*

Eight. Zoe looked around the living room; she was already on her third tin of lager. Sophia, now warm and dry, was sat cross-legged on the fireside rug in her pyjamas with Princess by her side watching cartoons. The little girl yawned, the usual sparkle in her eyes dulled, her eye-lids heavy with tiredness.

'Mum, can I go to bed yet?' she asked.

'No, you can stay up for a bit more.'

'I'm tired, Mum.'

'Do as you're told and watch 'telly,' said Zoe before taking another gulp of lager as the rain continued to batter the outside of the house. 'Have you finished your chocolate and crisps yet?' she added.

'I've had enough chocolate—' There was a knock at the door. 'Who's that?' asked a startled Sophia.

'How do I know?' replied Zoe looking at the clock. 'Don't worry, love, calm down,' she said as she elevated her tired body from the sofa. *It's only just gone eight. He's never this early.* She crouched towards the window and pulled back the curtain. There were no headlights, no waiting car. *Who the fuck is it?* The knock was repeated, not a stern, forceful knock, but definitely a knock. Her heart dropped. *What if there's no fucker there?* She stood still for a second and then realised that her hesitancy was spooking Sophia.

She asserted herself and approached the door as the knock was repeated for a second time. She steeled herself whilst spinning the latch and pulling the door open towards her.

There was no one there. The squalling rain blew into the house, wetting her face as she stared out into the storm. And then came a voice: 'Me mam said 'ave you any milk?'

Who the fuck? Zoe looked down and saw the middle lad from The Bottom House Kids, drenched, standing in the pouring torrent.

'What?'

'It's me mam. She said 'ave you got any milk cos she hasn't got any, and she's no money till Monday, and she said she'll get you it back when she gets her money on Monday,' he said in an unusually husky voice for one so young.

Zoe took a second for the bizarre request to sink into her fuzzled head. 'Come in, you're getting drowned stood out there,' she said as she unlocked the security gate to let the young lad in.

He entered the room and his gaze met Sophia's, which immediately brokered broad smiles on both accounts. He wore dirty tracksuit bottoms with a mismatching hooded top. His soiled trainers were cheap and worn. His fingernails were dirty, and his hair drenched and unkempt. 'Hiya, Sophia,' he said, beaming.

'Hiya,' replied Sophia sheepishly, unable to hide a smile from her illicit little playmate.

'Sophia, go into the kitchen and get a bottle of milk from the fridge,' said Zoe.

Sophia obediently carried out the order.

'What does yer mother want milk for?' asked Zoe as she turned and looked over the dripping wet scruff bag.

'It's for us supper cos she got visitors later and she wants us all in bed,' he replied. 'We're 'aving cereal.'

'Are you? You're wet. Why don't you sit in front of the fire for a bit and watch cartoons with Sophia?'

'Oooh, thank you,' he replied.

'It's *SpongeBob SquarePants*. Do you like it?'

'I've never seen it, but thank you,' he said with a smile.

'Sophia, get him a towel,' she shouted through to the kitchen. 'Do you want some crisps and chocolate?' Zoe asked the boy.

'Yes, please,' he replied, by now kneeling in front of the

blazing living-flame gas fire and beaming from ear to ear.

Sophia brought out the milk, placed it on the coffee table and handed the boy a tea towel.

'Sophia, get yer friend some chocolate and crisps and get him a drink of Pepsi.'

'Mum...I thought you said...'

'Never mind what I said, just get it,' replied Zoe, throwing Sophia a knowing motherly stare.

The little girl needed no further encouragement; the novelty of having a 'guest' round quickly dissipated any tiredness. Not only did she serve her friend the snacks, but she also went the extra mile and delivered them on her favourite SpongeBob serving tray.

Both the children were content and easy in each other's company, each with a smile on their faces as they chuckled at the cartoons and chattered away like little lifelong friends.

For Zoe, it was just a brief period of relief. The company and increased normal activity in the house took the edge off her anxiety. She relaxed just a little and resolved to enjoy it as much as she could; she knew it wouldn't last. She glugged away at the lager.

The wind and rain continued to batter against the windows. The thunder rolled and the lightning flashed as the children laughed and chattered. The mother guzzled and drank in silence.

Through the cacophony of the storm and the blazing antics of SpongeBob and his pals, there was another knock at the door. This time firmer and more forceful than the earlier one.

Zoe quickly looked up at the clock. Eight thirty. *Still too early. Who the fuck is it this time? It's like fucking Briggate in here tonight.*

Again, she jumped up and peeked through the curtains. This time she saw a shrouded figure hunched in the doorway. *Who the fuck?* She swung the door open.

'Is he 'ere?' cried the voice in a thick, flat Leeds accent.

Zoe recognised the huddled figure as the mother of The Bottom House Kids trying in vain to shelter from the torrid weather. 'Yeah, he's here, come in,' said Zoe, 'get out of the rain.'

The Bottom House mother ushered herself in and bent over shaking her shaggy shoulder-length curls with her hands after pushing the door closed behind her. 'This fucking weather, innit?' proclaimed the small, ample-chested woman with dark olive skin, soft brown eyes and natural beauty. 'It's never fucking stopped, 'as it? All friggin' day. I'm Tracy, by the way, honey. Some call me Racy Tracy, ha, ha! You know what I mean, love? And where've you been, ya little get? I only sent you up to borrow some friggin' milk. Where've ya been?' she asked with an impish grin on her face.

'Look, Mam, I've had some chocolate and crisps and some pop with Sophia, and we've been watching *Square-Bob Underpants*,' gushed the young lad excitedly with a huge grin on his thin, pale face.

'Aye, I bet you have, ya little fucker.'

Sophia chuckled. 'It's *SpongeBob SquarePants*.'

'Ha, ha, *SpongeBob SquarePants*, is it, love? Well, we've gotta get going now, so SpongeBob'll have to wait until next time. C'mon, buster, let's be 'aving ya.' She spotted the milk on the coffee table and picked it up. 'Aw thanks, darling. You don't mind, do ya? I'll get you some more when I get paid o' Monday.'

'Yeah...er...that's fine,' replied Zoe. 'You...er... You don't want to stay for a drink, do ya?' she asked, glancing down towards the remaining tins of lager standing up-right on the table.

'Oh, yer a darling, love, but I've got people coming round, an' I need to get these little fuckers to bed. Ya know how it is. Us lasses have got to have a bit o' time for usselves, an't we, luvvie?' She laughed and winked. 'C'mon, you fuckerlugs,' she said to the boy as he got up and walked towards her. She clipped him around his head not with malice but with love, and the boy beamed with pride. 'Right, we're off, darling. What do ya say?' she said, turning to the boy.

'Thank you, Sophia, and thank you, Mrs Cooper,' he said, still smiling.

'Can he come again, Mum?' asked Sophia.

'Er…yeah.'

'And thanks for the milk, darling. We're off – no doubt gonna get fucking drenched again, but, hey ho! Ta-ra now, and thanks again!' She darted out into the sodden dark-ness of the street with her happy young charge in tow.

Zoe pulled the security gate towards her and locked it before slamming the front door closed with the Yale lock engaged. She looked at the clock. *Twenty to nine. Fourteen hours.* Sophia yawned. *Better get her to bed.*

'Right, come on, you. Bedtime. Get yer teeth brushed, and I'll be up to tuck you in in ten minutes. Take dopey Jimmy with ya.'

'Night, Mum,' said Sophia as she gave her mum a hug.

Zoe squeezed her daughter tightly and caressed her flushed cheeks before kissing her on the forehead. 'Go on now,' she said, 'I'll be up soon.'

Princess dutifully followed his mistress up the wind-ing staircase with his usual boundless energy and bat-tery-powered tail.

With Sophia out of the way, Zoe stood up and opened the bifolding kitchen door. Without stepping over the threshold, she reached over to the cutlery drawer and grabbed a spoon and then picked up a bottle of vinegar which was on the worktop. The very fact that just her head and arm were technically inside the boundaries of, what she perceived to be, the horrible little room sent a tingling shiver down the length of her spine.

She rammed the door closed and sat on the sofa, carefully placing the spoon and vinegar onto the coffee table. Sliding her hand into her handbag, she pulled out a packaged hypodermic needle and placed it next to the spoon and vinegar. Further rummaging around the bag yielded cigarette filters, which, again, she placed neatly on the table. *Ten minutes.*

CHAPTER 8

May 1975

George's raincoat was damp, if not dripping wet, due to the intermittent rain showers he'd encountered on the way home from the club. Clutching his Saturday night supper, he shuffled through the front door and gently closed it behind him. With his wife lying motionless on the settee, he slunk past her and eased his bulk into the kitchen.

Stella's head was buzzing; her body wasted. Her dark, sunken eyes and purple, engorged nose stood out, distinct against her otherwise pallid features. On this particular Saturday evening, she appeared a little more subdued than was the norm, a little less forward, less animated. She remained still and listless with no inclination to engage or interact with her monotonous husband as he peered through a gap in the curtained partition.

East Moor Park Workingmen's Club had been the Saturday night drinking haunt of George for many years. Stella had ceased accompanying him due to the bland company he kept in the gloomy TV room. That was her story – the fact of the matter was that she'd been scratched, for being drunk and disorderly, during an incident in the more comfortable lounge, where the self-styled, discerning clientele chose to spend their weekend evenings.

George would never have been seen anywhere near the lounge, not with his gum line, and would certainly never venture into the concert room, where the early and late (bingo) flyers sandwiched the night's variety entertainment and where the atmosphere was more vibrant and upbeat. He preferred the TV room with his like-minded, easy-to-please pals. Not much conversation, not much thunder and well under the radar – just as he liked it.

One evening, bored with the company of 'the doylems' , Stella decided to spend an hour or two in the lounge, leaving George in the TV room. In her younger days, she'd been accustomed to a much higher tempo of socialising, always partial to a drink and a boisterous laugh with a large but tight-knit group of friends. Most of these were from her earlier life with Trevor, but over the years they'd subsequently moved on, away from East Leeds. Now she had no one.

She could never remember anyone joking or chuckling in the TV room. She needed more stimulation than she could ever hope to receive in the company of George and his pals. So, it was in the posh lounge where she'd attempted to fraternise with the elite, to impose her dormant charms on the unsuspecting patrons. Here, the gentlemen sat stiff-backed, suited and collared; the ladies lounged demurely, drinking Babychams and G&Ts, with pretentious eveningwear and immaculate hairdos. *This was more like it*, she thought as she found an empty barstool at the bar.

Sitting alone for nearly two hours, knocking back whisky and dry ginger, there had been no fraternisation of any order. She didn't speak a word to a soul other than the barman, and she was not spoken to by one person. She spent the first hour smiling and trying to fit in, awaiting an opportunity of eye contact, a chance encounter... with anyone. Even the bottle boys passed her by without a nod or hint of a pleasantry.

The second hour she sat and wallowed in self-misery, in seething silence, knocking back the whisky. She wished this crew could have seen herself and Trevor in their pomp. *That would've shown them. None of this lot in here could compare to my Trevor and me – none of 'em. There's no class, no warmth and no life in this lot. Not a patch on us and our crew.*

She staggered up and declared that they were a set of pompous, arrogant bastards, that they were no better than anyone else and questioned who the fuck they thought they were anyway! She'd been escorted out by a committee member and banned for a month.

Although the ban had been lifted, an embarrassed George had been reluctant to pass on the message that she was now eligible, on good behaviour, to have her membership reinstated. It didn't really matter as there was little disposition on her part to return to the club, or the TV room. The patrons, she declared, were all mild-drinking stiffs from the Sally Army hostel – not her type at all, never mind the up-their-own-arses crew in the lounge.

Instead, these days, a Saturday evening for her would be spent entertaining herself at home, alone with her granddaughter, in front of the telly and with a plentiful supply of alcohol, usually provided by George.

He placed the newspaper-wrapped chips and curry onto the cabinet worktop and then retrieved two dishes from the overhead cupboard. The pair neither sought eye contact nor registered acknowledgement of the other's presence. It wasn't quite the usual Saturday night routine. Stella was half-cut, but not at the stage, yet, where she'd sunk low enough to give her record collection an airing. As far as George was concerned, this unorthodox schedule put him slightly on edge. He looked down on her from behind the curtain with the hint of a frown and a slight purse of his bloated, fish-like lips.

He dished out the food and rubbed his stubbled chin as he deliberated over the current state of affairs – the highly irregular state of affairs, as he saw it. He served the meal by shoving it onto the coffee table with a fork protruding from the pile of chips.

'Here, come on then, sit up and 'ave your supper,' he demanded as he rounded the coffee table to collect a handful of Bell's miniatures from his overcoat pockets. He placed them on the table in front of Stella. 'Here, some Bell's for you. Are you not playing your music tonight? What's up wi' you?' he said in what was, for him, a rather forceful manner.

'Thanksh, love... Not feeling meshelf tonight,' she replied as her dulled eyes slowly shifted to make contact with his.

'You'll be reet,' reassured George, reaching over and grabbing one of the miniature bottles. 'Get some music going then, and get them there chips down ya. That'll settle you down.' He unscrewed the bottle and poured the sweet-smelling contents into a beaker which Stella had been using for the consumption of vodka.

'All right... All right... Shtop rushing me,' she replied in a slow drawl. She grabbed her teeth from the table and jostled them into place before attempting to rise from the settee, where she'd lain for almost three hours.

'Hell fire, woman, you're all over the bloody place. Stay there and get that down you,' said George impatiently as he handed her the beaker. 'I'll get it.'

Stella collapsed back into the settee and took a gulp of the whisky.

George lifted the record player from the alcove and set it down on the coffee table, plugging it into the socket. 'Who do you want? Ronnie Hilton? Dickie Valentine?'

'Slim,' she replied.

'Right y'are.' He shuffled through the small collection and eased the shiny black vinyl from its sleeve before carefully placing it onto the already revolving turntable. 'This is more like it, love,' he said as he lowered and positioned the stylus. 'Now, 'ave your chips, and you'll feel a lot better... Go on.'

'Not that hungry, love,' she replied. 'Don't feel too good...'

'Well, I've bought 'em for you now, so just try 'em an' see.'

She reached over and lifted the fork, which already had a lifeless chip attached. After staring at it for a second, she reluctantly shoved it into her mouth. She needn't have replaced her teeth as she almost sucked the soggy morsel straight down her throat in one. Having swallowed it, the sustenance, and perhaps the music, perked her up a little as she followed with two more mouthfuls.

'There y'are, look. I told you, din't I?' said George, as if encouraging a two-year-old to eat porridge. 'Good lass. Now come on, have another drink, it'll brighten your mood.'

Stella looked George in the eye before slowly turning away and succumbing to his persuasive demands. She took a large gulp, the effects of which went straight to her head, causing her to wince and her eyes to water. 'You'll be the death o' me, you will,' she slurred.

'Eh? What ya say, love?'

'Nowt,' she said, dismissing him with a shaking wave of her hand.

The two spent the next twenty minutes consuming the meal without communication, both content to listen to the constantly repeating 'Rose Marie' by Slim Whitman.

'Why don't you stay up with me an' have a drink?' asked Stella, suddenly breaking the silence.

'Aye-aye,' replied George, raising an eyebrow and turning to look at her. 'You know me, love. I'm off to bed when I've finished these. You stay up and listen to your dancing music, like y'allus do.'

'You allus go to bed, love. Stay up with me. I've been on my own all night... Trevor would've.'

'Well, Trevor's not here, is he? And I'm not Trevor. Anyway, you've had us granddaughter for company.'

Stella stared at George through sorry eyes.

He shifted his bulk and looked down at the dish.

'Well, she goes to bed early, and, you know, she doesn't say much... Are we going to church tomorrow?'

'You know we can't go back there, love. Not after the way you showed me up last time. I could never show me face in there again after that. Everyone looking and pointing at us,' he said, shaking his head. 'We're the pariahs of society around here now, thanks to you, can't show us faces anywhere.'

'I'm sorry, love... It won't happen again.'

'I know it won't cos we won't be going again, will we? You're scratched... You've been banned from... No, *we've* been banned from the church, not by Father Venables, but by me! I've banned us. We're not going, and that's that – and it's all down to your drinkin'.' George stopped abruptly. 'Anyway, just have your chips and your whisky. Have you had your tablets today?'

Stella didn't reply.

After a short pause, George muttered that he was tired and off to bed. 'I'll put yer dancing record on for you afore I go.'

With much effort, he rose from the armchair and returned his empty dish into the kitchen, sliding it into the sink. From behind the cover of the curtain, he once again carefully scrutinised the demeanour of his wife as she struggled with the late-night supper. He noticed the whisky was proving much easier for her to consume than the food; she'd already rattled through the first couple of bottles.

He re-entered the living area and replaced the 'Rose Marie' record with 'Lonely Ballerina'. The soft music soon filled the room and instilled in Stella her customary melancholy reminisces. She could barely sit up, never mind embark on her usual drunken 'ballet' routine, but, by waving her shaky arms in the air, she managed a feeble attempt at impersonating Mantovani's conducting style, albeit in the absence of his or any other live orchestra.

'Stay with me, love,' she murmured softly without even looking up at her husband.

'I'm off. I'll see y'in 'morning,' he replied as he lumbered over to the stair door and shifted his bulk up the first couple of stairs, gently pulling the door closed behind him. He purposely left it slightly ajar.

As her drained and delicate body lay listless on the settee, Stella couldn't face finishing off the food. Her mock conducting gradually diminished until she was completely still. Even the consumption of alcohol petered out as she eventually succumbed to the effects of the combination of strong lager, vodka and whisky, her eyelids laden with the weight of her miserable existence. As the tones of Mantovani continued to pervade the furthest corners of the pitiful little house, her consciousness ebbed away to a level of insentience. She was oblivious to the pair of bulging eyeballs staring hard through the two-inch gap of the slightly opened stair door.

As Stella's mindset ebbed from conscious into unconscious, George's senses remained on high alert. He stood silent and motionless. There were no desperate, awkward dancing moves from Stella tonight. Highly irregular, he considered, but he remained put until he was sure, absolutely positive, that she was out for the night. Once satisfied, he turned, clicked the door firmly closed behind him and began a slow, lumbering ascent up the steep staircase.

*

The Girl lay on her back in the dark attic bedroom with the bedclothes drawn over her head. There was no bedside table lamp, the main light had been turned off, and the only chink of illumination came from the street lighting which shone through a gap in the grubby curtains hanging in front of the dormer window. The decaying window frames allowed the wind to whittle through, creating a constant, low-howling whistle. The Girl hadn't slept at all; she never did in this room.

If, on the ground floor, Stella's consciousness had deteriorated into a mishmash of alcohol-infused madness, then the mindset of The Girl on the top floor was crystal clear. She listened to groups of kids in the street, shouting, laughing, joking and squabbling. She heard the revellers and drunks returning home. Some happy, crooning love songs; others abrupt, boisterous and aggressive.

She witnessed the thunder of the East Coast loco-
motive as it powered along the railway towards Selby,
but she never flinched. The rain showers softly pattered
against the window as she slowly sank into a desolate,
psychosomatic world where the haunting, whistling
winds never die and the black oppression forever suffo-
cates.

As the rotting window frames continued to be
breached by the mean-spirited, spiteful wind, the un-
lined curtains fluttered and buffered, casting irregular
dancing shadows on the inside walls. The Girl, though
still of tender years, perceived a cold and ominous atmosphere in this, the dormer attic bedroom. She always
did.

As the hours and minutes ticked away, The Girl's
breathing gradually became more laboured, her heart
rate accelerated. Her mouth dried out and her grip on the
bedclothes tightened. For a short while, the wind died
down and ceased – a time out. A lull ensued as The Girl
listened intently to the abject black silence. And then,
a distant click. Another click, and then a double click,
from outside and at some distance. The clicking got
closer and became louder and developed into footsteps,
laboured footsteps, the resonance of which she was familiar with.

She closed her eyes and clung onto the bed sheets as
the footsteps became louder and more distinct, louder,
clicking, louder, until they ceased directly beneath the
bedroom window on the old stone pavement two floors
below. Granddad George was home. The jangle of keys,
then the sound of the door being unlocked and closed.

The muffled high-pitched voice of Granddad George

could be heard from two floors above in the attic bedroom. Stella's voice was too weak to traverse the two flights of stairs, so it sounded like a one-way conversation to The Girl, not that she could hear distinctly enough to make any sense of it. She remained alert under the cover of the sheet as she listened. Her heightened senses picked up the nauseating aroma of greasy food integrated with the more permanent odours of alcohol and damp. It was a familiar routine. Muffled one-way conversation, the clatter of crockery and then music. Familiar music. Old-fashioned music. But not *the* music – not yet, anyway.

The wind resumed and continued to wail like a demented demon. The little dormer bedroom hadn't been touched or decorated in twenty-odd years, not since the days when a young Susan Wilson had occupied it. It was cold and damp, and the ominous blackness pressed itself upon The Girl, her anxiety steadily intensifying. Her delicate hands began to twitch – the only sign of life as she lay steadfast, stock-still and silent.

There was the distant clatter of crockery, a tap being turned on and the subsequent hissing of the lead pipes as the water tank in the bathroom below slowly replenished. And then a subtle change of music, and with it a further deterioration of the ambience in the draughty little bedroom. As the stifled tune of 'Lonely Ballerina' by Mantovani and his orchestra slowly filtered up the two flights of stairs, The Girl stiffened and slammed her eyes closed. Alone, all alone in the whole world, she remained rigid, her delicate body consumed with fits of sporadic twitching.

The intensity of the music increased and became clearer amid the incoherent mumblings of Granddad

George, and remained so as his monotone drone slowly petered out. A negative mist seeped beneath the sheets and infiltrated The Girl's defenceless psyche as she clung onto every sound, every smell. The click of the door being closed two floors below. Mantovani and his orchestra returned to a muffled resonance. The Girl recoiled and retreated deeper into her silent, blank world.

The heavy, sweating bulk of Granddad George began his upward journey, his leather brogues producing a hollow thud on each of the threadbare steps as he lumbered upwards. Step by step, each laboured, each an incremental juncture closer, slowly reducing the distance between himself and The girl. She shuddered as each thud on each tread sent a splinter-sharp shard of ice-cold revulsion reverberating through her vulnerable frame. Louder, more succinct, closer. She listened, her eyes now tightly closed, her desperate grip on the bedclothes so tight that her clenched fists trembled, her pulsating heart beat like the piston of an overworked steam engine. The music continued on and on, continuous and insensitive, as the wind whistled with increased vigour and the curtains quivered with portentous anticipation.

The footsteps stopped, just for a moment. First-floor landing. Hard rasping of Granddad George as he hesitated, taking a moment to regain his breath and compose his overweight and overworked body. The footsteps resumed, slow and lumbering, until The Girl heard the creaking of the landing door hinges. The second flight of stairs. Around the twisting corner, one dull thud after another.

Granddad George now struggled with every step, stopping to regain his breath on each, further cranking up the intensity of the atmosphere. The Girl's attempts at remaining deathly still were foiled by the constant and un-controllable tremor of every nerve in her delicate young body. The steps continued, nearer, louder, each one more concise, more terse, than the last.

The music meandered in and around The Girl's head whilst the constant low wind hummed like a perpetual dammed soul. Three steps to go. The Girl's mouth was now arid dry, her forehead dripping, as his rasping breath, his rancid, rasping breath, edged nearer and nearer, sharing and soiling the very same air particles that she was forced to silently draw into her young un-sullied lungs.

The footsteps stopped. Granddad George heaved and swayed. Sweat ran down his matted back as he poked the creaking door open. Silence. The Girl intensified her concentration, her agitated heart threatening to break loose from her ribcage as she sensed his burning eyes in the darkened room. Granddad George composed himself and wiped his streaming brow with the back of his hand. He scrutinised The Girl's quaking body, shrouded within the bedclothes like a corpse awaiting ceremonial sacrifice. She sensed his approach before his bulk eased onto the bed next to her. Her grip on the sheet intensified as she clamped her eyelids as tight as a pair of limpets on a far-away Flamborough rock.

'Right y'are, lass...right y'are,' soothed Granddad George in his high-pitched, soft voice. 'Come on now, love, it's only me... Granddad George's come to see you.'

The Girl smelled the stomach-wrenching combination of alcohol and body odour, causing her to flinch as she slammed her head sideways away from him.

'Come on, luvvie, let's have a look at you. I know you're awake, love,' he said in between large gulps of air.

'Come on now, you've nowt to be scared of…it's only me.' He attempted to separate the sheets from The girl's determined grip.

She clung on for dear life, but she was only six years old and no match for the bulking strength of Granddad George.

'Right y'are, love.' He intensified his efforts to remove the sheet. 'Come on, luvvie, you've nowt to be scared of, it's only me, your granddad, Granddad George.'

The Girl struggled and put up a brave fight but eventually acknowledged the inevitable. She realised the futility of resistance and gradually gave up, slowly releasing her grip as Granddad George gently but firmly eased the bedclothes down to the very bottom of the bed.

His black malevolent eyes scanned every inch of the slight, vulnerable form of his six-year-old granddaughter. 'Right y'are, love,' he whispered as he ran his dirty fingers through her soft shoulder-length hair. 'It's only me, love. Granddad's here.'

The Girl remained stock-still as tears broached her iron-tight eyelids and ran down her soft cheeks.

Granddad George cupped and caressed her face with his gnarled, filthy hands. He lowered his head towards hers and licked her face before forcing his brutish, stinking tongue between her lips, into her mouth and down her throat to the extent that she began choking. His rank breath made The Girl's stomach turn as she physically retched, but he continued, groaning and rubbing his bloated, orange-peeled snout against her soft little button nose.

She flailed and flapped, but what strength she could muster against that of her grandfather soon diminished. She eventually gave up, her body listless, her eyes clamped closed and her mind jettisoned to another realm, beyond an impenetrable psychological shield. She was his to do with as he pleased.

Contorted shadows played out on the darkened, desperate walls as the wind wailed and hollered around the tiny attic bedroom, in the tiny house, on the tiny street in East Moor Park.

*

Stella's consciousness raised its hazy, fuzzled head. The sounds of Mantovani and his orchestra continued to reverberate around the cluttered sitting room. She opened her misty eyes and mustered as much strength as her frail body could facilitate in order to sit up. She looked around the room in a daze. Just for a fleeting moment, she searched for Trevor before realising that she was stuck in the 1970s not the 1950s. She was alone, and it was George who had left her...again.

Trevor, her first husband, would never have done so. He would have held her hand and stayed up with her. He would have danced with her; he would have kissed her. He was a gentleman, a kind-hearted, quiet and gentle caring man, tragically taken away from his small family whilst in the prime of life. They'd made such a handsome couple as they frequented the dancehalls of Leeds in the early 50s, jiving, jitterbugging and bopping almost every night and without the need of alcohol.

Such happy memories; such happy carefree times. She was an elegant, beautiful woman who exuded a sparkling energy and an irresistible personality. He was, in the eyes of Stella, the most handsome and striking of any man she had ever laid eyes on, always immaculately dressed with gleaming white teeth and jet-black hair. They'd been so happy when Susan came along, with the astute Trevor insisting they buy a family home rather than rent.

Although the house in Reginald Street was small, it was still almost unknown in those days for a young couple to buy their own home. But that was Trevor. He decorated the whole house from top to bottom, built the small dormer bedroom in the attic and converted the small bedroom into a bathroom with an inside toilet. They were the first ones in the street to have this modernisation carried out. But that was Trevor. They'd been so happy those first few years in their little home with their daughter and the whole world in front of them. That was until two days before Susan's fourth birthday, when her doting daddy was knocked down and killed by a lorry in Leeds town centre.

The following period had been Stella's first venture into the dark world of depression. Although Trevor had been savvy enough to take out insurance to pay off the mortgage, there was little left for his wife and daughter to live off. These had been the wilderness years for Stella. She'd never come to terms with how the happy family unit, with a husband she adored, had been abruptly reduced to single-parent status, struggling to make ends meet.

The spark in her eyes was lost forever; her confidence, pride and self-worth slowly eroded away. She was never to be the same woman again. She'd met George at The Palace pub on the edge of town two years after Trevor had passed. He'd seemed a nice enough fella, a bit dull and unexciting, but he had a job and Stella had decided that Susan needed a father figure in her life. He'd proven to be a poor replacement for her true love. Trevor would never have left her downstairs in the late hours in such a state.

He would have caressed her and cared for her. But that was Trevor, and this was George, and George wasn't here. George had gone. He'd left her, alone.

Just for a moment, she allowed her heart to lord it over her head as she felt the pain of many years of emotional neglect along with the huge emptiness she still harboured over the loss of her first husband. However, it wasn't long before it smacked home just how physically ill she felt as the effects of the alcohol reared to the fore.

She staggered up and stumbled into the kitchen before heaving the noxious contents of her stomach into the sink. The violent gagging tested her physical resolve to the limit as she began sweating and shaking. She held onto the sink for dear life as her overworked heart tightened and struggled with the sudden burst of stress and physical activity. Her mouth tasted like the inside of a toxic waste bin as she spat and spluttered before grabbing a mug and filling it with water. She first sipped and then rinsed her mouth. After swallowing a couple of mouthfuls, she managed to compose herself.

Lurching back into the sitting room, she decided she couldn't face any more Mantovani. It was nauseating her woozy headspace. She stooped down and yanked the plug out of the socket. The turntable slowed down and stopped. All was silent. She took deep breaths and felt her heart pumping, harder than usual, harder than was good for her. The water and retching had not only helped to sober Stella up, but it had the effect of enabling her to think rationally, just for once.

'Bed,' she croaked, 'got to get to me bed.' She swayed towards the bottom door and began climbing the stairs methodically, using the banister to steady herself as best she could. As she reached the top three winders, she had to stop just to catch her breath. Once she managed to regain reasonable control, she continued around the bend, faltering past the bathroom door and passing the slightly opened attic door before staggering through to the bedroom and collapsing onto the bed.

After closing her eyes as the room began to spin, she felt the need to sit up and kick off her slippers. As she did so, she heard a noise, not anything particularly unusual, just a noise, something that made her take note. She tried to make sense of it and was just about to dismiss it when the noise was repeated. A muffled whimper. She then realised that George wasn't in the bed.

'Where the hell is he?' she muttered. 'He can't be down the bloody cellar at this time o' night.' Her mind began to clear itself of muddled thoughts and alcohol-induced confusion. Again, she heard a muffled whimper; and again, through the bedroom doorway, she noticed the attic landing door slightly open.

She cocked her head and narrowed her eyes as she stared at the door. The mists of confusion began to lift. George. She slowly got to her feet and began walking towards the bedroom door opening. This time she heard muted grunting and groaning and more whimpering. A dark sentiment of dread trickled into her heavy heart. She turned to face the landing door and opened it fully, causing the dry, rusting iron hinges to creak.

Sinister thoughts peppered her headspace, thoughts she dare not expand on, thoughts that made the hairs on the back of her head and neck stand to full attention. She slowly ascended the stairs, quietly, refusing to accept the scenario that was being created and enacted inside her head.

As she continued, the grunting reached a stifled crescendo, followed by heavy breathing. The whimpering stopped, but Stella didn't. Stella continued. As she reached the top landing, she stood and gripped onto the banister. The sight that befell her made her knees buckle.

Through the wide opened doorway, in the gloomy light of the dormer bedroom, she saw the corpulent, sweating backside of her husband. She saw him ease himself away from the naked body of her granddaughter. Unaware of the presence of his wife and oblivious to the fact that Mantovani had packed in, he softly pulled down The Girl's nightdress from around her neck and lifted the bedclothes back over her limp body. He pulled up his dirty drawers and trousers and re-engaged his braces before lowering himself onto the bed where the listless body of The Girl lay, her eyes still tightly closed.

'Right y'are, me luvvie...right y'are,' he murmured in his sickly, soothing manner. 'Thank you for that, my little love. You know I love you, don't you? And don't forget that this is our little secret, just you and me.' He kissed her on the lips and stroked her forehead. 'This is for you,' he said as he forced open her hand, placed an object inside and then firmly wrapped it back into the original clenched state.

Stunned, Stella looked on silently. Her mind became clearer; the effects of the alcohol had evaporated and the gravity of the situation smacked her in the heart. She was broken in half.

'Night night, luvvie,' he said quietly as he struggled to ease himself up from the bed. 'Right y'are.' He picked up his shoes and turned around to exit the room. He then suddenly stopped dead in his tracks as he came face to face with the frail, hunched figure of his alcoholic wife in the dismal darkness of the doorway.

She stood wide-eyed and open-mouthed, seemingly sober, with her wrinkled face and stooped gait, staring him straight in the face. Both stood in silence. A look of puzzlement masqueraded his perverted countenance. Just for a split second, husband and wife faced each other off, not moving, not speaking.

The whistling wind continued, with the patter of intermittent rain striking the dirty dormer windows. There was a brief moment of mutual acknowledgement. Just for a second. And then George regained self-control. He breathed in deeply, his features returned to the simple and untroubled look of his everyday life; and without a hint of emotion or any further acknowledgement, he casually lumbered straight past her and descended the top flight of stairs.

Stella didn't flinch. She was mesmerised by the scene she'd stumbled across, by the scene she was not meant to witness. The drink, the music...it all began to make sense. Things began to fall into focus.

She heard his laboured bulk struggle down to the first floor and enter the bedroom, panting and wheezing, before eventually clicking the door closed behind him.

It was now just her and her corrupted granddaughter, her beautiful granddaughter, the granddaughter who kept her going, who kept her sane, the one she lived for. She didn't know what to do or what to say. She stood entrenched on the landing as her mind brought together incidents and signs that, looking back, she'd been aware of, but through her insensible mind she'd discounted as mere piffle.

But now she could see. And the more she thought, the clearer things became. She looked down at The Girl who lay still and stiff with eyes tightly closed and hands clenched. Stella approached her granddaughter. She saw the trail of tears that ran down her little cheeks and under her chin. She herself began to sob as she sat down on the bed and leant over to embrace the girl, holding her head to her own, cheek to cheek, with the tears from both merging into a hot, sticky liquid.

The Girl didn't respond. She refused to respond and kept her eyes and mouth clamped shut, but she couldn't hold back the tears.

Stella rocked and she cried and she kissed and she wept. Her heart beat rapidly through guilt and sheer love for The Girl. 'I'm sorry, my darling,' she sobbed. 'I'm so sorry... I'm so sorry...it's all my fault. I wasn't here for you was I love? I wasn't here when I should've been.'

The Girl remained unresponsive, clearly conscious but unwilling to acknowledge her grandmother. The only movement she did make was to unclench her fist to release the object that Granddad George had so carefully and forcefully placed there.

Stella removed the object and brought it up to eye level. 'The dirty bastard! He's given you a shilling. The dirty, dirty bastard! Love, I know you can hear me, darling, and I don't blame you for not wanting to talk to me or look at me. I don't blame you one bit, my little love,' said Stella, now tenderly caressing the girl's forehead. 'I've failed you, love, and I'll take that with me to me grave. I'll never forgive mesen for that, but I can tell you one thing, my love, I'll make sure that...that evil bastard will never *ever* touch you again. He won't ever come near you again, my love. He's had me as a right kipper, he has, but never again, my love. Never again. If I've to use me last breath and me last ounce of energy on this earth, I'll make sure he won't ever come near you again. I promise you that, else God strike me down dead right here and now.'

The Girl remained stiff bodied and unresponsive, but Stella never left her side for the remainder of that night. She tightly embraced her before eventually drifting off into an uneasy slumber in the dark and musty little attic bedroom amidst the howling wind and the dancing curtains.

The Girl remained conscious. She couldn't, didn't dare, fall asleep. She'd never been able to. Not in this house.

*

George returned from his early morning walk to his allotment, which was just at the end of the street over the railway wall. However, in order to access the plot without scaling the wall, he'd had to walk almost to the top of East Moor Drive, turning left to the bottom of Glensdale Road, and then through a lockable timbered door. He was glad of the walk. It had given him time to clear his head and take stock of the situation.

After spending an hour there ruminating and pottering, he walked back down East Moor Drive, calling in at Jack's newsagents for his usual copy of the *News of the World*, and then took a right turn back into Reginald Street. His eyes darted from side to side, he kept his head down and he maintained a pace a little swifter than his usual. The last thing he wanted was to stumble across his stepdaughter, Susan Wilson, in the street. But if his timings were right, and they usually were, then their paths shouldn't cross and he'd be able to scuttle his way down into his subterranean bolthole, out of sight, until the heat was off. He had a plan, a story, and he was confident that he could pull it off, given time.

On his return, he was relieved to find the downstairs living room unoccupied, so he niftily slid through the kitchen doorway and crept down the old steps into the cellar. He was comfortable down there, in the company of his animals, with his fascination of their simplicity, how he was able to exercise total control over them. He found it calming – exactly what he needed on this morning as he plotted his way out of what he perceived to be the 'tight corner' he felt he'd got himself into.

He sat in the great battered armchair and awaited the arrival of Susan Wilson. She duly arrived within five minutes of his estimation. He sank back into the chair as she passed by above him and walked into the house. After hearing Stella's sad voice greet her, he turned up the volume on his radio. He didn't wish to be privy to whatever their topic of conversation was; he didn't want his script to be in any way modified or tainted by anything he overheard from them.

He sat steely eyed and determined whilst keeping a firm, controlling grip on Samson, stroking his underbelly with his index finger. There was no deep eye-to-eye contact today, though; George had other things on his mind.

Although Susan Wilson was to stay only twenty minutes, George remained in the cellar for a further hour and a half. Once again he'd shrunk back into the armchair as he'd silently observed Susan Wilson and The Girl walk past the window on their way to the bus stop. They couldn't see him, he lurked below pavement level in almost pitch darkness, but he could see them. He watched them closely until they were out of the street and out of sight – and out of the way. He bided his time, plucking up the courage to face his wife, reciting his story, contemplating whether or not she'd buy it, whether he'd get away with his sickly misdemeanours.

He'd fed all the animals but hadn't bothered cleaning out the stinking cages. Stan and Hilda were no bother at all, but Samson was overly fussy at cage time, as was Maggie, but eventually he'd settled them down. He now stood at the bottom of the cellar stairs and stared upwards. He shook his head, took a gulp of dank air and made his slow ascent.

Stella was ready for him. She'd received her daughter, explaining that she couldn't, under any circumstances, have The Girl stay over any more.

'Is it owt to do with George?' Susan Wilson had asked, nodding her head downwards in the direction of the cellar.

'It'll all come out in 'wash, love,' repeated her mother, shaking her head. 'That's all I'm saying. You'll both 'ave to go now. Leave it to me. I'll be in touch.'

Susan Wilson, although perplexed and concerned, had no stomach to scrutinise her mother further on the issue. She had other domestic problems that she was already unable to cope with. Stella tearfully hugged her granddaughter before sending mother and daughter on their way.

Since their departure, Stella had sat glued to the settee, awaiting the appearance of George, who she knew was in the cellar, and who she knew was plucking up the courage to come up and face the music. She sat upright with arms folded and stared straight ahead. She heard the cellar door open.

George entered the kitchen and quietly closed the door behind him. She listened to him fumbling about, opening and closing drawers, clanking and clinking about. The sound of water from the tap filling up the kettle and the gas stove being lit. The chinking of mugs retrieved from the drainer, tea caddy lid removed, tea caddy lid replaced. The curtain drew open just enough for George to push his head through. Stella stared straight ahead.

'Ah, there y'are, love. Just putting 'kettle on...fancy a brew?' he asked with his usual semi-docile demeanour. Stella didn't answer, but George decided to make her one anyway. He brought a mug of tea through and placed it carefully on the table in front of her and, still not having the confidence to brazenly sit down in the armchair, he scuttled back into the kitchen, preferring to conduct any further 'chit-chat' from behind the curtain. 'Get that there tea down you, love,' he said, 'an' then I'll get 'dinner on. We can have that piece o' brisket I picked up from 'market yesterday. Is that all right? Wi' some nice mash, Yorkshires, carrots an' peas...and some onion gravy. What do you think? I'll do it. You just settle down and rest up'.

Stella didn't respond. She remained silent and impassive whilst staring straight ahead at the fireplace. She was determined that it would be her controlling this situation, not the booze, nor her sly, deceitful husband. She was to blame for the whole sordid affair. So she would resolve it, one way or another.

After a while, George skulked through the curtain and sat down on one of the armchairs.

Stella didn't move.

'You're quiet, love, everything all right?' he asked. 'How was Susan? Was she all right?' George was used to being on the end of Stella's sharp tongue, especially the day after she'd been on the razzle, but today was different. Circumstances were different. He was unsure, unsure how best to deal with her. It was still in the balance, he decided. Just push her a bit more, he thought, just see how much, if anything, she can remember. *I might still be in the clear yet.* 'Aren't y'aving your tea, love? It'll be getting cold,' he probed.

Still no reply, but this time she slowly unfolded her arms, rubbed her chin and lightly tapped her cheek with her index finger.

'You'd had a few last night... You were in a right state when I went to bed. You were on about all sorts... I cun't make head n' sense of half o' stuff you were on about.' After a short pause, he carried on. 'Can you remember owt, love? You don't look too go—'

But before he could finish his sentence, Stella slowly turned her head ninety degrees and looked him square in the face.

As soon as George saw the flash of venom in those eyes, the way she was in total control, the way she was sitting up straight, her whole demeanour, he knew the game was up. She hadn't said a word, had hardly moved a muscle, but that determined, fierce glint in her eyes sent shock waves through every cell in his body, causing him to almost piss himself there and then.

'You!' she fired.

'Who? Me, love?'

'You dirty, filthy, repugnant bastard!'

'What...? What's up, love?' he stammered.

'You filthy, conniving bastard... Don't you dare "what's up, love" me. You know exactly what's up.'

'Why...? Wh... What's happened, love? It'll be the drink... I told ya, you were all over 'place last night. It'll be 'drink, love...'

'Drink my fucking arse!' fired back Stella with a vitriol that sent tremors reverberating throughout the whole house. She now turned her shoulders to face him and without losing eye contact, she stabbed her bony finger straight at him. 'YOU KNOW what happened, you dirty bastard freak. And I'll tell you what's *gonna* happen, shall I? Do you want me to tell ya what's gonna happen? Eh? Do you wanna know, eh?'

'What, love,' replied George in a high-pitched whimper.

'You're gonna be out o' this 'ere house in half an hour... And do ya know what'll happen if you're not? Do ya know? Eh?'

'No, love...what?'

'Well, d'ya know that bread knife we've got in the kitchen? Eh?'

George sat spellbound.

'I'm talking to you...you thick-headed bastard,' she screeched. 'Do you know the bread knife we've got in the kitchen? Yes or No?' she persisted.

'Yeah,' replied George, his hands and face now clamming up, his heart racing.

'Well, do ya know what I'm gonna do with that fucking bread knife if you aren't out o' this 'ere house in half an hour? Do ya? Do ya know what I'm gonna do with it? Eh? Eh?'

'No, love,' said George, shaking his head and shifting around in the armchair, almost reduced to tears.

'D'ya wanna know what I'm gonna do with it?' she continued, pointing and jabbing her bony finger towards him and still glaring at him with widened eyes and a manic stare. 'D'ya wanna know? Eh? Eh?'

'What, love, what? What ya gonna do with it?'

'I'm gonna slice your bastard throat open with it! That's what I'm gonna do with it. I'm gonna slit your fucking throat from 'ere to 'ere,' she fired, indicating on her own throat where her plans to slit his would start and finish. 'From 'ere to fucking 'ere,' she repeated. 'What do you think about that then, George fucking Wilson? Eh? What do you think about THAT!'

'It... It's a bit harsh, love, is that—' he whimpered, scratching his head.

'A bit harsh! A bit fucking harsh, he says. The dirty bastard who's been plying me wi' drink for months and months so's he can have his filthy way with his innocent six-year-old granddaughter, *my* innocent six-year-old granddaughter! He thinks it's a bit harsh, does he? I'll fucking harsh ya, you dirty fat bastard! GET OUTTA THIS FUCKING 'OUSE – NOW!' Stella was shaking with rage as George shot up from his seat. 'You've 'alf an hour...or else!'

'Right y'are, love,' he said as he immediately began flitting around in a stunned daze, attempting to work out which items from his few meagre belongings he could muster in the timescale he'd been assigned.

His plan had been unsuccessful.

*

Half an hour later George stood in the kitchen. He wore his grubby donkey jacket with a bulging duffle bag and two carrier bags lying on the floor by his side. He was worried about the welfare of his beloved animals but had been told to 'fuck 'em' when he'd meekly enquired whether Stella would look after them.

He shuffled about nervously, not knowing exactly how to make his exit. He bobbed his head through the curtain. 'Do ya mind if I take this lump o' cheese wi' me?' he asked.

'Fuck off!' came the immediate reply from his determined wife.

He left the cheese in the cupboard and eventually ushered himself through the curtain with the duffle bag over his shoulder and a carrier bag in each hand. 'Right y'are then, love… I'll be off then,' he said softly.

'Aye. Fuck off, and don't come back.'

'Right y'are, love. Right y'are,' he repeated before exiting the tiny room and gently closing the door behind him.

Without moving from the settee, Stella sat stewing over her situation for hour after hour. The way that George had manipulated her. The way that she'd neglected and failed her granddaughter. It didn't sit right in her fuzzled head. She reflected on the numerous occasions when she'd been too pissed to pick up on the little signs. Too preoccupied with herself, lamenting over the past, when she should have been ensuring the welfare of her granddaughter.

Trevor would be turning in his grave, she thought. She was his granddaughter, not George's. The way she'd fostered the relationship. It was she who had encouraged and pushed George to form a bond with his 'step' granddaughter. It was all her fault. She was to blame. *He's a dirty, filthy bastard, but I've stood by and let it happen, right under my nose. I'll get my granddaughter justice. That evil pig won't be getting off that easily. I haven't finished with him yet.* She slipped on her stained anorak and lurched the short distance to the end of the street towards Ken's off-licence. She needed a drink.

CHAPTER 9

May 1975

Two days had passed since Stella's suggestion to George that it may have been prudent if he sought shelter outside and away from the family home. Since that highly charged episode, her mental and physical well-being had deteriorated. The only sustenance of any kind passing her thin blue lips had been of the alcoholic variety. With eyes dulled like a dead sea bass, her withered body lay languid; the intermittent tremors which had invaded her hands and fingers struck with increasing vigour. It hardly seemed worth the hassle of lighting up, but she persisted, puffing away as she lurched from periods of lucidity to irrational, incoherent ramblings and back again, puffing the fags, supping the liquor. She found it impossible to comprehend her own behaviour. Whilst George had been gratifying his immoral lust, by means of his clandestine molestations of their granddaughter, she'd been getting layered two floors below.

She asked herself how this could have happened, how she could have behaved so blasé where the welfare and well-being of such a cherished love of her life was concerned. She challenged the principles and motivations of those around her: her own daughter, the church, even the neighbours. More importantly, she interrogated the complete lack of veracity in her own actions, her own integrity, and the lack of responsibility towards the one she was there to protect. She'd allowed her dim-witted husband to play her like a puppet, but *she* had been the dimwit. She was the dummy, the baby whose candy had been so easily confiscated. She felt humiliated. The sense of guilt sliced through her broken heart like a cold steel carving knife.

She had developed a rocking motion, sitting hour after hour, huddled and hunched on the settee, at one point gouging a cross in the arm of the vinyl couch with her nails. Rocking, back and forth, back and forth. Constant rocking and ruminating and smoking and drinking.

The few people she had encountered during her daily traipse to the off-licence had been abruptly informed that George had been 'kicked out', irrespective of whether they'd enquired about his, her or their combined welfare in the first place.

In reality, those who assumed local knowledge of the odd couple had presumed that it was George, the dull but henpecked, long-suffering husband, who had walked out on her. Nevertheless, everyone who crossed her path was looked upon with a deep-seated mistrust, including those she'd previously never set eyes upon.

On the Tuesday lunchtime, as she lurched home clutching a plastic bag stuffed full of beer, she stumbled across Peggy Bowden standing outside her front door, an empty laundry basket by her feet.

'Oh hello, Stella. Is everything OK, love?'

Stella stopped. She swayed, slowly twisted her head and looked up. She glared at Peggy through dark, narrowed eyes. 'I've kicked him out,' she crowed. 'He's gone!' She sniffed at her neighbour and continued her way over the cobbled road towards number 10 with no further pleasantries.

'Oh dear, I thought I hadn't seen him lately. Is everything all right, love? Is George all right?' Peggy persisted, now addressing the back of her disappearing neighbour.

'He's gone!' bellowed Stella, throwing up an arm behind her before entering the house and slamming the door closed.

Peggy stood silent with hands on hips and slowly shook her head. 'What's the bloody world coming to?' She hoisted up the washing line, picked up the empty basket and retreated into her pristine little house of regimentation and order.

The words 'regimentation' and 'order' would not have been used to describe the house opposite at number 10. The standards of cleanliness and organisation had already been dubious, even when George had been in residence, but at least he'd afforded some semblance of order. With him out of the picture, and in her current state, Stella didn't stand a chance.

She was deeply depressed, permanently intoxicated and had no inclination towards the mundane practice of housekeeping. She was living, sleeping, drinking and smoking in the sitting room, which reeked like a 1950s tap-hole on a Bank Holiday Monday. Neglect was the order of the day as junk and clutter lay scattered throughout. Her personal hygiene had also taken a hit. She hadn't washed, bathed, or changed clothes or underwear in days.

She figured there was no need to clean the house and no need to worry about personal hygiene. *There's no one here and there's no one coming.* Her state of health was hardly improved due to her stubborn refusal to take any of her prescribed medication. She'd been secretly stockpiling her pills for months on the top shelf of the kitchen wall cabinet. They included medication for blood pressure and, amongst other stuff, Valium, prescribed by her doctor because of his ambiguous diagnosis of depression.

*

During his unceremonious departure, George had grabbed food and water, hastily ramming it in the cages of his beloved animals, until he could work out his next move. It had been a rushed affair, and he worried as to whether he'd overdone it. Their welfare was a cause of anxiety for him, but he'd have to live with it; there was little else he could have done given the tone and aggressive nature of his wife. He reckoned he just needed a few days to sort himself out.

It had been spitting with rain when Stella had presented him with the graphic ultimatum involving the kitchen bread knife and his throat. He'd found himself on the street, deliberating his next move. His pals from the TV lounge would have put a good word in for him at The Salvation Army hostel, he had no doubt about that, but his pride dictated that this wouldn't be a path down which he was likely to venture. However, timing and opportunity knocked for George, as a seemingly ready-made solution to his problem suddenly popped into his head as he'd loitered outside the off-licence with the spitting rain turning into light drizzle.

The previous week he'd been chatting to an old kid, Arthur Thompson, who lived at the top end of East Moor Drive. The two had become acquainted over the years with Arthur being a well-established member of the allotment community, who, with his father before him, had worked the same strip of land for the last forty-odd years. Furthermore, and providentially for George, in this, his hour of need, the Thompson plot was one of only a handful which housed a decent-sized shed – albeit a decrepit rotting timber structure with a patched-up roof, but a shed nevertheless.

Arthur would be absent for a while, due to minor routine surgery, and he'd asked George to keep an eye on the plot (and shed) until such time that he was fit and mobile enough to return. George had been more than happy to oblige, and now, in his current predicament, he'd been presented with a dry place to lay his head, just for a while. His luck and good fortune had returned.

Arthur had not left a key, but the cheap padlock to the shed was easy for George to break. He'd worry about the lock and Arthur's return later on. But for now, he could get his head down for a couple of nights, giving him a chance to work out a plan. He'd worked Stella in the past, and he was confident he could do so in the future, given time.

That first night proved to be a traumatic experience for George, a reality check, a wake-up call. In the pitch-blackness with only a small handheld torch for light, he'd attempted to sleep by slouching on a rickety old rattan seat covered in a dirty anorak and resting his feet on a milk crate.

The shed was dilapidated, reeked of damp and festooned with webs, dust, spiders and bugs. Draughts were flying in from all directions; he was freezing cold and his back had seized up. He couldn't sleep, and every bone and joint in his body began to ache after just a couple of hours.

His sandwiches and flask of tea had ran out, as had the chocolate and coconut mushrooms he'd picked up from Jack's on his way up. By midnight, the only provisions left for him to fall back on were a half packet of polo mints. At around one in the morning, the intensity of the rainfall increased dramatically. Well, to put it succinctly, it started to absolutely fucking piss it down!

*

In her perpetual intoxicated stupor, Stella mulled over her life path, how she'd degraded from a vivacious beauty into a worn-out, wrinkle-faced, old hag. How, from being a loving mother and wife, with a thriving social life, she'd turned into a foul-mouthed, embittered, old pisshead, without a friend in the world.

She had rooted out a number of black and white photographs, some of them lone portraits of Trevor, others with the pair of them as a handsome couple, and positioned them around the room as a reminder of happier times. Her internal monologue had developed into an external one-way conversation as she rambled and mithered to her own silent shadow.

She continued to knock back the alcohol. On that first night alone in the house, she rocked herself into drunken oblivion as she struggled, but failed, to rid her head of the appalling scene she'd witnessed the previous evening.

Images of The Girl flashed through her mind, without warning, over and over again. In her attempts to rinse her memory of the haunting imagery, she gazed at the photographs of Trevor, extraditing herself back to the 1940s and '50s, dancing, jitterbugging, twisting and jiving. Happy times, laughing and joking to the popular tunes and swinging sounds of the dance halls. And then she'd switch back to the here and now, the horror she'd been privy to, the shocking sight of that 'fat, evil bastard' as he pulled up his dirty drawers, his sickly countenance as their eyes had met.

Thus, it continued, back and forth, from good to bad, from dark to bright, hate to love, hour after hour after hour. At times, her sense of reality became blurred as she questioned which characters and loved ones in her life belonged to which era.

She picked up one of her favourite photographs of Trevor and pulled it up to her face. He was dressed immaculately in a dark tailored suit, collar and tie, light coloured overcoat, with polished shoes and jet-black hair slicked back. He was grinning at the camera, showcasing his beautiful teeth and tanned, perfect complexion.

'And where are you now then, Trevor? Eh? Even you left me... You went and left me, din't you? If you hadn't o' left me, I wouldn't have ended up with the shithouse of a man I did... I've no one down here now... I'm on me own... I bet you're up there with yer mother an' yer father, and yer brother and yer pals, living it up, without a care in the bleedin' world... And look at me down 'ere... I've got ball all down 'ere, me. Ball bleedin' all... I've lost the love o' me life... I've lost God... I've nowt to offer us daughter, can't go to the bastard church and I wish I was dead. And I bet you're dancing your balls off...up there... living it up while I'm down here...in this bleeding hellhole...having the time of me bastard life... Well, thanks for that, my love...thanks for that, darling... Cos at the end of the day...you're just like the rest of 'em, aren't ya? Eh? You left me...just like the rest of 'em, and so, my love...YOU can piss off with 'em!' She cried as she tore the photograph in half and threw it to the floor. In a further angry outburst, she launched a half-full can of lager at the row of photographs on the drop-leaf dining table. 'You're just the bleedin' same as the rest of 'em!' She missed the photographs by a mile and cried herself to sleep.

*

The rain had pooled in a dip in the tin roof and eventually located a weak spot through which it meticulously dripped into the shed. The drops fell onto George's shoulder and spattered over his stubbled chin. He pulled his anorak-cum-blanket over his head but was eventually forced to move further into a tight corner of the little six-by-four shed. He cupped his hands to his mouth, his hot rancid breath condensing in the cold shed air like heavy plumes of white smoke. Although he didn't know it at the time, the rain wouldn't cease for three whole days, non-stop. He never managed even one minute of sleep.

He was relieved when, through the tiny broken glass window, the pitch-blackness had lightened into a dark, menacing grey. At least it signalled the break of dawn and gave the opportunity for him to escape the shed and make his way to work in Leeds city centre.

He walked into town, his lumbering gait and dishevelled appearance attracting little interest from those out at such an early hour. His working day largely involved operating to his own devices. He was used to skiving and hanging about under the radar within the maze of nooks, crannies, arches and tunnels that were abound in Leeds Central Station.

After clocking off, he collected a handful of well-used pornographic magazines from his work locker, eagerly stuffing them into his bag. He then called into Kirkgate Market and bought cheddar cheese, sliced tongue and a pork pie for supper. He looked skywards towards the dark, leaden clouds and donned his battered flat cap as he headed off on foot and in the pouring rain back to Arthur's tiny rain-soaked shed in the allotments, barely fifty yards from his own house, as the magpie flies.

He managed to stumble into work on the Tuesday, albeit in poor physical condition, but by Wednesday morning he'd deteriorated to such an extent that there was no possibility he was ever going to make it to the depot. He was cold, wet, exhausted and broken. His knee joints had seized up, his back was stiff as sheet glass and his gout had flared up with uric acid crystals taking permanent residence in the toe joints of the whole of his right foot. On top of that, he had developed a bad cough, a condition which he only usually picked up during wintertime. Initially, he'd been peeing up the outside shed walls, but his reduced mobility gave him the excuse to piss exactly where he sat, aiming the steaming spray as far away as he possibly could, because of hygiene, he reasoned.

Although George was in a bad place both mentally and physically, 'living it up' in Arthur's shed had given him time to think. He'd let his guard down the other night, that was for sure. He wouldn't let that happen again. He mused over Stella's foul temper and shook his head. He worried about the welfare of Samson, Maggie, and Stan and Hilda, and whether or not Stella was looking after them. He figured she wouldn't be. He never once considered the welfare or well-being of The Girl. He did consider how, not so long ago, he was marching up East Moor Drive every other Sunday morning in his suit, overcoat and brogues looking resplendent on his way to church. The fact was that his alcoholic, dishevelled little wife tagging along hadn't been a problem for him as it had made him look good and feel good. But he didn't look good or feel good now. He couldn't face spending another night at Chateau d'Arthur. He didn't think he would survive it.

*

The alcohol in Stella's wizened frame had reached saturation levels. By Tuesday afternoon she was merely topping herself up, which didn't require much further intake. She fazed in an out of consciousness as her mental state and physical body cowed to the effects of the booze and lack of food. In one of her rare lucid states, she'd forgiven Trevor for kicking her into touch, taped the torn photograph back together and replaced it on the table-top, back amongst the others. It was around teatime when she'd awoken from yet another blackout. She took in the scene around her as the reality of the situation, once again, struck home. She was back in the '70s. The black cloud descended.

Humph! You're still here, lass... I remember now... Aye, this is your 'ouse... Where you live. Shithouse of a husband... kicked out, gone...molested me granddaughter... It's all here, all real...not a bad dream...it's not gone away...

She shook her head before looking around to see what, if any, alcohol was at hand. The previous night's whisky had gone and there was only one can of lager left on the table, already opened and warm to the taste. She took a sip. 'Ugh,' she uttered, grimacing, 'bleedin' shite!' She didn't really feel up to another trip to the off-licence but knew she'd have to if she were to obtain further sustenance. After shakily lighting up another Woodbine, she took another gulp of the warm lager and looked around for her purse.

'Where the hell is it?' she croaked, searching the table-top before feeling around the settee just in case she'd been lying on it. She found it on the floor and opened it up to check for cash. After fumbling around, she pulled out a small dog-eared photograph. She stared at the image and brought it closer to her face, dropping the purse onto her lap.

She stared intently, her eyes glazing over, and then welled up. Tears slowly descended and meandered down the rutted complexion of the dejected little woman as she stared at the tiny photograph. They'd spent a week together in a caravan on the outskirts of Bridlington the previous year. Herself and George, Susan and The Girl. The weather had been terrible, but it had been a holiday, a family holiday.

As she looked at the photograph, she thought about that week back in July. There hadn't been much laughter, not that much fun. They'd sat on the beach in their coats and scarves trying to engage The Girl in the usual family beach activities like sandcastles and shell collecting. It had been too cold for her. They'd dressed up and gone to the campsite family cabaret club for a couple of the evenings, but they hadn't been able to persuade The Girl to participate in the fun and games with the children's entertainers.

It hadn't been a great holiday, but the photograph, of The Girl and Stella, a photo booth snap of just the two of them, had reduced her to tears. Stella was smiling in the image, crouching cheek to cheek with her beloved grand-daughter, but there was no such smile from The Girl, no mirth, no holiday excitement, not even a hint of merriment. Just the same sad little face – the image of which Stella couldn't get out of her head. The sad little face that would aggravate her mother when she collected her. The same sad face she'd witnessed just a couple of days ago. Stella tried to remember, tried to visualise, her grand-daughter with a happy face, a smiling face, a contented face. There was no such memory. Just a lasting image of that forlorn expression.

'I know now, love?' she whispered tearfully. She thought back to the week at Bridlington and the times George had taken The Girl to the shower block, just to give herself and Susan a 'bit of peace.' She remembered the night when George suggested that he and The Girl stay in the caravan whilst she and Susan went to the bingo. 'Enjoy yourselves,' he'd said as they left the cara-van, 'you're on holiday.' She cried as she held the photo-graph to her chest. She looked around at the shithole of a room and shook her head. Then something clicked in-side.

'I'm no good like this. What good am I to you, my love? No good, that's how good…no bloody good at all. I've got to be strong for you, my little darling. I was strong when I kicked him out. I was up to it then. I didn't buckle… And I need to be strong now… I need a backbone, and if it's the last thing I do, my precious, I'll make sure you get your justice… I've failed you once, but not again, I prom-ise you. I'll be strong…just for you… Just wait and see.'

Stella dragged herself out of the house and up towards the off-licence at the end of the street. She bought six tins of lager but left the hard stuff firmly lodged on the top shelf. She purchased bread, margarine, Spam and corn-flakes. Hardly a feast fit for a king, but she realised that she needed a measure of solid sustenance if she were to build up her strength.

On her return, she ran herself a bath, had a long soak

and then dressed herself in clean clothes. She could only stomach a spam sandwich supper, but it was a start. Even though she demolished half of the lager and still slept on the settee, she had a relatively restful and peaceful night's sleep.

She awoke on the Wednesday morning feeling more refreshed and clear-headed than she had done for quite a while.

*

It was around seven o'clock that evening as Stella sat upright on the settee facing the television. It was a cold, wet and miserable night outside. The rain had continued unabated since Sunday; although not heavy, it was light and persistent. She'd regained a little physical strength, and the improved sleep and afternoon nap had settled her mind a little. Even though she'd downed a couple of lagers in the afternoon, and was planning a trip to the off-licence for more that evening, she was still thinking straighter and clearer.

She sat with a straight back and puffed on the Woodbines with purpose as her eyes flicked from the clock to the window and back to the clock. The gas fire glowed a dark, cosy orange, with the only sound being the methodical tick-tocking of the mantelpiece clock. Stella had tidied up the house, taken the rubbish out and washed up. A collection of underwear hung drying on the small clothes horse in the alcove next to the fire. She glugged away at the last tin of warm lager, putting off her trip to the off-licence as she looked outside at the dismal weather. All was calm inside the house. She waited.

It happened just after a quarter past seven. She didn't flinch. She'd been expecting it. Without moving her head, her eyes flitted towards the rain-spattered window through which she observed Peggy Bowden's quivering curtains on the other side of the street. Her vision toggled between the fire and the window opposite as she remained stock-still and silent, not moving an inch from the orange settee.

Nor did she move on the second knock to the door, barely six feet away from where she was sitting. On the other side of the narrow street, the curtains from number 11 continued to shimmy, but Stella remained cool and calm. The rain was incessant, continuous. Whoever it was knocking on the door, she figured, was getting one hell of a soaking. By the time the third knock came, louder and more desperate than the previous two, Stella decided that she'd injected enough devilment into the situation.

She eased her body up and lurched to the door, unlocked and slowly opened it. She needn't have guessed who was stood there, stooped over in the pouring rain.

Dripping wet, bent over double with duffle bag slung over his shoulder and his weight supported by a rickety old stick, George stared down at the pavement. He'd checked out of Arthur's and now stood, wet through, on the front doorstep of his own home as the rain dripped from the peak of his saturated flat cap. His breathing was laboured. It had taken him almost half an hour to stagger from the allotment to the house – a journey that would have normally taken just ten minutes. He was shattered and in pain, but he couldn't bring himself to look Stella in the eye or make the first line of conversation.

In an awkward stand-off and with her hand still on the door handle, Stella looked down at the sight of her pathetic husband, hunched over, soaking wet and wheezing, as though he'd just run a four-minute mile.

George maintained his hard stare at the wet pavement before Stella eventually broke the silence.

'What do *you* want?' she asked forcibly and succinctly.

George began to shake his head, finding it difficult to muster a reply.

'I said, what do *you* want?' repeated Stella, but this time with added zip and vigour.

George stuttered. 'I...I... Can I come back, love?' he asked quietly. 'I've been sleeping rough, and I'm not feeling we—'

'What? What did you say?'

'Can... Can I come back, love?' he repeated. 'I'm sorry. I'm sorry for what I did, love.'

'Oh, I see. You want to come back, do you? Eh? After what you did to us granddaughter? You wanna come back, do you?'

'Yeah, love. Can I?' His faltering voice was barely audible against the constant light patter of the rain. 'Can I come back, love? I'm sorry.'

Stella entered into another silent stand-off as she pored over the pathetic sight in front of her.

George, conscious of the intense, close scrutiny, nervously awaited her response and remained hunched over, not daring to look up.

'I'll have to think about it, won't I,' she said before slamming the door closed, turning the key and resuming her resting place on the settee. She lit up another Woodbine, plucked the can from the table and stared into the fire.

Peggy Bowden's curtains danced like a magician's cloak as she struggled to make sense of the highly succulent and scandalous incident being played out right opposite her own front door.

'Nosey bastard,' muttered Stella. She remained on the settee with a determined straight back and arms folded facing the warm, toasty fire. She puffed on the cigarette and finished off the remaining dregs of lager. She had plenty of time on her hands.

Ten minutes had passed before Stella, with her rigid back and new-found confidence, again rose from the settee and again unlocked and opened the front door.

George had remained in exactly the same position and stance as she'd left him, sodden.

She scrutinised him from head to foot and shook her head. 'Get in!' she fired.

George was caught unawares as he mumbled some manner of humble gratitude before shuffling through the doorway into the warm and welcoming little living room.

Stella slammed the door closed.

'Thanks, love,' he said meekly.

'Don't stand there dripping all over the bloody carpet, you bleedin' idiot, go on,' ordered Stella, ushering him into the kitchen. 'Get in there – drip on the bleedin' oil-cloth.'

George did exactly as he was told whilst continuing to avoid any measure of eye contact.

His wife stood facing him, Woodbine in one hand, the other resting on her hip. 'So, you wanna come back then, do ya? You dirty bastard. Well, I'll tell yer summat, shall I,' said Stella. 'I guarantee here and now, you'll never ever touch or even get near that girl, or any other girl for that matter, ever again. Cos I'm gunna make sure of that. Do you understand? Has that sunk into your thick skull? Has it? Do you understand? Eh?'

'Y-Y-Yeah, love. I understand. Right y'are, love,' replied George.

Stella continued to look him up and down, her top lip curling, with a surreptitious shake of her head. 'Right,' she said. 'If you're serious about wanting to come back into this 'ere house, there's gunna be some rule changes. Understand?'

'Right y'are, love,' replied George, still dripping but now offering minimal eye contact, his head remaining bowed.

'Firstly, you'll never leave me on my own down here... Do you understand?'

'Aye, love, I-I understand.'

'Secondly, we do things together, like man and wife... Do you understand?' she continued.

'Aye, love, right y'are.'

'Never mind them brain-dead doylems down at the club, d'y'ear? Your place is here, wi' me...'

'Aye, love...'

'If I have a drink, *you'll* have a drink...'ere...wi' me. Do *you* un...der...stand?' she fired with bulging eyeballs and a fierce frown.

'I u... I understand, love, right y'are,' stammered George.

'So I can keep my beady little eyes on you, so's I know what you're up to... You get me? Eh?'

'I get yer, love. Yeah, I get yer,' said George, who was nodding in agreement to whatever terms and conditions were being laid out by Stella, irrespective of whether he considered them reasonable or otherwise.

'And it starts tonight. You are gonna get your stinking backside up them there stairs, you are gonna get a bath and you are gonna get changed. And then we, that's you and me, are gonna have a drink together. Right?'

'Right y'are, love,' replied George. 'Me back's gone and I've been coughing and me gout's flared up—'

'I couldn't give a cat's cock-hair about your ailments, ya bleedin' middin bin y'are – ya nowt else. You've brought it all on yerself. Now get up them there stairs and do as I tell you. You've half an hour, and bring them filthy wet clothes down an' put 'em in 'basket,' she said, half pushing, half slapping her hapless husband through the bottom stair door.

'Right y'are, love,' he said as he lurched up the stairs with Stella slamming the door shut behind him.

'Right yer-bleeding-are, love,' she mocked. 'That's all the gormless get can say – right yer bleedin' are.' She sat on the settee and once the fire in her belly began to die down, she again began to ruminate, hypnotised by the glow of the gas fire as it quietly hissed its warming radiance in defiance of the atrocious weather outside. She picked up the photo booth picture from the coffee table and pored over it, as she had done so constantly over the previous two days. 'Don't you worry, me lovely... Don't you worry one cotton-picking little bit.'

*

George dared not take a second longer than the thirty minutes he'd been assigned to take a bath, get changed and get his arse back downstairs. He'd niftily ventured down to the cellar to check on the welfare of his animals and left them suitably fed and watered. He now sat on the armchair next to the fire, warming his gouty feet on the tiled hearth.

The front door opened and in walked Stella. Wet and agitated, she dragged off her headscarf before removing the soaked anorak. She hung it up behind the door.

'Is it still raining, love?' piped up George. 'You should've taken the brolly. It's hung up on 'back o' cellar door.'

Stella bit her tongue. Her default reaction was to discharge a barrage of acid-flavoured put-downs, but she simply glared at him.

He looked away sharply and dropped his head, staring directly into the hot, fizzing gas fire. He realised he'd spoken out of turn and decided, at this delicate juncture, to speak only when spoken to, until such time that Stella became intoxicated – then he could play her a little.

Having refrained from retaliation, Stella planted her carrier bags, laden with lager and whisky, onto the settee. 'Here,' she said, handing him one of the cans, 'start on that while I make us summat to eat.'

George didn't really like the modern lagers; they didn't agree with him. He didn't even drink draught bitters. He preferred mild, preferably Tetley's mild, from the club. 'Thanks, love,' he replied, 'lovely.' He removed the ring-pull and started to drink. He grimaced on the first gulp. It was strong and tasted like metal, but from where he'd been since Sunday, he wasn't complaining. Although still in much discomfort and pain due to his arthritic joints and glass back, he was warm and dry. He could put up with a couple of tins of warm, metallic rat piss.

Stella clattered around in the kitchen preparing the meal. There was no conversation. It was now her turn to scrutinise George from behind the curtain, his countenance, his demeanour. She could see that he was in pain and could hear his wheezing and coughing. He sat expressionless, a blank canvas, as if nothing had happened, as if it was just a normal day.

He stared into the hot fire and carefully rubbed his feet together, the good one comforting the gout-ridden one, warm and toasty. He offered nothing to Stella. No reassurance, no regret, no sense of shame, no meaningful conversation.

Having finished the meal of steak and kidney pie with tinned potatoes and peas, Stella continued to set the pace with the consumption of alcohol – well, where George was concerned, in any case. After she'd 'forced' four cans of lager down him, she detected a change. Slurred speech and just a slight hint of familiarity.

With the ordeal of the previous few days, George's resistance was already low. It hadn't taken much alcohol to have an effect on him.

She walked into the room and slammed a mug of whisky and dry ginger onto the small table adjacent to where George was sitting. 'Now, get that down you,' she fired.

'What is it, love?'

'It's whisky and dry. Now stop chelping and get it down ya.'

'Well, you know I'm not one for spirits, love,' said George, picking up the mug and staring down at the contents.

'What did I bloody say to you earlier, when you came through that there door? What did I say to you? I said, din't I? We're gonna do things together, and we were having a drink tonight... Din't I? Eh?'

'Aye, love, you did. Aye,' George replied slowly.

'Well, get it supped, then. What's up wi' ya?'

'Right y'are, love,' he said, nodding his head. 'Right y'are.' The tail end of his uttering tapered off into a whisper. 'Aren't you having one, then?' he asked.

'Aye, I am, mine's in 'kitchen. Don't you worry about me, laddie. Just get that down ya an' give me 'mug back so's I can get you another.'

The ever-submissive George immediately complied with the order and necked the full concoction in one, causing him to wince before handing back the mug.

Disdain was etched across Stella's face as she grabbed it and proceeded towards the kitchen for a refill. 'I told you,' she bellowed, 'if you wanna come back here, me and you are gonna do things together, like man and wife, as we should be... D'y'ear?'

George heard all right, but he didn't answer. The strong liquor wasn't in agreement with his bland constitution. He felt queasy, tired and light-headed.

'Did you hear what I said?' cried out Stella. 'Like man and wife!'

'Yeah, I heard you, love,' replied George. 'Right y'are... like man an' wife, aye.'

Stella dispensed another mug of whisky and dry with, if anything, more whisky and less ginger than the first.

George, too browbeaten to refuse, took a large sip before imparting an offensive, gut-wrenching belch.

'Charming,' muttered Stella before sinking into the settee with her own mug in hand.

For the first time that night, George looked his wife straight in the eye.

'What's up wi' you?' she asked.

He didn't answer but struggled as he attempted to rise from his chair with the mug still in hand.

'What you doing?' she asked.

He lumbered up, limped and lurched over to the settee where he slumped down and attempted to slide his arm around his wife.

'What the friggin' hell d'ya think *you're* doing?' she demanded, shrugging his arm away in disgust. 'Get your bleedin' hands off me... What's your game?'

'I thought you said...er...man and wife...'

'Man and bleeding wife! Get back over there, you silly get! You're bleeding mental, you are... What the hell do ya think you're doing?'

'I thought you wanted—'

'I know what you thought, you dirty old bleeder! That's what's got you into this mess in 'first place, you and your bloody filthy mind...'

'No, it wan't that, love. I just thought—'

'Well, think again. Go on, get back over there, ya simple-minded get, and don't come anywhere near me,' yelled Stella, spitting vitriol like an exploding nail bomb.

A dejected George lurched back into his alcove armchair, looking both perplexed and sorry for himself.

Stella followed. Then, with a face like stone, she lashed out, aiming a glancing blow with the palm of her hand towards his balding head. 'I'll bleedin' man and wife ya.'

George cowered and flinched, holding up his arm in defence in case she followed it up with further hostility.

She refrained and stepped back. 'Lunatic!' she cried. 'Now finish that off!'

He quickly guzzled down the whisky just to get her away from him.

She grabbed the mug and threw in another dagger-like glare before turning for the kitchen.

The quick intake of alcohol plus the shock of Stella's reaction towards his ill-timed advances had George wondering if he'd have been better off staying at Arthur's place after all. He was in constant pain, he felt ill and now his head was beginning to spin. 'All this booze is no good for me gout, love,' said George as Stella prepared more whisky.

'I wouldn't worry about your gout, laddie,' she fired back, as she crushed half a dozen or so Valium tablets firmly between two spoons.

'I don't feel well, love,' continued George. 'I'm feeling a bit dizzy.'

'You'll be all right – stop mithering. You're not used to it, that's all...but you will be.' She emptied a spoonful of the now chalky substance into the mug of whisky, added dry ginger and administered a brisk stir.

George's speech was now markedly indistinct; his head lolled from side to side and his heavy eyelids were beginning to drop.

Stella had been gradually increasing the dose of Valium with each of George's servings, whilst her own whisky and dry had been devoid not only of any trace of Valium, but also of whisky.

'Oh God. I feel like shit, love,' slurred George as she swished the curtain aside and entered the living room.

'Never mind that. Here, get that down you,' she demanded. 'I'm putting some music on, and we're gonna listen to it and have a nice drink...together... Understand?'

'Do I have to, love? Don't feel well at all,' garbled George, who scanned the room through blurry eyes as Stella knelt down by the coffee table fumbling with her cherished record player.

'Yes, you do,' she fired. 'Just have that one, and then you can have a rest. Now, be quiet whilst I put me Slim Whitman record on.'

'A rest, love? I wanna go to bed...'

'Well, if you don't want to end up back on the street

in the bloody rain, then you'll shut up and get that there whisky down you.'

By now, George's head was hanging and his eyes were closed, but he could still hear the sharp, menacing tone of his determined wife. 'Right y'are, love,' he mumbled, jerking his head back and half opening his eyes. His hand shook as he raised the mug to his mouth just as the sounds of Slim Whitman began to fill the room.

'Go on then, get it down ya...in one,' commanded Stella, glaring through devilish eyes and now standing directly in front of him with hands on hips.

He just about managed to complete the instruction before mumbling incoherently and collapsing sideways against the arm of the chair. The mug slipped from his grasp, landing softly onto the carpet, with a residue of the noxious concoction trickling from the side of his mouth.

'George!' barked Stella. 'George, wake up!' She approached the slumped body and slapped his face as hard as she could.

George half opened one eye. 'Right y'are, love... What...is it?'

'Come on, get up. We've got to go feed your ferret...in 'cellar. Simon yer call it, in't it?' she hollered.

George managed to raise his head and tried to focus. 'Sam... Sam... Samson?'

'Aye, that's it, Samson. He's poorly and needs feeding. So, come on, let me help you up so we can go see him... come on,' said Stella, as she struggled to coax him into a standing position.

'Samson? What's up wi' 'im?' replied George, who attempted to coordinate himself in accordance with his wife's instructions. His eyes were almost closed, but he just about managed to raise his bulking form before collapsing once more into the armchair.

'George! Come on, try and get up...it's for Samson,' she cried, grabbing him by his shirt collar.

Once again, the insensible and incoherent George attempted to get to his feet as he stumbled and grabbed hold of his frail wife. Once upright, she guided him towards the kitchen doorway as he lurched backwards and forwards and tottered from side to side.

'Come on, that's good,' she said, following behind him with both hands on his back.

He'd only managed five or six shuffled steps when the spinning room sent him crashing through both the kitchen doorway and hanging curtain. He clunked his thickset head on the linoleum floor. There was no further movement. He was out.

Stella tutted. She slapped his face and threw a mug of water over him, but nothing; there was no way she was going to revive him in this state. He was still breathing, but there was no response. She looked down at the comatose heap in front of her. The immovable object would have to be moved, no matter what. She subsequently set about the task.

She wedged the cellar-head door open and bent down, grabbing his shirt collar. She yanked it. It was clear that the shirt would tear before any movement of George's bulk would take place. A rethink was needed.

She tried gripping him by his greasy head but was unable to get a firm hold. She grabbed his left arm. With a tight grip, she heaved and yanked and pulled with every ounce of energy she could muster. Stella wasn't built for strength, and her current health was certainly not conducive to hard labour, but, through sheer bloody-minded resolve, she managed to shift the hulking body just an inch.

Inspired by this small measure of success, she continued to heave, utilising the full seven and a half stone of her body weight. Her heart raced and the veins in her arms reached bursting point, but she wouldn't give up. Inch after inch after inch, she slowly dragged the dead weight of her husband towards the cellar-head.

With her chest burning, she took a time out, pouring herself a mug of cold water. Sweat oozed from her purple head like rainwater dripping from a stone ledge as she struggled to catch her breath.

She drank the water and re-entered the living room before picking up the tiny photograph. The melancholic image of The Girl, her only granddaughter, reaffirmed her resolve to complete the only aim she had left in life and one that she *would* accomplish – whatever the cost.

To the unrelenting sounds of Slim Whitman's 'Rose Marie', she carefully placed the photograph into her cardigan pocket and paced back into the kitchen with a straight back and a bolstered determination.

It had taken Stella the best part of half an hour to lug George's limp body to the cellar-head, just about managing to get his head and shoulders over the top step. She realised that if she continued as she was, then it was possible his body could tumble down the stairs on top of her, causing her injury, if not totally crushing her. That wouldn't do, and she certainly couldn't push him, as the greater part of the bulk was still lying horizontally on the kitchen floor.

She remembered a coiled rope in the cellar. After flicking on the light switch, she descended the murky depths in order to retrieve it. The place stank of piss. The inky black rainwater had risen through the collapsed corner section of the earthen floor, resulting in the whole basement being flooded with an inch of liquid filth.

Stella grabbed the rope, which hung from a rusty nail in the brick wall, and reclimbed the stairs. She wheezed like a ninety-year-old as she stood over George, surveying the job in hand. Deciding that it would make the job of yanking him down the cellar stairs easier if he was lying on his back, she set about turning him over. She tugged, shoved, pulled and rolled – she swore and cursed – but she didn't give up.

With that mission accomplished, she next tied the rope around his torso and under both his arms before tying it fast with a crude knot. Having tugged on the rope, she was satisfied that the rope would hold and do the job, if she could find the strength.

Back down the steps, taking the rope with her and standing in the water, she took up the slack. She leaned back and pulled on the rope with all her strength and might. Nothing. She pulled again, hard. The rope cut into her hands. But no movement.

She looked around and snatched a rag from the stone table and wrapped it around her right hand. And this time she bound the rope around her waist. Again, she took up the slack and pulled as if her life depended on it, straining every muscle, every sinew. Her head felt as though it would explode any second, such was the pressure exerted, but she wouldn't give up. That wasn't an option.

At an angle of almost forty-five degrees, she utilised every ounce of her body weight to counter that of George, who was more than twice her bulk. She continued on and on until, after taking in one huge gulp of air, and through sheer belligerent determination, she managed to muster up one last mighty haul. She screamed as the body shifted just a notch. Sensing momentum, she intensified her efforts with short jerking, pulling and tugging motions, each exertion being matched with dynamic blasphemy. Each yank moved the load in short increments until, after one last desperate heave, the whole bulk of George's body slumped around the corner.

The natural forces of gravity then took control as he tumbled down the stairs. By the time he reached the bottom, his whole body and limbs lay twisted and contorted. The back of his head lay in the water on the earthen floor. His backside was stuck in the air with his left arm trapped beneath him. His other arm lay out in front and his legs were splayed open at odd angles.

Although he'd been rendered cataleptic by the powerful combination of drink and drugs, the sheer physical shock to his system caused by the fall brought him round. He began to mumble. As the pain began to register, his mumblings turned into groans.

Stella immediately jumped at the opportunity. 'George! George!' she yelled. 'Come on, George. You've had a fall. Come on, let's see if we can get you up.' She began to untie the rope and unravel his limbs whilst still breathing heavily from her own exertions. 'Come on, George,' she coaxed, slapping his face.

George groaned and muttered insensibilities as Stella continued to badger him.

'Come on now, let's get you up and into your chair,' she said whilst untangling his battered arms and attempting to help him to his feet. It was a miracle that she eventually managed to stand him up, with his legs buckling beneath him and his mind a mass of confusion.

Maggie had begun chacking, and Samson charged around his coup in a frenzied excitement.

'Shut the 'ell up, will you?' fired Stella at the magpie. 'Bleeding thing!'

With much encouragement, shuffling, barging and sheer physical willpower, she somehow managed to get George to the huge leather armchair, positioning him to sit upright and resting his arms on the arms of the chair.

With Maggie chacking, the excitable ferret squealing, and Slim Whitman's vocals ringing out from the floor above, Stella took a step back. She was exhausted. Although she'd managed to get George to his feet and onto the chair, he hadn't opened his eyes as he remained half delirious and still rambling like an imbecile.

She took a succession of deep breaths before firing a further tirade at the excitable, disabled magpie. 'Shut it, I said, ya noisy little bastard!'

Stella then grabbed an old rusting chain she'd discovered in the side coal bunker room earlier and looped it twice around the large girth of her husband and around the back of the chair. She pulled it as tight as she possibly could before slipping on a padlock.

Next, she retrieved two pieces of strong twine, using them to tightly bind each of his bare feet to the front two legs of the chair. This had the effect of his legs being splayed open. She then tightly bound the end of a length of rope around his left hand and pulled it tight, fastening the other end to an iron ring fixed into the wall adjacent to the chair. This yanked his arm upwards and at an angle of about forty-five degrees, causing blood to drip onto the chair arm from a cut to his elbow.

His right arm was a little more complicated. This

time, after tying the rope around his wrist, she then had to loop it over a hook that had been driven into a ceiling joist some five or six feet away. She pulled down tightly before pulling the rope back towards her and securing the rope to the chair leg.

The incapacitated and bloodied George sat tightly bound to the huge leather armchair. His legs were spread apart and arms crudely suspended in mid-air with thin rope that dug deep into his skin. This took place against the backdrop of the dingy cellar with a deranged magpie and, by now, the tedious, continual rendition of Slim Whitman's recording of 'Rose Marie'.

Stella was bushwhacked. She'd been at it, tugging and straining, pulling and yanking, for over an hour and was struggling to breathe freely, her tight chest heavy and painful. She turned away from her captive and leant on the stone table with both arms. She felt dizzy and took in large gulps of air. Her back was still straight; she hadn't buckled. She stood there until she'd restored some self-possession.

Maggie's manic screeching eventually subsided, and Stella managed to filter out the repetitive drone of Whitman. She delved into her cardigan pocket and plucked out a packet of cigarettes. Pulling one out, she lit it with a match. A deep drag calmed her nerves. She placed the packet onto the stone slab and then carefully pulled out the photograph. Bridlington, less than twelve months ago, just her and The Girl. She brought it to her lips and kissed it before leaning over and placing it up against the cigarette packet so that the image of their granddaughter was facing George.

Next, she reached over and grabbed a chunky candle from one of the shelves and positioned it next to the photograph. She lit the candle and then waded through the dirty black rainwater and turned off the main light switch. The candle gave off a dim, low light as the flame flickered, initially struggling to establish a hold on the wick. Once the flame had settled, Stella's eyesight became accustomed to the darkness, although she still couldn't make out the darkened extremities of the inky black cellar.

She looked around. She could perceive the shimmer of the floodwater at her feet. The dim candlelight revealed the shallow dips and hollows, strike marks and imperfections of the stone table. The flickering shadows cast by the dancing flame conjured within her an abject mental desolation. The simple shrine to The Girl, in its soft yellow light, illuminated the innocent beauty of a soulless angel.

Stella turned; her line of vision directed her to the base of the old leather armchair. She looked up at the bizarre roping which held the feet and arms of her captive firmly in place. She then glanced up at his face and received the shock of her life. She gasped and held her hand up to her mouth. Her weakened heart missed a beat as the energy drained from her like an electric charge zapping out in a short circuit.

George, just a few seconds ago a delirious and rambling wreck, was now sitting up, alert, conscious and staring directly at Stella through widened eyes, the whites of which shone in the dim light against his wretched, pallid face. There was no expression, no physical movement, just a knowing stare with a distant look of resignation in his eyes.

The shock reduced her to slouching back onto the stone table, but this was a new, hardened Stella. She quickly asserted herself and stood up straight. She walked over to George and leaned over so she was staring him straight in the eye. At that moment, she knew that George was lucid and conscious. A spark of light in his eye connected them, just for a split second. She took a step back, arched her wizened frame and then aimed a fully fledged blow to his face with the palm of her hand.

'Bastard!' she cried. George's head flopped backwards. She grabbed a shilling coin from the pocket of her cardigan. 'A shilling!' she cried. 'Is that what my granddaughter's worth, eh? A fucking shilling? You dirty, filthy bastard!' She threw the shilling at George and glowered into his empty, cold eyes. 'Not so clever now, are ya? You fat bastard!' she continued before reaching over and slapping him a double whammy combination, this time using both hands.

His head flopped and his eyes closed as he returned to the state of a slumped, spent mass.

'You've me to contend wi' now, George fucking Wilson, never mind a six-year-old... You won't be getting anyway near her ever again,' she panted. 'And you, you can go to hell as well!' she cried as she ripped the silver cross and chain from around her neck and threw it over her shoulder into the far corner of the room. 'There's no God in this world – it's all a bastard con!'

Panting heavily, she reached over to the wooden crate and grabbed the radio. She clicked it on. It was tuned to BBC Radio 4; she turned up the volume before placing it back onto the crate. She hesitated, and then grabbed it back and fumbled as she tried to focus on the controls before clicking it to long wave. She fiddled about with the tuning dial before selecting a foreign news channel. She calmly placed it back onto the crate top.

'Fuck you, George,' she said quietly and without emotion.

The commotion had set Maggie into a further orgy of guttural chacking.

Stella turned to face the tiny shrine to her granddaughter and blew a gentle kiss. 'I told you, my love, I won't let you down again…ever…if it's the last thing I do.'

She waded through the water past the stone table and picked up a large pickaxe handle which rested against the wall. She lifted it and aimed a slicing sideways glance at the flimsily built cage that housed Maggie.

'And I'm sick of hearing you, ya fuckin' black-eyed freak,' she cried as the door to the cage flew open. She made her way up the old stone steps, her feet sodden and dirty, whilst her husband sat battered and bloodied, unconscious and on the brink of death. 'And if you think you're getting off that lightly, George Wilson, then you've another think coming. I haven't even started with you yet.'

CHAPTER 10

October 2016

I t had turned eleven thirty. Zoe had infused the substance delivered direct to her door at bang on the prescribed time of nine o'clock. Her coy invitation for the dealer to join her inside for a drink of sorts had been met with hysterical laughter and a definitive rejection, so, with Sophia now fast asleep in bed, she slouched on the sofa, determined to get through the night one way or another.

She'd already fizzed her way up to the high echelons, and now, on the way back down, she wished she'd doubled the order and intake. However, there remained a plentiful stock of alcohol for her to fall back on. The clock was scrutinised every five or ten minutes, although she was now unable, or unwilling, to compute the number of hours before Phil's arrival back home.

She ploughed on with the consumption of alcohol, now on the Bacardi, the lager already consumed and consigned to history. The 24/7 news channel blared out in the background which, Zoe believed, would give a grounded ambience to counter the unmitigated negative atmosphere that hung thick in the little Edwardian back-to-back. The plan for mind-numbing obliteration hadn't quite materialised as planned.

Although mentally shattered, she remained painfully conscious of her surroundings. The expectation of impending, sinister undertakings was unrelenting and lodged at the back of her throat, like a Billy Goats Gruff lurking under the bridge. She was unable to shrug off this shroud of pessimism no matter how much alcohol she downed. With each glass, she sank lower and lower. Morbid visions of the cellar, dragging her down, inhaling her soul into the blackness, the toxic womb of obscurity, into the dark unknown.

The strength of the storm intensified with wave after wave of booming thunder and exploding lightning as it seemingly homed in on its target: Reginald Street, East Moor Park, LS9.

Zoe picked up the iPhone and checked her Facebook account but was too pissed to consider posting a status. Instead, she blindly scrolled through her timeline. Discarding the mobile, she took another gulp of Bacardi and surveyed the room, her attention again being pulled towards the area under the window. The house still had her by the throat, unrelenting, perpetual. *What the fuck do I have to do? I should be slaughtered by now, out of it... What the fuck...?*

A flash of light illuminated the whole street before the house rocked as another clap of thunder cracked like scene from an epic biblical movie. But this wasn't epic, it wasn't biblical; and it certainly wasn't a movie, this was East Moor Park!

Zoe flinched and cursed as her mind oozed back to the space beneath her, the chair, the musty smell, the murky collapsed corner, the little coal bunker room. She shook her head and protested that it wasn't fair, it just wasn't right. The high from the cocaine hadn't lasted that long and the after-effects had dragged her down a little, but still, the alcohol should have rendered her impervious to such negative contemplations, but it hadn't.

She was hazy, her head was buzzing, but she was aware, well aware and too aware for her liking. She picked up the phone, pressed the contacts icon and scrolled down until she reached Phil's number. She called him. The phone rang and rang. *Pick up the phone, Phil, you twat!* He didn't, so the phone was once again jettisoned to the end of the sofa.

A glance up at the clock revealed that it was almost midnight. Zoe just about managed to work out that the night was still young, the middle of the night was some distance away and morning was miles away. She poured a further boisterous measure of Bacardi into the glass and topped it up with Diet Coke before gulping almost half the contents in one go. The storm now raged directly above the impoverished little street as the thunder and lightning struck in unison with the squalling winds sending a shower of rain hammering onto the window like a spray of bullets.

'Aw fuck off!' pronounced Zoe nonchalantly. 'Do what you fucking want.' She threw her hand in the air, wafting away at what she perceived to be God's mischievous attempts at stoking up the tension. 'I don't friggin' care!' She again reached over and grabbed the phone, pressing the contact number for Phil. The phone rang continuously, but still no response, nothing. Just as she was about to fling the unit in disgust yet again, she spotted the power icon at one per cent and realised that she'd neglected to put it on charge that morning as she had planned. The phone went flying with increased revulsion as she dropped her head into her hands. *Twat! Fuckin' thing!*

*

All light sources in the room slowly dim as a soothing cloak of velvet blackness descends over the little sitting room. The sound of the TV, the ticking clock and the storm dissipate, leaving the atmosphere shrouded in an ice-cold silence. A chink of light appears in the dark far corner of the ceiling and slowly draws to the fore, gradually increasing in size as it reaches the centre of the room. A spotlight from above focuses a harsh light onto a figure in the pitch-blackness.

The figure, an old female, is now centre stage and sits on a bar stool which slowly revolves. The stiff-backed figure is slumped to one side, her emaciated limbs hang loose. Bedraggled grey hair is scraped back into a bun. The figure sits stock-still on the revolving barstool. The head is bowed with eyes closed. Her wrinkled, white-grey face is embellished with garish red lipstick and heavy black eyeliner. The figure is dressed as a ballerina with grey tutu and bodice, loose-fitting tights and worn, scuffed ballet slippers. The listing, stiff-backed figure is dead. It sits on the revolving barstool.

Zoe watches, she observes, she witnesses. She sees. Slowly revolving, dead, spotlight, soothing blackness, front, side, back, side, over and over, silence, revolving, slow. Limp limbed and stiff-backed. Dead.

*

Zoe had dozed off in an upright sitting position still clutching an empty glass firmly in her grasp. She opened her eyes to the shrill ringtone of the iPhone with the image of a dead woman revolving on a barstool still sharp in her mind. She didn't know whether to shit, shave or shampoo. By the time she'd worked out where she was, what was happening and traced the whereabouts of the phone, the ringing had stopped. She harboured a deep, sad sentiment in her heart as she looked around the room. There was no soothing blackness, just a harsh light, a droning TV and a foreboding ambience. The emotional impact of 'the vision' lingered as she struggled to attune herself to the prevailing circumstances.

The clock told her that it was quarter to one; she hadn't been out for that long, she figured. She was still groggy as she lifted the phone up to her face, confirming that the missed call had been from Phil. *About fucking time.* The thunderstorm had not moved on and lingered directly overhead, still as lively and volatile. She took a second to collect her thoughts. She knew she'd rang Phil but couldn't quite remember why.

She pressed the recall button and listened to the ringtone. She let it ring five or six times. 'Answer the fucking phone, Phil, you dopey fuckwit!' she said out loud. As she was about to throw down the phone, yet again, she heard a voice.

'Zoe...everything all right, love?'

She slammed the phone back up to the side of her face. 'Phil! Phil!' she screeched. 'Phil!' There was no further answer. As she looked down at the phone, her panic turned to disgust as the blank screen indicated that the charge had totally expired. 'I don't believe it!' she cried. 'Fucking thing!' She threw down the phone and threw back her head, closing her eyes and clenching her fists tight. *What a fucking night this is turning out to be. For Christ's sake just let me get through it, just let me get through to the morning... that's all I ask. For fuck's sake, it's not much, is it?* She remained in this position, quietly contemplating, quietly cursing as the pressure in her head began crank up. Eventually, from the depths of her deepest subconscious, her fighting spirit once again surfaced. She took a deep intake of breath.

Right. You need to go upstairs, get the bleeding phone charger, come back down and plug the fucking phone in. That's not hard, is it? You can do that. What's your problem, lass?

She convinced herself that the task was indeed no problem at all, but the negative ambience and the howling wind and rain immediately suppressed the outbreak of confidence. She decided to have another drink before embarking on the inevitable expedition upstairs.

Pouring Bacardi into the glass, she topped it up with coke and took a large glug. She didn't fancy the short journey to the bedroom but knew it had to be made. Even if she couldn't contact Phil, she regarded a fully charged phone as an essential piece of survival kit, her contact with the outside world, the rational world. So if she was to get through the night unscathed, she'd need it, fully charged. But for now, she'd just knock back another drink, and then she'd go.

She stared at the TV. She watched and listened but saw and heard nothing. She made a concerted effort to engage in the Brexit news story being aired. The country was still reeling from the result of the EU referendum but, even as a fervent Brexiteer, she found it impossible to focus on the news bulletin. She admonished herself for being so weak and pathetic, shook her head, sat back and took in another mouthful.

A far away noise, a howl, focused her attention, but it was too distant and indistinct for her to take on board as anything to worry about. Another shower of rain battered against the window in unison with a flash of lightning as another burst of thunder rocked the house and street. Again, an image of the beaten, leather chair in the cellar seeped into her mind's eye like a black smog perco-lating her expectant headspace.

She shrugged off the thoughts, physically shaking her head and shoulders. She looked at the clock. Five to one. Finishing the drink, she planted the glass down on the table as she mustered up the confidence and energy to retrieve the phone charger. Scratching. She stiffened up. Her immediate thoughts were channelled towards the hideous witch doll, Sophia's pride and joy. There'd been an identical scratching noise during that incident earlier on.

She fired a look at the empty mantlepiece before muting the television with the remote. More scratching, muffled scratching. This noise was not distant – near, but muffled. *The witch doll! I threw the fucking thing out!* She sat, wide-eyed, entrenched on the sofa, not daring to move an inch, senses on high alert. The scratching con-tinued, so near... She sensed a presence. She sensed a con-sciousness. She was being watched.

More scratching, delicate scratching. Thoughts of the macabre effigy raced through her mind. A nasty, evil entity sent to taunt her by some depraved force, a force wicked beyond her comprehension. The scratch-ing stopped, but the sound that ensued sent every nerve cell into a frenzy as the energy drained from her already weakened body. Her heart pumped hard and fast.

The unmistakable creak of the dry metal hinges on the bottom stair door slowly grated, barely four feet over her right shoulder. Slow, terse and cranky, the sharp grinding echoed throughout the little room. Her nerve ends jangled, her stomach churned, her heart thumped.

Without moving her head, through the corner of her eye, her periphery vision, she could make out the slow opening movement of the door. She sat stiff. The creaking continued, excruciating, as she tracked the tortuous, slow movement not daring to move. *What the fuck! God help me, for fuck's sake! Almighty God, help me!*

The creaking stopped. She could make out that the door was now half open. She was sure, one hundred per cent certain, that there was someone, something, watching her. She could sense it, she could smell it, she could hear the breath.

As the newscaster continued her muted news report, Zoe stared straight ahead at the mantlepiece and wall clock. A downdraught from upstairs produced an ominous chill, which slithered into the room like a python descending upon a potential kill.

You've got to turn around and confront it, whatever it is. There's no other way – you've got to do it! Do it! She remained motionless, spellbound and stunned. *Do it! If it's the fucking doll just go for it, kill the fucking thing!*

She couldn't move, her chest heaved and her heart thumped. There was a stand-off between herself and the 'thing' that she was one hundred per cent certain was now standing at the foot of the stairs burning a hole in the back of her neck. Every neuron stood to attention. Every hair bristled with anticipation. Every mental process was super sharp. *Fucking do it! Turn your fucking head around now!*

Knowing she had to look, Zoe cried as she began to turn. Slowly, inch by inch, she twisted her shoulders, neck and head before finally coming face to face with the wicked presence playing such a cruel, tortuous game. She almost fainted.

'Jimmy! You little bastard! I'll fucking kill ya! I'll skin you alive, you little twat!'

Princess gave out a sharp yelp and wagged his little Yorkie tail.

'Get up them fucking stairs, you dopey little twat,' screamed Zoe, her heart still pounding and a fire now raging in her belly. 'No, get the fuck down here,' she bellowed as she rose from the sofa, cocking her thumb back towards the room.

Now it was Princess who didn't know whether to shit, shave or shampoo as he sat on the second bottom step panting and wagging his tail.

'Get in here now!' demanded Zoe as she reached over and grabbed him before slamming the door closed. Her heart raced as the pressure in her head slowly released, the sense of relief leaving her drained and woozy. She was so thankful to hold the little bundle of fur close to her chest as she slumped onto the sofa. Tears began to flow down her cheeks as she held him up to her face and kissed him. 'You're a little twat, you are,' she said softly as she continued to kiss and caress him. 'Do you know that? A little fucking twat.'

She sat there for ten minutes pinning Princess close to her breasts as her heart rate returned to normal. With Princess now in tow, she was more confident about the prospect of retrieving the phone charger. Unmuted, the TV continued to churn out news, sport and weather reports as the designer wall clock slowly ticked away. The rain still lashed against the living room window and as she looked up at the curtains, the mother of all lightning strikes exploded in a frenzied rage directly above the house. The crack of thunder shook the whole building as every property on the street plunged into instant and total darkness. The power cut immediately expunged all sources of lighting and the television zapped out, leaving Zoe disorientated and clinging onto Princess as he yelped in the pitch-black darkness.

She couldn't believe it. She'd only just calmed down from the creaking door episode, and now this. She grabbed her phone to utilise the torchlight feature before remembering it was on zero charge. *I'm fucked...* She was fucked. *What am I gonna do now?*

Princess yapped away incessantly.

'Shut up for God's sake,' she growled, clutching the little dog whilst thinking hard about her next move. She knew the fuse box was located at the top of the stairs at the cellar-head. *There's absolutely no fucking way I'm going there to check that out – no fucking way!* She shivered at the thought.

She crouched in the blackness, mentally and physically shattered. She traced the day back from the minute she'd woken. From the time Sophia had roused her and made her grumpy with her constant nattering. How she'd snapped when all her little girl had wanted to do was help tidy the house. The flying witch doll and the walk around the desolate park in the pissing rain and the subsequent encounter with Mrs Patel at Sally's. The Bottom House family, the rough diamond she now knew as Racy Tracy, and 'Geoffrey' the dealer who had declined her kind invitation for a nightcap. The phone charger, the creaking door and now this.

As she thought, with the effects of the substance and alcohol now seemingly spent, it occurred to her that nothing odd had really happened – nothing that couldn't be explained rationally. The storm had undoubtedly made things appear a little more daunting, the ambience a little more sinister; but in reality, nothing had happened. Furthermore, nothing had happened the previous night, either. Nothing had happened, and nothing was going to happen. *Phil's right, it's all in me friggin' head.* She rebuked herself for being so weak and feeble-minded. *All that anguish, all that nervous energy for fuck all. He'll be home in a few hours anyway, you gormless bitch. Pull yourself together!* This new-found rationale once again instilled a confidence as she felt a large burden of anxiety slip away from her tense shoulders.

'Come on, Jimmy, let's go check that fuse box...it might just be a trip switch.' She stood up holding Princess under one arm and faced the kitchen bifolding door in the dark as she listened to the patter of rain against the window. The eye of the storm seemed to have passed with that last outburst, so perhaps things were just about calming down a little, at long last.

She placed one hand on the handle before stopping dead. A bolt of fear smacked her in the face as she realised a flaw in her premise. *Nothing had happened that couldn't be logically explained.* She realised that this wasn't actually true. It was false. *The fucking witch doll. That bastard thing flew from the fireplace over to the fucking door. I felt it whizz past me, for fuck's sake. There's no way that could have happened naturally. No way! No fucking way at all.*

Immediately, the negativity, which had taken such a hold over her since the departure of Phil, returned – but this time with an added dimension. This time it was fuelled by her own rational thought, not feeble-minded nonsense.

She removed her hand from the handle and took a step back. She looked around her, at the hazy black shapes and then the digital battery-powered clock which gave just a hint of a green light showing the time as half past one. Zoe couldn't take any more. She made the decision there and then that the best thing to do was hit the sack and be done with it. *It'll still be dark whether we're up there or down here… Whatever will be will be.*

'Let's just go to bed,' she said wearily. Clasping the sleepy little dog, she trudged up the stairs and around the dark winding corner at the top. She lurched towards the main bedroom and paused at the attic steps, deliberating whether to check on Sophia before deciding against disturbing her. She proceeded to enter the open bedroom, kicked off her slippers and, still clinging onto Princess, she slid under the duvet pulling it tightly over her head. She closed her eyes. She was shattered, so tired, so weary and, whether she wanted to give one or not, at this particular juncture in her life, she didn't possess a fuck or a care in the whole world. She'd given up.

Her overactive mind initially resisted the notion of slumber, but it wasn't long before the mental fatigue took hold as she quietly slipped into a deep sleep, giving her tormented soul just a measure of respite. For the time being at least.

CHAPTER 11

May 1975

I t had been over four hours since Stella had returned to the living room from the murky depths of the cellar, where a lifeless and battered George remained, trussed up and insensible. Apart from his superficial physical injuries, far more serious was the damage caused by the overdose of narcotics, surreptitiously administered by his wife. However, Stella's only concern was that it was she who was now in control. She was as confident as her befuddled head would allow that there wouldn't be a murmur from George at any time in the near future.

During those four hours, Stella had gravitated towards the only pursuit she was capable of: the consumption of alcohol. She was slaughtered and as the sounds of Mantovani's orchestra, once again, rang throughout the little house, she was up to her usual shenanigans. She'd increased the volume so George could share her enjoyment of the music, should he regain consciousness.

'Trevor, my darling, dance with me!' she pronounced as she half waltzed and half lurched around the little room. 'Come, my love,' she said as she performed her gauche dance routine with total abandon. She arched her back and stretched her arms, her trembling fingers reaching for the far corners of the ceiling. She pointed her slippered feet towards the furthest echelons of the dingy little room as she tottered and floundered, but she didn't care. As far as she was concerned, it was as consummate a performance as any *Swan Lake* production. The alcohol had elevated her aloft a floating cloud, in a world where the drudgery of her wretched existence was left behind, out of sight and forgotten about. She stumbled between photographs of Trevor, kissing each one in turn as she clumped her way around the room.

'Trevor, my beautiful Trevor,' she repeated. 'Come with me, my love, and dance.' The drama was palpable and had been fine-tuned over many years, but the cracks were deep, the paper tissue thin. No matter how much undying love she declared for Trevor, or how much whisky she consumed, and regardless of the happy vibes that manifested in her fragile mind, the pain was overtly evident deep inside her sad grey eyes.

Trevor sat in the armchair and looked up at his wife. A handsome, slim man with jet-black hair and a soft, tanned complexion. He smiled at her and then grinned, showcasing his gleaming white teeth. He was dressed impeccably in dark suit, crisp white shirt and blue silk tie. He sat cross-legged with his right hand resting on his knee. Consummate, confident and compassionate, he smiled, causing his piercing blue eyes to sparkle like finely cut crystal.

Stella twirled around the room as blissful and content as she had been in many a year. She held her outstretched hand towards Trevor as an invitation to join her. He was content just to sit and watch, but Stella didn't care. She carried on, carefree and untroubled. Mantovani and his team continued to orchestrate the beautiful but austere background harmony, as they had done so many times before.

The alcohol had empowered Stella with an energy

surge well above the levels that would be deemed normal for someone of her age and condition, especially after the exertions of earlier that evening. Even so, after a while, her disjointed movements slowed to the point where she was forced to flop down on the settee. She gulped the stale air and closed her eyes as her head fizzed and popped. As an image of the girl flashed into her mind, an all familiar vacant expression proliferated across her haggard features.

She began to rock whilst digging her nails into the plastic arm of the settee. A look of consternation appeared as she lifted her head and turned to face Trevor.

There was no Trevor; Trevor had departed.

Her heart dropped a beat as she panicked, her eyes darting around the room in search of her one true love and soulmate. She found him, standing behind her, just inside the kitchen entrance. The exact spot where, just a few hours ago, George had stumbled and crashed to the floor knocking himself unconscious.

The huge, toothy grin had disappeared from Trevor's face, but he looked down at Stella with a sympathetic smile. His eyes conveyed compassion, understanding and love.

Stella's acute suspicion turned to adulation as she returned the smile. The rocking ceased as her heart warmed and the nails were retracted with her mind now at ease.

'She's our granddaughter, Trevor. Ours...not his. It's all my fault, my love. All my fault. It's up to me now. I don't want you to get involved, love. I'll sort it – I promised her... I won't let her down, love, I can't...not again.' She sat up, lifted her head and straightened her back.

Trevor silently turned towards the cellar-head and

disappeared from view.

Stella stood up and followed him into the kitchen. The small chair that she'd wedged in front of the cellar-head door had been moved aside with the door now half open.

Trevor stood at the top of the stairs. He turned to face Stella. A trace of a smile remained, but this was now accompanied by a more serious countenance. He looked her in the eye before turning away and descending the dark stairs. Stella looked on lovingly.

She turned to the cupboard unit and slid open the top drawer, pulling out an oversized pair of tailor's scissors. They were large, well used and sharp. She placed them onto the worktop and then retrieved the bread knife, the same one with which she'd threatened to slice open George's throat, 'from here to fucking here', just a few days previously. She ran her hardened finger up and down the jagged blade and placed it next to the scissors. Next, she bent down and pulled out a small bag of hand tools from under the kitchen table before rummaging and pulling out a rusting pair of wire cutters. A ball of string was plucked from the top shelf as she stood and surveyed the odd assortment of tools and kit. She then calmly gathered them all up.

She took a step towards the cellar-head door and stopped. She listened to Mantovani's orchestra and smiled. Trevor had descended the cellar steps ahead of her. She was happy. They were together. No more round shoulders.

Stiff-backed and self-possessed, she stumbled down the cellar steps to find the candle still alight, flickering next to the photograph of The Girl. She waded through the flooded basement and placed the assembled apparatus onto the stone table before looking over towards

Trevor.

He stood, silently lurking in the shadows of the far corner, the one with the collapsed floor. The dim dancing light gave him a more gaunt expression, less vibrant with a more serious tone to his face. She could barely make out the black form of his body; the fine detail of his suit and strong hands were now indistinguishable in the dark. Only his face with piercing cobalt-blue eyes stood out clearly in the far reaches of the gloomy corner.

Stella was unperturbed. She smiled at him. This time the smile was unreciprocated. Instead, it was returned with a grave, still stare. She remained untroubled and turned towards George. He was still out cold, but the slight movement of his chest indicated that he was still alive, just.

She reached up to turn down the volume on the radio, which enabled the music from the living room to pervade the basement and override the nonsensical jabbering resonating from the little transistor. She once again looked over to the corner where the image of Trevor appeared to be slowly withdrawing into the very fabric of the house.

'Trevor,' she said, 'this is our granddaughter, my love. We're both here for her now. We can both look after her, just the two of us.' She picked up the photograph and held it to her heart.

The shadowy figure slowly ebbed away as she looked on. It was now just a black shapeless form with a lingering outline of a pale grey face with blue laser-sharp eyes glowing through darkened eye sockets. The amorphous form continued to slowly recede into the dark, inky black corner.

'Trevor! Trevor, my love, please don't leave me...don't

you dare leave me,' she said, increasing the gravity and tone of her voice. 'You've left me once, love, don't do it again...Trevor!'

As she spoke, the black form became even blacker than the surrounding blackness. All that remained was a reducing shimmering black vision with a fixed pair of pinprick-sharp blue eyes, which were now laced with malicious intent.

'Trevor! Trevor!' Her cries turned into a whimper. 'Trevor, please...my love.' As she stared at the disappearing apparition, the piercing blue eyes abruptly and sharply turned blood red as an icy blast of foul air from the corner extinguished the candle, plunging the whole cellar into total darkness. The black form and eyes were no more, and a deathly silence descended throughout the cold, subterranean chamber.

*

Stella's consciousness resurfaced. The inside of her mouth was caked in a nauseas crust which tasted like shite. She smacked her lips, attempting to hydrate her arid-dry palate. Her head throbbed. With her eyes remaining firmly closed, she became aware of a harsh light from above pressing onto her sensitive eyelids. She determined that her body lie in the foetal position – but where and in which realm, she was unsure.

As her brain began to boot up, she recognised the undulations and contours of the base she was lying upon. It was the trusty little plastic settee, the one with the chocolate brown cushions. She correctly presumed that she'd been drinking and had eventually flaked out. A standard aftermath of a heavy night on the booze, which had been played out many times before, but this time it was different.

A deep negative sentiment hung over her like a dark, distant nightmare. An awareness of her innermost emotions being compromised, but with no tangible memory, no detail, just a deep-seated essence of negative depravity.

She opened her eyes and rubbed away the encrusted sleep before massaging her wrinkled face with the palms of her hands. She surveyed the room; her heart sank as reality slowly enveloped her. She prayed to God that he might teleport her into another world, another realm, any but the one she now found herself in.

The curtains were closed, but she could see by the shaft of light streaming through the central gap that it was daytime and quite bright outside. The mantelpiece clock told her that it was a quarter to three in the afternoon. She grimaced as she sat up, the blood rush compounding the heavy throbbing sensation in her head.

Again, she attempted to wet her parched lips by licking them before rubbing her feet together and wiggling her toes in search of her slippers. She located the first and hooked it on. It felt cold and damp. The second one also, but it was more than damp. It was soaking wet. She looked down to discover that not only were the slippers sodden, they were soaked in a red dye.

As she bent over to scrutinise the situation further, she noticed her hand, and then the other hand, and then her forearms. She threw off the anorak she'd been using as a blanket. Her slacks, blouse and cardigan were the same. Red. Blood red. Covered in it. From head to toe, all over the place. She didn't move. She sat there calm and untroubled but confused.

A cool draught meandered through the kitchen. From

the musty, damp odour, Stella recognised it as deriving from the cellar. She remembered George. The husband whom she'd dumped and left trussed up downstairs in the musty little basement.

She looked around the room for any signs of his presence, but as more and more details from the previous night surfaced, she remembered it being almost impossible for him to escape.

She rose unsteadily from the settee and walked over to the mirror above the fireplace. She looked at the old hag staring back at her. She raised her hand to a cut on her forehead, the blood still fresh, moist to the touch, daubed over her neck and face.

She turned and methodically walked into the kitchen. The chair with which she remembered wedging the cellar-head door had been moved to one side, the door now being partially open. She calmly walked over and peered down into the dark, malodorous cellar. There was no flickering candle. She turned on the light switch, immediately swathing the room in a dull, artificial light, before slowly descending the stone stairs, her anaesthetised headspace devoid of emotion.

Most of the water had receded by now, with small pools of water lying sporadically around the earthen floor. Only the far corner remained fully submerged in a dirty black liquid. She reached the bottom of the stairs. In the dim lighting, she casually looked over at the body of George, still in the chair, exactly where she'd left him in the early hours.

A large pool of blood covered the ground around the front of the armchair. George's bulk was slumped to one side with his head hanging from his limp neck. Stella was oblivious to the erratic scuttling and squeaking from the caged ferret behind her. She stood silent, mesmerised by the sight that lay before her.

She became aware of the transistor radio still playing, but barely audible. George's slashed underwear and trousers lay in shreds around his ankles. His exposed and shrivelled manhood was now lacking the collaboration of his debauched gonads. They were certainly redundant now as they lay severed, mashed up and mutilated in the seat of his soiled drawers which lay slashed and blood-soaked around his ankles. Blooded string hung between his legs, attached to what remained of his scrotum. His limp arms hung in mid-air where two of his finger ends were missing from each hand, with another crude attempt to remove a third one on his left. His shirt and vest were covered in blood.

As Stella looked on, she detected a slight movement from his chest. 'George!' said Stella firmly. 'George, can y'hear me? It's me.'

George began to groan in pain and then slowly rose his head. Blood mixed with saliva oozed out of his mouth where the last inch from the tip of his tongue had been cleanly sliced away. The groan turned into a guttural growl as George suddenly listed forward. He cried out with all the pent-up energy his pitiful mass could muster.

Stella shrieked as she took a step back. His eyeballs had been removed in the most crude and horrific manner. A viscous liquid dripped from his eye sockets, now hollowed and bloodied.

Again, George lurched forward; a blood-curdling scream echoed around the cellar. The cord and chain which bound him were drawn taut but held firm as the sudden burst of energy re-rendered George back into a lifeless mass. He flopped back into the old leather arm-chair as Stella looked on. The only sign of life from George now was a subtle rattling emanating from the back of his ripped-open throat.

The shocking sight left an already numbed Stella in an even deeper state of disorientation. She was unaware of the photograph of The Girl, which now lay flat and face down on the stone table, beneath the crushed and flat-tened carcass of the dead magpie. Across the table, ad-jacent to the spent candle, lay the pickaxe handle, now matted in blood and feathers.

She stood and stared at George, numbed, without dir-ection, without any comprehension of the scene which lay before her. She reached over to the radio and in-creased the volume before turning her back on him. As she did so, she stopped and listened to the scratching and scraping. She calmly bent over and released the catches on both hutches, and then, with serene composure, she slowly climbed the stairs, turned off the light and closed the door behind her, shutting away the scene, closing it off, out of sight.

As she wedged the chair in front of the cellar-head door, George continued to whimper as he edged towards a slow, lonely and painful death in the dark cellar be-neath.

*

Stella hadn't moved from the settee since witnessing the horrific spectacle of her mutilated husband. She slouched round-shouldered and detached from reality. Silence shrouded the little room, the only sound being the tick-tocking of the mantelpiece clock. She stared at the unlit gas fire, then at the still curtains which had remained drawn all day. There was no attempt to figure out what had happened.

She remembered tapping George up with the Valium and the immense struggle in heaving him down to the cellar. Stringing him up and slapping his smug face. Wedging the cellar door with the chair. But nothing after that. She had no idea how the cut to her head had occurred, or how much blood she'd lost.

Stella assumed that it was she who was responsible for the mutilations – her blood-soaked clothing and blood-caked hands bearing testament to that theory. That and the deep-seated negative sentiment, the black hole which now dominated her psyche. But she didn't know for certain. She'd only planned to slap him about a bit, take the edge off his sickly demeanour, in honour of The Girl, her granddaughter. She sat quiet and motionless and waited, the assumption being that the answers would slowly percolate her muddled headspace. But the answers never arrived. She finished off the previous night's whisky.

It was eight o'clock. Stella had mulled over her predicament for hours but was no nearer to a plan of action. The only certainty in her head was that she'd be paying the off-licence a visit sometime before ten o'clock.

There was no single person on the face of the planet to whom she could turn to for guidance or advice. She was too ashamed to talk to her daughter, and her two husbands were unavailable. Her first, Trevor, had done one yet again; and the incumbent George was obsolete and currently being held in storage. She had no friends, no mutual acquaintances with George and was certainly not on speaking terms with any of the neighbours, Peggy Bowden included.

However, the more she contemplated her situation and the more she ostracised herself from those around her, the more a tiny glimmer of hope began to light up from the darkest corner of despair. Conceivably, one last-ditch attempt to make sense of her existence. Maybe one last chance that the person emerging in her mind's eye could tender some answers, guide her back onto the straight and narrow. It's worth a shot, she thought. *Last chance saloon.*

She'd recently had a spat with this fella, but previously they'd had a close relationship for as long as she could remember. She'd always placed her trust in him, confiding in him both as a child and during the rockiest times in her adult life, but his latest act of betrayal had sliced her soul open to the elements. Under the current circumstances, however, she was prepared to forgive, deciding that he deserved this one last chance to redeem himself. The fella in question answered to the name of God.

*

Having cleaned and tidied both the house, and herself, as best she could, Stella embarked on the short journey to the church, battling her way up East Moor Drive against the blustery May winds. It was dusk as the weary sun began to dip below the grim city nightscape. The strong winds buffeted her light frame; the fact that she was already half-cut and unsteady on her feet didn't make the journey any easier. She wore a headscarf, which covered the gash to her forehead, and the dirty blue anorak as she staggered up the Drive, passing the closed shops with her head held low and her mind lost in a dark, lonely apprehension. She fought not only against the wind but also against the weight of her troubled, confused mind. She carried on. She had to.

Clusters of youths wearing star jumpers and bell-bottomed jeans loitered on the street corners, offering no direct confrontation towards the strange little woman, just a knowing sneer and the occasional dry witticism once she'd passed out of earshot.

'Fucking 'ell, it's Old Mother Riley,' quipped one.

'March the Taylors dress you well!' said another with a snigger to his vacant-looking pal.

She reached the top of East Moor Drive and slouched past the Slip Inn, which reminded her of the happy times she'd spent there in the company of Trevor and friends. She allowed herself to reminisce. She'd never been in the place with George, but it wasn't the pub or any other establishment that reminded her of him, it was the dog shit that littered the street corners like pungent landmines. Through more luck than judgement she managed to avoid treading in them, though there had been a couple of close calls.

She turned left onto Ascot Terrace and then right onto Pontefract Lane. Pausing for a brief respite, she looked up towards the magnificent blackened stone spire of All Saints Church, silhouetted beautifully against the orange and crimson darkening skies. The church sat at the bottom of Pontefract Lane, just before the York Road junction. At over 150 feet high, the iconic church spire had dominated the local skyline for 140 years. To Stella, the sight and sanctuary of this beautiful building opened her heart and filled it with pure love and sentiment. Ever since she could remember, since her days as an infant at the school many years ago, the church had symbolised the security and decency of a warm and loving community, a caring community.

Not for much longer, though. This was 1975, and the church was in the final throes of its own death rattle as a result of ongoing regeneration of the area. It was only a matter of time before the tired, old structure would follow in the footsteps of the old school and be replaced with a modern, soulless construction, one that would prove to be more economical to run.

However, on this particular night, the spectacle of the church was an inspiration to Stella as she lurched down the hill past The Shepherd pub and the former Princess Cinema, now a thriving bingo hall. She shuffled by the numerous corner shops, which had loyally served the community for so many years, but were now, one by one, succumbing to the noose of redevelopment – the end of an era.

The church grounds were bordered by sandstone walling, which had been blackened by many years of industrial pollution like thousands of other stone structures in the grim northern cities. As she approached, the unmistakable and distinctive aroma of common oak wafted through her sensitive nostrils. The sweet, comforting fragrance evoked fond and cherished memories. She had married Trevor here; both she and Susan had been christened at the church. She reminisced over past Christmases and Easters, the harvest festivals and the summer garden parties. The church had always played an important part in the fabric of Stella's life, and now, abandoned by all around her, she was back, back at All Saints, and never in more need of divine salvation than on this blustery May evening.

She walked up the dark cobbled lane, either side of which stood the huge oak trees which formed an ecclesiastical guard of honour, towards the church entrance.

She turned the iron ring on the huge oak door and pushed. The door was locked. The church had never been locked before; it had always been open to anyone, at any time of the day or night. But this was now, this was 1975, and this was East Moor Park. She shook her head and turned around, slowly retracing her steps back down the shadowy lane.

The photographs of her wedding to Trevor had been shot in this area of the church grounds on that happy day in the blazing June sunshine, many years ago. The memories brokered a quiet smile upon the troubled little woman as she sought out the services of Father Venables and his access to God.

At the end of the cobbled lane, she turned right, opened a sturdy low wooden gate and made her way up a gravel path, which ran to the front door of the modern brick-built vicarage.

The lights were on as she watched the shadows and movement of a number of souls through the downstairs windows. She approached the porch, climbed onto a raised paved step and leant over to press the doorbell. The wind whistled through the neatly cultivated vicarage gardens against the gentle rustle of the millions of leaves from the church oaks, but there was no response from the vicarage.

Again, Stella reached up and rang the doorbell, this time pressing it three times and each for a longer duration than the last. She could hear muted activity and voices from inside as she waited patiently, still unsteady on her feet.

Eventually, a figure approached, unlocked the door and slowly opened it. A neatly dressed, slightly built woman stood in the entrance and looked down at Stella, slightly puzzled as to why anyone would be ringing her doorbell at this time of the evening.

'Er, hello,' said the woman in a soft, educated voice. 'Can I help you?'

'It's Father Venables,' answered Stella. 'Can I see him, please? I need to see him.'

'I'm afraid he's engaged at the moment. Er…is there anything I can help you with?' asked Mrs Venables.

'No, no, I need to see Father Venables. I need to see him tonight, now. It won't take long, just five minutes… I just need to see him…please…it's urgent.'

Mrs Venables relented with a sigh and was just about to invite Stella into the vestibule when she noted the state of the woman: headscarf skew-whiff, grubby anorak and dishevelled in general appearance. 'Well, just wait there a second. I'll see if he's available,' she said. 'Who shall I say it is?'

'Mrs Wilson… Stella Wilson. He'll know who I am.'

'Right, Mrs Wilson, if you'd just like to wait there for a second.' She smiled and gently closed the door, leaving the late-evening visitor standing on the step in the blustery cool wind.

The night was closing in as Stella looked up at the beautiful dark skies and the ever-looming black church spire. Standing within the confines of the church grounds, she felt comforted, protected and at ease. The consecrated breeze seemed to cleanse her soul of the badness, the decay and the day-to-day rottenness of her life.

The crescendo of rustling leaves caressed her inner soul as she stood and waited patiently. As far as she was concerned, right there at that moment, standing in the shadow of the magnificent church spire, she was at the centre of the world. She wouldn't want to be anywhere else. Holding her head high, and although physically exhausted and in mental turmoil, she was satisfied and convinced that she was in the right place. The church – All Saints Church – her church.

The door suddenly opened to the tall, slender figure of Father Venables. He looked down his long, angular nose at Stella, unable to conceal his displeasure at being ousted from the activity he had been otherwise engaged in. 'Mrs Wilson! What on earth are you doing here at this time? What is it?' demanded the vicar. 'You can't just show up here at any time of the day and night. I'm in the middle of entertaining guests, woman! What is it? What's the problem?'

'Well...Father,' stammered Stella. 'Something's happened, and I just need someone to talk to...just a few minutes...'

'What?'

'Just a few minutes of your time, Father... That's all I—'

'This is preposterous, Mrs Wilson,' he replied, looking over his shoulder. 'I have a houseful of guests round for dinner, and we're halfway through serving crème brûlée cheesecake, and *you* arrive in your dishevelled state and demand an impromptu chit-chat! It's outrageous!'

'Well, I'm...sorry, Father. I just—'

'I'm afraid it's just not on, Mrs Wilson. How dare you come round here—'

'No, Father, it's not that... It's just that it's George... I've... He's...'

'Ah, the long-suffering Mr Wilson. I feel for him, I really do, but I'm afraid this is highly irregular, Mrs Wilson, and totally unacceptable...' Father Venables stopped in his tracks as he raised his head, his cavernous nostrils twitching. He looked down at Stella. 'You've been drinking again, have you, Mrs Wilson? How dare you turn up at this time of night disturbing my guests, my family and I in such an intoxicated state? You ought to be ashamed of yourself—'

'Just five minutes, Father...'

'Out of the question, woman. I suggest you get along home and sort yourself out. Walking the streets in the state you're in at this time of night is asking for trouble. Come back tomorrow morning between nine and nine thirty, and I'll see you then and not a minute before. And make sure you're sober, do you understand?'

A dejected and defeated Stella stood with her head bowed as she realised her last chance of any type of salvation in this, her pitiful little life, was slowly ebbing away. She remained silent.

'Well, go on, then. Run along, woman. It's no good hanging around here. I'll see you tomorrow, nine to half past. Sober!'

Stella turned and walked slowly towards the gate whilst Father Venables stood in the doorway with his arms folded glaring at her. As she closed the gate behind her, she turned around to hear the vicarage door close and watched as the dark figure of Father Venables ghosted back into the vicarage, no doubt to attend to the needs of his ravenous guests.

She trudged back up Pontefract Lane. Alone, without hope, without a plan and without salvation. She turned left at Ascot Terrace and then right onto East Moor Drive. The star-jumpered youths sniggered, the local wits quipped and the dog shit endured. But the troubled Stella was lost as she lumbered down the long incline of the Drive, round-shouldered, with her hands stuffed tightly into her pockets and her skew-whiff headscarf concealing the cut to her head. She was a beaten woman. Through sheer automation, she called into Ken's off-licence and picked up more whisky before trudging back to the little house at number 10 Reginald Street.

*

It was sometime later that night, in the small hours, when Stella's pitiful life on this earth plane finally expired. She drew her last lungful of breath as her over-worked, broken heart pumped the last few drams of alcohol-infused blood before seizing up completely. She lay dead for four days before Susan Wilson discovered her stiff-backed body sat up on the plastic settee – this after Peggy Bowden had raised the alarm.

Resolute to the end, she gripped an empty glass in one of her dead hands and a spent Woodbine wedged in between the fingers of the other. The crackling tones of Lonely Ballerina by Mantovani played quietly in the background. It's impossible to say whether George survived his wife. His rotting remains lay undiscovered for another five weeks.

CHAPTER 12

July 1975

'I dentify a body! What body? George? Is he all right? What's wrong with him? What's happened? I can't take much more!' Susan Wilson buried her head into the palms of both hands as the two officers remained silent, closely scrutinising her reaction. She sniffed and snuffled and wiped her brow before rummaging through her cluttered shopping bag in search of a tissue, her efforts yielding no success. Dejected, she sat up and faced the detectives, her eyes red-rimmed and watery.

Manley turned and grabbed a box of Kleenex from an adjacent cabinet and passed them over the table. He received a feeble nod of appreciation in return, as she dabbed her eyes and wiped her running nose.

'Can you tell me what's going on, please?' she said quietly after a short pause.

'You're not a well woman, Susan, are you?' asked Manley.

'What do you mean?' she replied, looking him direct in the eye.

'I mean what I say. Are you on medication? Do you take tablets for owt, you know, from the doctor?'

'Well, I'm bad wi' me nerves, if that's what you mean... I'm on Valium. I'd be lost without 'em.'

'We know you're bad wi' your nerves, Susan, and we

know you take Valium – dependant on 'em, as I understand. Bit o' depression, is it, dark moods and stuff? A lot o' people take 'em. It's nowt to be ashamed of, love. Help you get through the bad days when you're not thinking straight – that kind o' thing?'

'How do you know all this?' she said, her eyes slightly narrowing.

'It's us job to know.'

Once again, she bowed her head. She didn't know where the questioning was heading or what fate, if any, had befallen George, or even whether or not the body in question was *his*.

A further silence ensued as both detectives stared intently, attentive to every squirm, every twiddle and every twitch. The poker-faced Taylor remained as still and cold as marble, despite the sensitive nature of the questioning and the nervous reaction of the interviewee.

'Do things get on top of you, Susan?' continued Manley.

'What do you mean?'

'Well, we know you've just lost your mam.'

She nodded.

'And we know you've got a little 'un who you're bringing up on your own wi' no man behind you... Things must be difficult for you just now – no wonder you're on the bloody Valium.'

'Things are difficult. I've only just buried me mam, an' it's hard being a single parent wi' no money...it really is,' she replied softly.

'How did your mam pass away, then? It was you who found her, wasn't it?'

'Heart attack. To be honest, I think she was an alcoholic—'

'You think?' fired in Taylor with a curt sneer.

'...She must have had a fall and cracked her head. There was blood all over the place... She was on her own... I think the shock of the fall must 'ave had summat to do with it, but they gave the cause o' death as a massive heart attack.'

DS Manley continued, 'Tell me about your daughter.'

'What the hell has she got to do with owt?'

'Is she in good health?'

'Aye, o'course she is. Why shouldn't she be?'

'She been to the doctors recently? Or the hospital?'

'What do you mean?' she asked.

'I mean what I say, Susan. I'm not here to mess about, love! Have you taken your daughter to the doctors for any reason, or the hospital...in, let's say, the last couple o' months?'

Susan Wilson dropped her head again as she struggled to answer the question.

'Listen, Susan, love, you don't have to tell us if you don't want to...if you've got owt to hide... We can stop the interview right now if you'd prefer. We can get you a solicitor, you're entitled to one, but at the end of the day, we'll eventually get to the truth one way or the other. This way it just saves time. Let's us get on wi' things, and you can get yourself back home... You know what I mean, love?'

Susan Wilson nodded her head and then burst into tears.

DC Taylor remained indifferent as he sat back in the new state-of-the-art swivel chair and continued to dissect Susan Wilson closely with no break in his cold, hard stare.

Manley expressed a little more empathy as he offered at least a few token words of comfort: 'Settle down,

Susan, love. Can I get you a cup o' tea or owt? Do you want a few minutes?'

She shook her head and after a short hiatus, the interview resumed.

'All we're looking for, Susan, is the truth, said Manley. If you've nowt to hide, then let's just get this over with. I know it's hard for you and that you're going through a rough patch, but we've got a job to do, and the sooner we get to the bottom of things, then the better for everyone. You know where I'm coming from?'

She nodded and attempted to compose herself. 'She has mental issues; she has had for a couple of years. She's really introverted, shy – she won't even speak to me sometimes, an' I'm her mother. A few weeks ago, I picked her up from me mam's...and when I got her home, I noticed some blood on her knickers. She wouldn't talk to me about it, and so I took her to the doctors.'

'Blood on her knickers? What did the doctor say?'

'He examined her an' then sent us to St James' Hospital.'

'And what did they say?'

'They said either that...that...either she'd been pushing things inside her...or that...'

'Or what?' pressed the detective sergeant.

'Or that someone had been abusing her. She wouldn't say a word about it – either to me or the doctors – and she hasn't since... She's booked in for child counselling... They said that I should go to the police.'

'Well, why didn't you?'

'I'm bad wi' me nerves. I just couldn't cope with it. I didn't know what to do. I just hoped it would all go away...that in time everything would blow over... I was thinking that they might have been... I was hoping that they were wrong, that they'd made a mistake.'

'They don't usually make mistakes, Susan, do they?'

Susan Wilson stayed silent and stared down at the table.

'Earlier, when I asked you why your mam kicked George into touch, you said that she didn't want to talk about it and that they hadn't been getting on.' Manley stared at her hard. 'What did she really say, Susan?'

Susan Wilson rolled the anorak drawstrings and continued to stare downwards, her clammy face and neck now blotchy red. After a short pause, she answered, 'She wouldn't say owt; she said it'd all come out in 'wash. She said not to take her back there and that she was ashamed and blamed herself. She told me she was sorry and cried her eyes out. She was wracked with guilt.'

The two detectives exchanged a quick glance.

'Why was she wracked with guilt?' asked Manley.

'I-I dunno.'

'Well, why do you think she was wracked with guilt, then? What did you think at the time?'

A silence ensued before she eventually answered the question: 'I thought it might have had summat to do wi' George, but she wouldn't say. Me mam loved my daughter; she wouldn't have knowingly let owt bad happen to her.'

'That's interesting, Susan. You say your mam was wracked with guilt, presumably because she'd been getting pissed downstairs whilst her husband, George, your stepfather, abused your daughter behind her back. Is that what you're saying? But your mam's now passed away, and there's no way of us checking with her that what you're telling us, that what you're saying to us, is correct, is there? She's not here to corroborate what you're saying, Susan…is she?'

'Well…no…but…'

'So, what are we supposed to think, then? Just take what you say at face value? Is that what you think we should do, Susan?'

'Well…that's what happened. I'm just telling you… I… I don't know what you want me to say.'

After a further pause, Manley left the thread hanging in mid-air as he changed direction once again. 'And what about you then, Susan? Is George a good stepdad to you? Is he…affectionate towards you? Did you suffer any kind of abuse from him when you were a kid? Did he try it on with *you*, Susan?'

'No, definitely not. I can't really remember much of my real dad. George has always been there for me, but… he's allus been quiet… But he's all right… There's never been any abuse…none at all.'

'When you were a young 'un, Susan, who was it who usually gave you a bath? Was it your mam or was it George?'

Susan Wilson hesitated. 'Well, it was George, but he never did owt.'

'Why didn't your mam bath you?'

'George was always hands on wi' things like that…'

DC Taylor raised an eyebrow and turned a cheek.

'…He always got me ready for bed and stuff, but nowt ever happened that shouldn't o' done. Me mam was allus on 'settee. Looking back, I think she were bad with her nerves as well, even in them days. And she usually liked a drink on a night-time – just a couple o' bottles o' stout, nowt heavy. I don't think she ever got over me real dad getting killed.'

'What about sitting on his knee and stuff like that?'

'I used to go down in 'cellar and sit on his knee. He's allus kept rabbits an' stuff down there, and I used to sit on his knee and hold 'em while he listened to his sport on the wireless. That were all, nowt else.'

'Did he ever ask for mutual favours, Susan, you know, like if he did little things for you, little favours, little treats, and then you might do little things for him? Did any o' that sort o' thing go on?'

Susan Wilson looked down at the table and continued to yank at the coat drawstring. Once again, she hesitated just for a split second. 'No, never...ever.'

Manley sighed and relaxed. He sat back in his seat. 'And what about now, then. How do you feel about your stepdad now?'

'I don't know,' mumbled Susan Wilson.

'Well, do you hate him, or what, for what he's been doing to your daughter?'

'I...I don't know,' she replied quietly.

'You don't know?' fired back the detective sergeant. 'You don't know? I don't know about you, Baz, but if it was my daughter who'd been fiddled wi' by someone, whether it be me stepdad or anyone else, I'd want to kill the bastard, wun't you?'

'Wun't half, Bob. I'd smash him to pieces if it were one o' mine, anyone would,' answered Taylor in a dry, sinister monotone.

'Is that how you felt, Susan?' continued Manley. 'When you found out that George had been abusing your daughter? Eh? Did you want to harm him?'

Susan Wilson shook her head and mumbled.

'What was that, Susan?'

'I'm not like that. I didn't know what to do, did I? I'm bad wi' me bloody nerves, I keep telling you... I shoulda come to 'police. I didn't, but I shoulda done.'

'Do you know what my problem is, Susan? Eh?'

'No…what?'

'You're telling me that your mam was wracked wi' guilt for allowing her granddaughter to be abused, right under her nose, yeah? That's what you're saying to me, in't it? But I think that it's you who's wracked with guilt – and if you're not, you bloody well should be. Because from what you've told me, I think your stepdad did abuse you when you were a kid. Maybe not to the same extent that he abused your girl, but he abused you nevertheless. He did, didn't he, Susan?'

'No!'

'Well, I think he did. And my problem is that you… knowing what type of a person he was, what kind of an animal he was, you still took your innocent little daughter round to your mam's house and let her stay there, knowing full well that in her pissed-up state your mother was incapable of looking after her, didn't you, Susan?'

'No!'

'You left her there, abandoned her, just so you could have a bit a peace and quiet. That's what happened, in't it, Susan?'

'No! It wan't like that at all—'

'Just like when your mother abandoned you as she sat on her backside watching the bloody telly and supping ale whilst he did exactly the same to you as a young 'un. Your daughter was left to the depraved devices of your abusive stepfather, wasn't she? You knew she was at risk, didn't you, Susan? You knew George was abusive, didn't you? It was you who was wracked with guilt, wasn't it, not your mother, but you? And like any other decent parent would, you wanted to harm George, didn't, you Susan? You wanted revenge for the abuse he'd inflicted upon you as a girl, didn't you?'

'No! I don't know—'

'And revenge for what he'd done to your daughter. Abuse that could have been avoided if you'd been a little bit more attentive, a little more responsible as a mother! Isn't that right, Susan? I don't blame you for wanting to get your revenge on George, love, but don't give me that old chestnut, "It was me mam and she's dead, so there's nowt you can do about it".'

'No!' screamed Susan Wilson. 'I don't know what you're on about… What d'y'mean it was me mam? What was me bloody mam? And no, he didn't abuse me.' With tears in her eyes, she stood up and hammered her hands on the table before facing up to the detective sergeant. She stared him straight in the eye. 'Now, just tell me straight… Is he fucking dead or what?'

The two detectives looked at each other. 'You can decide for yourself, Susan, love,' said Bob Manley after a short pause. 'Cos you're coming with us to pay him a visit.'

*

It was in a side room at the city morgue where a lurching Susan Wilson doubled up whilst violently retching over a metal bowl provided by the mortuary assistant. The cynical DC Taylor stood by her side offering no more than bare minimal support. Her eyes were streaming, due in part to having witnessed the mangled, putrefied body of George, cold and dead on the mortuary slab, but due also to the sheer physical intensity of her reaction.

Although the morgue attendants had taken steps to

mask the smell of decomposition and covered up the horrific state of the cadaver as they saw fit, on first sight Susan Wilson had collapsed in a heap. The eye sockets had been found writhing with maggots, with part of the brain and surrounding soft tissue eaten away. The mortician had prepared the corpse wearing oversized sunglasses in a bid to spare Susan Wilson the horrors of the spectacle, but unfortunately he hadn't taken equal care with the concealment of the sliced open throat, which had been crudely sewn up. The macabre display, like a gruesome waxwork model from a Madame Tussauds sideshow, proved too much for Susan Wilson, who was all but carried from the room.

*

Once again, the indomitable Peggy Bowden had raised the alarm after detecting a low buzzing from the cellar of number 10 during the early hours. This after earlier noticing a profusion of bluebottles in the downstairs windows the previous day. Such had been the commotion when Stella had been discovered that the low hum of the radio in the basement had gone unnoticed, and with it the body of George.

Susan Wilson, already on Valium due to her nervous disposition, had been in no state to inspect the house. She was barely able to facilitate the services of an ambulance. On the removal of her deceased mother, she'd subsequently turned off the living room light, locked up the house and hadn't the stomach to return since.

Unable to contact Susan Wilson, Peggy had consulted with Terry the milkman and a couple of the neighbours. In view of the local gossip surrounding the disappearance of George, they'd concluded that all was not proper or correct and decided to inform the authorities.

Once inside, the police had made the grim discovery of the mutilated corpse of George, still trussed and bound up in the cellar. The stench had driven both coppers and detectives out onto the street, much to the intense curiosity of the neighbours, headed by Peggy. The mutilations to the body were self-evident but had been exacerbated by a suggestion of interference by a small carnivore.

It had been presumed the perpetrators were probably rats, but it was possible that Samson, George's beloved ferret, had been forced, by starvation, into the carnivorous consumption of his dead master. Samson was never seen again, dead or alive, but the decomposing bodies of Stan and Hilda were found nestled side by side in a dark corner of the side coal room. The remains of the emaciated magpie lay on the stone table directly in front of her master's rotting remains.

Susan Wilson would eventually confirm the identity of the body by virtue of a faded tattoo of a star on the mutilated right hand of her stepfather.

*

Susan Wilson was never charged with any offence. She'd never been regarded as a realistic or viable suspect in the mysterious death of George Wilson, but the authorities neglected to give her the peace of mind of being totally and officially exonerated.

She would carry the cloud and burden of guilt over the whole affair for the rest of her life. With the little money she eventually received from the sale of 10 Reginald Street, she was able to move away from East Leeds and start a fresh life in Middleton, another sprawling Leeds council estate, south of the River Aire.

As a young teenager, The Girl descended into the murky world of drugs and prostitution. Somewhere amongst the myriad of dark and shady Leeds terraced streets, all traces of her whereabouts would eventually evaporate, her memory consumed to a lonely, sad and empty history. Susan Wilson never cast eyes upon her daughter again – she herself being dead by the age of fifty-two.

CHAPTER 13

October 2016

Z oe stirred. She half opened her eyes and slid them left and right. The dark room, the bedside chair, the light patter of rain – the dog. She came to and realised that she was still wrapped up in her warm bed and that it was sometime in the middle of the night, although she had no way of verifying the exact time.

The bedroom door stood wide open with a dim light pushing through the bathroom blinds onto the small landing area. It dawned on her that the street lighting must be back to normal, and the flashing alarm clock confirmed that the power to the house had also been restored.

She contemplated hauling her weary body out of bed in order to sort out the phone, but she opted to remain within the warmth of the thick duvet and the comfort of her hazy mindset. However, it wasn't as straightforward as that. It never was with Zoe.

Now awake, her mental airwaves were laid bare and declared open for business. Her precarious state of mind soon became immersed in a swirling mass of nonsensical junk. There was no way she was sinking back into a restful sleep anytime soon. Nevertheless, she persisted, attempting to empty her head of the negative crap as best she could. *At least I'm resting. Jimmy's here, so just chill out, girl. Let nature take its course. The phone can wait – what happens will happen. Fuck it.*

Over the next half an hour or so, she fluxed in and out of consciousness, aware of her surroundings but never descending back into full sleep mode. She was conscious of the light rain lapping onto the windows, the storm now having passed over. She listened to the leaching rainwater from the decayed eaves guttering three doors up. A constant deluge cascading onto the Yorkstone pavement. And there was a pang of rejection as Princess decided to go walkabouts and disappeared from the room. But Zoe remained still.

Although the soft, distant melody had been audible to her for a while, it only registered as it grew in richness and sonority. She recognised it as Mantovani. The one Phil had played on the first day she'd set foot in the house; the same one that had often woken her in the early hours since. Caught unawares, the music had stealthily crept into her head, like the swathing, slithering tentacles of an assassin octopus, gradually infiltrating and suffocating her every deliberation.

Fuck me. Not again. She fought hard to remain positive. *It's only music – hasn't harmed you in the past. Just sit tight, girl. They can play the fucking death march if they want, but music can't harm you. Sit tight and hang in there. Fuck 'em.* And sit tight she did.

The intensity of the music escalated until it became relentlessly purposeful. Despite Zoe's initial resistance, she ultimately succumbed to the haunting composition, her emotions crawling back inside her headspace as a light grip on reality began to slip away.

She felt an empathy, just like she did on that first day in the house. It was the same music, the same sentiments. Images began to filter into her head, an impression of

loneliness, sadness. Movement in the darkness, a soothing darkness, flowing movement, the sense of a human
form, a female in the dark, moving, graceful, alone. She
sensed a bond, a commonality, an emotional attach-
ment.

The more she relaxed, the clearer the images and the
deeper the connection. She felt at ease, awash in a sense
of freedom and tranquillity. However, the feel-good fac-
tor, the wild flower meadow and the oasis of compassion was short-lived, as the positive vibes and emotions
abruptly ceased. The flowing form drew back and faded
away, but the darkness, the sinister darkness, remained.

An indistinct cloudy image began to appear within her
headspace. As it materialised, it became clearer and then
into full, sharp focus. The battered armchair and the dark
ominous space in which it existed, the dark cellar two
floors below, now occupied centre stage in her mind.

She realised that she'd let her guard down, that the
forces which had besieged her ever since she'd moved
into this house had penetrated her mind once again. Her
heart beat fast, but now she was angry. She shrieked out
loud, 'No! FUCK RIGHT OFF!'

She opened her eyes. Everything was calm. There was
no music, no representation of battered leather armchairs, no boding sentiment. The gutter leached onto the
stone pavement and the street lighting continued to im-
part a dim illumination onto the landing area. She hadn't
moved a muscle, her heart beat slowly and calmly, yet
just seconds previously she'd been struck with panic and
fear, her heart pounding like a piston. *What the fuck is
going on? This can't be right, Am I mad or what?*

Whilst pondering the sanity of her existence, she realised something else decidedly odd. As she lay on her

back, in exactly the same position as when she'd fallen asleep, she looked around the room. The only parts of her physicality over which she had any control were her eyes. They flitted from side to side giving her a panoramic view of the whole room, through the open bedroom door and down the landing corridor. She could see the attic door and the top of the winding staircase. She looked at the walls, the bed and back to the landing, yet she could feel that her eyes were still firmly clamped closed.

She had presumed that she was in sleep paralysis. She'd encountered this phenomenon many times before, but this time she could see, as clearly and concisely as the dark setting would allow. Her eyes were physically closed but psychically wide open. *What the fuck!*

Zoe attempted to turn over and reach for the bedside lamp but was unable to move even an inch. She was physically paralysed, with the use of only her darting, apprehensive eyes.

She lay there, captive and useless, listening to and watching the world around her, although she now had misgivings about every aspect of her existence. Despite her dubious practices and obvious weaknesses, she regarded herself as a sharp cookie, a cut above most when it came to being streetwise and looking after herself – after all, she'd been born and bred a Seacroft lass.

But this whole episode, this last three months or so, had her beat. She lay under the duvet, stock-still, her destiny in the hands of some unknown force. Condemned. Her only option was to sit tight, hang in there and wait. She didn't have to wait long.

Fluttering. At first, soft as the flurried wings of an agitated moth on a hot, humid summer evening. Then a flapping sensation, like a line of damp washing strung out on a windswept Yorkshire dale. Zoe stared down the landing, half expecting the source to appear from the staircase or around the corner. Instead, a black shape materialised from behind her periphery line of psychic vision, flailing around the bedroom, erratic and irregular in motion. She recognised the anomaly from the recent encounter at the foot of the stairs. The same bird-like creature, but not of a type that had ever taken wing on this earth plane, the one in which Zoe existed.

Her eyes zipped around the room tracking the dark-feathered beast as it swirled and looped, closing in on her with its sharp beak, vicious talons and pinprick red eyes.

Each time it rounded on her, the creature emitted a guttural screeching chack – and each time, Zoe responded with an internal tirade of profanities.

Anger now superseded the confusion as she summoned an energy and inner strength to flay her arms and fight for her life. She connected with one swipe, causing the creature to disintegrate and disappear mid-air. Once again, the room descended into peaceful silence. Zoe's heart, racing just one second ago, was now calm and operating at a slow, undisturbed tempo.

Again, she surveyed the dimly lit room and landing, conscious of her eyelids being closed. Her arms and nails, with which she'd fought her corner just a moment ago, were tucked beneath the duvet in the same position from when she'd climbed underneath. Her body was dormant, but her mind was active and sentient. Zoe was also raging with anger.

I don't know who's doing this to me. I don't know if I'm possessed or if it's some kinda joke, whether someone up there's fucking me up, but I'm telling you this, and I'm telling you

*now, whoever you are, whatever you are, you've got a fight on
your hands, cos I don't fucking give up, and I'll catch up with
you eventually and fucking God help you when I do, cos you're
messing with the wrong one – I'm telling you now! So just back
the fuck off messing with my head, you bastard!*
The city buzzed and the gutter leaked. Her anger
ebbed. No matter how aggravated she became in her
head, her body remained struck with paralysis, inert. Her
overactive mind should have been numbed beyond rec-
ognition, in total oblivion, that had been the plan, but
it was her physical body which lay insensible and untroubled. Or, so she thought.

As her line of vision descended from the wall to the
bed, arms lay on top of the duvet. Large, masculine arms,
covered in matted hair, with gnarled hands, chunky fingers and uncut, dirty nails. She couldn't move them.
They felt as much a part of her anatomy as the nimble-
fingered limbs which lay undisturbed and intact beneath
the duvet, of which she was still acutely aware.

The pendulum of rational thought shifted once again,
as she convinced herself of a possession, that an entity
had taken residence within her soul, intent on harming
her – or at the very least toying with her – for the purpose
of a spiteful, twisted gratification.

The spectacle of the masculine arms slowly faded
away whilst a spellbound Zoe looked on. As they did,
she became aware of the temperature. It had dropped.
She could feel the chill as it swathed over her face and
slowly filtered down to her body and limbs under the
duvet. She observed the swirling clouds of breath as
the temperature slumped. Her vision was clear, but the
noises around her, which, to a degree, had kept her sane
all night, became muted before totally dissipating, leav-

ing the bedroom in silence. There was an impasse. Zoe looked, listened and smelled as she waited; her suspicious mind on high alert.

At first, it sounded like scratching, the same light scratching sounds she'd been freaked out by with Princess earlier that evening. It stemmed from somewhere beneath the bedroom, clear as frozen ice, such was the tomb-like silence in the house.

This time the scratching expanded into a dragging sound, the dragging of a heavy object, with short bursts of concentrated endeavour. The heaving and tugging continued, intermittent, clear and concise, from below, somewhere below. She listened intently, eliminating all possible rational explanations. Zoe didn't know what to think. She couldn't do anything except watch and listen and sit tight.

After a while, the noises petered out to nothing, but the total silence and freezing temperature remained. She offered no further resistance against the paralysis, fatigued and battle weary, her mental capacity enervated.

She scanned the room. The only discernible signs of any movement were the ghostlike clouds of vapour expelled into the cold air. A muffled bump from a deep part of the house broke the stillness for just a moment, but the silence returned. She took the opportunity to embark on another round of self-reflection, of self-conviction. All that had happened thus far this evening, she reckoned, she'd experienced before, and each time she'd come through it relatively unscathed. *If that's all you've got to offer, then I can take it. Just do what you've gotta do, and I'll take it. Come on, let's get it over and done with.* She lay, unable to budge with only her own mind as a point of reference in this, her mad world.

The bottom stair door creaked, the stiff steel hinges grated through the ice-thin atmosphere like a device from a medieval torture chamber. A heavy thud, a short gap, and then another.

Zoe immediately 'opened' her eyes, fully alert – but like before, she felt the sensation of her eyelids being closed. Footsteps, thudding footsteps. Louder, intense and foreboding, laboured footsteps, each muffled thump accompanied with a rasp of heavy breath. After attempting to shift her body, she was met with an iron-like resistance. The slow galumphing continued as she sensed whatever *it* was, was now nearing the winding turn at the stair head. Her heart raced. *What the fuck now?*

A black mist appeared at the head of the stairs, gradually seeping around the corner. She lay frozen as the footsteps ceased and the black mist took the hazy form of a human-like creature. A stooping figure emerged, with its head bowed, gasping for breath. She watched in horror as the misty, black form wheezed hot air into the cold atmosphere.

The figure lumbered towards the bedroom door, directly towards Zoe as she looked on, powerless and vulnerable. The mist took on a more defined form, that of a large, heavy male. She observed the laboured movement of limbs as the form shuffled forwards, heading her way. The figure, blustering and wheezing, creaked closer as each footstep reverberated around the room, irrespective of the sumptuous carpet over which it appeared to be slowly progressing.

Zoe attempted to close her eyes, but they were already closed; she was forced, against her will, to witness the lumbering horror approach. On reaching the opened bedroom door, the figure stopped. Zoe's heart strained like never before as the form, with bowed head, paused, as if catching breath. What happened next sent an ice-cold chill down the entire body of the already transfixed and terrified young mother.

Gasping for breath, the figure slowly turned away and reached up to take hold of the doorknob to the attic staircase door. The attic, where, in the dormer room above, lay her beautiful and innocent little daughter.

In the intensity of the evening, Zoe had all but forgotten about her baby upstairs, too self-absorbed by her own fears. She never thought for a minute that the safety of her Sophia would be compromised. She felt a numbness of the head, her emotions churned with helplessness and guilt.

The figure hesitated. It appeared to acknowledge the presence of Zoe, sensing the pure emotion of fear. It turned to face her, slowly raising its head in the process. Zoe tried to escape, but she couldn't. She tried to shut down her psychic eyelids, but she couldn't. She couldn't do anything but lie there, watch and see, stiff as a corpse.

The features came into focus: the skin a pale whitish-grey, the head disfigured. They faced each other, but the ghoul had no eyes, only sockets, empty and black. Zoe felt the sensation of hot piss trickle between her legs. She watched the figure then turn back to face the attic door, open it and continue a lumbering journey upwards, up towards the dormer bedroom.

Zoe attempted to snap out of the physical lockdown. She struggled to rock from side to side. She strove to concentrate intensely on the movement of one hand, one finger, anything to switch on the bedside lamp and break the spell of paralysis. She tried shouting and screaming, but nothing, just the haunting sound of the slow, thudding footsteps and a residue of the black mist which disappeared as it filtered through the now opened attic stair door. She never stopped fighting.

For fuck's sake, what are you doing to me? You don't go anywhere near my fucking daughter, you horrible bastard. Leave her alone... I'll fucking kill you... Almighty God, give me the strength to protect my baby from these evil bastards... Help me, for fuck's sake! Help me! HELP ME!

The hollow footsteps continued as Zoe fought with her inner demons that they might coalesce to engage in battle with the external demons. Physical tears squeezed and pushed out through her ironclad eyes as she realised how powerful the forces were that she was up against and how useless her pathetic efforts were in return.

I'll never forgive you, you fucking twat, for putting me through this. All that church shite, and you're letting this happen to my fucking daughter. Release me NOW, so I can help her...do something to help... Please, God, please...

The next sound that Zoe heard tore her heart to pieces and made her wish that she was dead there and then. The pitiful cries for help from Sophia broke her in half.

Amid high-pitched screaming, she could hear her daughter shout, 'Mummy! Mummy! Mummy, please...! Mummy help me...!'

A powerless Zoe closed her eyes and once again appealed to God. This time in a soft, non-confrontational manner. *Lord Almighty, please help me. Please, please help me.*

She then felt herself slumping down the side of the bed towards the bedroom floor, a sensation of descent, downwards, down and down, slumping downwards, between the floors, through the sitting room and through the cellar and downwards into the dark unknown beyond. The desperate screams became weaker, fading into a distant faraway echo as Zoe found herself descending dimly lit stone steps, narrow, steep steps, deeper and deeper, downwards into the dark. Downwards and downwards, deeper and deeper into the unknown black bowels of the earth, the distant cries of her daughter becoming weaker and more remote by the second.

The sensation of falling then ended abruptly. Zoe's manic eyes refocused. She found herself manacled with chains and rope to the old leather armchair. The chair stood within a small, black, claustrophobic pit carved out of natural bedrock in a dark place somewhere deep within the heart of the earth's core. She couldn't move.

In front of her stood a stone altar. Suspended above with an otherworldly luminance, the body of a young girl lay horizontal in mid-air and dressed in white night-clothes. The girl, with an ashen, tear-stained complexion, slept silently. In the far corner was a niche carved out of the rock face, in which stood a glowing white cross.

Zoe stared spellbound at the scene in front of her. Against the distant echoes of Sophia's piteous cries for help, the levitating luminescent girl slowly turned her head towards Zoe. She faced her square on and opened her eyes. They were empty, soulless and gloss black. Zoe found herself being drawn towards them, lured into the dark inky blackness of an unknown malevolent world. The black eyes turned blood red; the glowing white cross simultaneously collapsed into a liquefying crimson mass and copiously dripped with thick blood.

It was too much for Zoe as she clamped her eyes closed. She summoned up one last effort as she expended every last ounce of energy, every last grain of mental sway. She resorted to the Christian religion, the one that she'd been brought up on and the one which she'd callously derided for most of her adult life.

She conjured up a vision of Jesus Christ on the crucifix and appealed directly and intensely to the Son of God against the continuing backdrop of Sophia's own pitiful faraway cries for help. *Please, please help me, for fuck's sake.* 'Jesus Christ! Please!'

Suddenly, an intense flash of brilliant pure-white light engulfed the chamber. Then, in the blink of an eye, the ambience in the little house descended into one of glorious serenity.

*

It had been eighty-seven-year-old Peggy Bowden who raised the alarm having been awoken in the early hours by the piercing and desperate screams from across the street. It hadn't been the first time the now bulbous-eyed, white-haired old woman had frantically requested the attendance of the authorities to number 10.

A bemused and unhurt Sophia had been carried out of the house in the arms of a policeman and into a waiting ambulance. The physically untouched but rambling, wide-eyed Zoe had been carried out on a stretcher. After a thorough search of the house, the officers discovered her ice-cold, shivering body curled up on the oversized leather armchair in the squalid little cellar. Unnoticed by the authorities, a single flame had flickered from a solitary candle which stood on the stone table. They never noticed the tiny black and white photograph propped up against it, facing the maniacal Zoe.

Despite exhaustive enquiries, it was never determined exactly how Zoe had accessed the cellar whilst managing to reinstate the plywood sheeting and American-style fridge-freezer back into place behind her. It would be many months of soul-searching, and many more in rehab, before Zoe would eventually convince those around her that the incidents she claimed she'd experienced in the house had not being fuelled by the effects of drugs and alcohol.

*

'Well, at least they lasted longer than Cameron and Osborne,' piped up Jock to Nathan as they cleared up after fixing new plywood security boarding to the windows and doors of 10 Reginald Street. 'I'll give 'em that. Four months they lasted 'ere. This is what I mean. Look, most of 'em in this street are foreigners, an' I bet most of 'em get their rent paid, by us, the taxpayer. That'll be why these lot 'ave left, cos it's like a foreign country round 'ere. No wonder we voted to get out. We need to get back to where we were... That's what I say, old love. I'm tellin' ya.'

A magpie swooped down to land just a couple of feet away from him.

'Go on, fuck off,' he cried as he aimed a swiping kick, the bird instantly launching itself airborne with its chacking cry.

Nathan threw the ladders onto the back of the pickup and securely tied them.

'When I were a lad, it were all right around 'ere,' continued Jock. 'It were like it should be. British, English. Cos that's where we are, innit? In bleedin' England!'

Nathan looked over. 'Jock,' he said quietly but firmly whilst shaking his head, 'shut the fuck up and get in the bloody van.'

*

As the white pickup truck pulled out of the tiny street of back-to-backs, Peggy Bowden peeked through her net curtains. The street was deserted. She surveyed the house opposite, once again boarded up, as it had been for so many years.

She looked up towards the roof. At the side of the dormer was a small low-level chimney stack. A striking magpie lurked behind and poked his head around the corner delivering a cold, hard stare.

A stand-off ensued as each glared at the other, stock-still and silent. The small gloss-black eyes of the mysterious corvine met with the large, white, bulging eyes of the old woman.

They connected and just as each became transfixed, the draw curtains at number 11 were hastily swished closed, shutting away the scene, closing it off, out of sight.

The End

Printed in Great Britain
by Amazon

38746260R00158